THE GIRL FROM MAGNOLIA STREET

THE GIRL
FROM
MAGNOLIA STREET

Aimee Spring

Always Spring Publishing

Cover design by Damonza. (AI-generated image, with extensive editing. Tools: Photoshop, Midjourney)
Interior design and formatting by Always Spring Publishing.

First Edition
ISBN: 979-8-9873674-3-8
Published by Always Spring Publishing, Savannah, GA U.S.A.
Printed in the United States of America

For information or permissions, please contact:
www.aimeespring-author.com

"Ar scáth a chéile a mhaireann na daoine."
—Gaelic Proverb

It is through the shelter of each other that we survive.

FLY

Obedient songbird, meant to delight
Sing me a song, happy and bright
Don't sing of the woes that trouble your kind
Or sing me a song that tells me I'm blind

Sing me a song that tells me I'm right
That's all I want to know, that I'm right
Never challenged or questioned
Obtuse, you may say
But ignorance is sweet, as Adam did pay

Knowledge is evil
Eve surely taught
Making things murky
Getting you naught

Sit there and sing, stop being a pest
I'll beat you and flog you,
Or what's better yet?
I'll tether your soul, yes, that's what I'll do
Cage you and keep you, control you; I will

Rise up, weary birds
Songbirds unite
Give up, not ever
We'll march, and we'll fight!

—Helen O'Donnell, 1915

PROLOGUE

November 20, 1915

I looked back one last time at Rochester, New York, home of my childhood, as the train pulled away from the station bound for Chicago. My stubborn eyes began to water, and I lowered my head, trying to hide my tears.

"Boys don't cry," I told myself. "You mustn't cry, or they'll surely know."

My mind raced. What if no one was there to greet me in Chicago? What would I do? Where would I go?

Through murky eyes, I glanced down at the bulky men's boots on my feet. Rosalie Kelly had worn them on her 150-mile march from New York to Albany with the other brave suffragists a few winters back. They had belonged to one of the most courageous women I knew. Just thinking about that made me feel stronger, more assured, and my vision sharpened.

I pulled the heavy pillowcase Olive had packed onto my lap. Inside were chunks of bread, strips of dried meat, *The Woman's Bible: A Classic Feminist Perspective* by Elizabeth Cady Stanton, a journal, and a pencil. I chuckled when I saw *The Woman's Bible,* a Kelly household favorite. Olive quoted from it often. I opened the cover and found the message she had scribbled inside.

> *Helen,*
> *Fly upwards, toward the heavens, and when your wings become tired, and you feel you can't go another foot, go higher anyway. And when you really can't go another inch, stop and look in your pocket, have a butterscotch, and think of me, for I'll always be there.*
> *Remember, a caged bird will never know its true potential. Fly high.*
> *Your best friend,*
> *—Olive*

I checked all my pockets and found a butterscotch that Olive had snuck into my jacket. I held the golden-wrapped candy to my nose and imagined how sweet it would taste. With all the strength of Job, I slipped it back into my pocket.

I could go further.

"Tickets!" the man called down the aisle.

I kept my head down and mouth shut as I nervously reached into my jacket and handed him the small piece of paper. My palms began to sweat when the man stared at me longer than seemed appropriate. He looked at my bag and then back at me again.

"You got work in Chicago, lad?" the man asked.

Olive had told me to speak to no one.

"Your girlish voice will surely give you away," she had said.

What would happen if someone discovered I was a girl of thirteen years traveling alone? Would they send me back?

"Going to meet my pa," I muttered in a voice I barely recognized.

The man looked at me again and hesitated. He knows, I thought. I closed my eyes, put my hand in the pocket with the butterscotch, clenched it tightly, and said a quick prayer.

My breath caught.

Then—click—I heard my ticket punch. The man moved on to the seats behind me.

I exhaled deeply.

I removed Pap's cap and scratched my itchy head. The touch of my short hair startled me. I turned to look out the window to keep anyone from seeing my tear-filled eyes. Everything outside was moving so fast. It reminded me how quickly the past four years had gone.

Once content to live in the shadows of others, I now found myself set ablaze, determined to pursue my own hopes and dreams, no matter the cost.

Olive had suggested I write my story on the long ride. I put my cap back on, fixed my vest and jacket, and pulled out the pencil and pad. I opened the small journal to the first blank page and pressed the sharpened tip to the crisp white paper.

The words came easily as my heart melted onto the pages, thinking about Magnolia Street.

ONE

October 7, 1911

Gram opened my bedroom door, saying, "Today is the big day." After months of hearing Grandma talk about Uncle Peter's anniversary in the priesthood, the special celebration was finally upon us.

"We must make sure everything is perfect when guests arrive, so your uncle will be pleased. Wash up and dust the downstairs for me. Grandma is moving a bit slow this morning, and Pap is out running errands with Nell."

Nell was my grandfather's old Dutch Harness horse who pulled his coal truck. Pap's soul mate, Gram would say.

"Gram. Do I have to?" I moaned as she poured steaming water into the large bowl on my washstand.

I was nine and a half years old and still hadn't been assigned chores by Grandma. Friends, relatives, and even

Uncle Peter had told my grandparents I was spoiled. Gram didn't like this and would firmly retort, "She'll be cooking and cleaning for the rest of her life, and by God's good grace, may she have a long one."

After losing two of her children, her response usually shut people up, and housekeeping was never expected of me.

I turned to the blue frock hanging in my closet that Gram had been sewing for the past four weeks. A smile lit up my sour face as I forgot about dusting and imagined showing off my new dress to my hero, Uncle Peter, and all the guests later in the day.

"Gram, can I put my new dress on now?" I begged, springing from my bed and tugging on her well-worn apron. "Oh, please, Gram," I insisted.

"No, Helen. It will get dirty," Gram said.

"No, it won't. I promise," I said, ignoring Gram's annoyed tone. "Please?"

"Helen, stop!" she bellowed, startling me.

I stood pouting as Gram touched her shoulder. She grimaced.

"Helen, I need your help today. Please wash up and get yourself downstairs."

I quickly cleaned myself. Grandma rarely complained or asked for help. I put on my play clothes with some assistance and picked Sadie off the bed before heading out of my bedroom door.

Santa Claus had given me Sadie two years prior, and I named her after my mother, the lovely woman in the framed photograph hanging on the parlor wall. My doll was made of porcelain and had red hair and blue eyes just like mine, with a big bow on top of her head that I would match with whichever dress I chose to put her in for the day.

I didn't get along well with other children and as a result,

Sadie was my only friend.

I started down our wooden stairs while Gram made my bed and tidied up after me. My nose filled with the aroma of some of Gram's specialties, and when I turned the corner I found a room fit for nobility. I had never seen our home look so elegant. The red flowers sitting on the lace cloth of the dining table were the perfect finishing touch. Uncle Peter would be pleased.

Father O'Donnell, as he was known in our Irish parish, was not only my grandmother's favorite son (though she tried to hide it) but also one of my favorite people. Gram always said he was a man of great importance, and with any luck, he'd get us all into Heaven.

A loud crash of pots and pans startled me while dusting. I rushed into the kitchen.

My grandmother was lying on the floor, motionless, and food was everywhere. I pushed the dinner goose that had landed on her to the floor and shook her firmly to awaken her. I ran to the larder for the smelling salts, hoping Gram had only fainted, but they didn't rouse her. I poured ice water onto her face, but still, she didn't move.

I panicked and ran outside, screaming for help. But who would help me? Neither Uncle Peter nor Gram allowed me to speak to the Kellys next door, and the Hamilton children down the street still hated me from a year ago at the quarry when I fibbed to save my own behind.

It took only a minute for Mr. and Mrs. Kelly to run over. I had no idea why the Kellys were "not our type of people," but it had been made clear to me that I was never allowed to be friendly to them or their granddaughter, who came to visit with her mother occasionally. On those days, Grandma insisted I play inside.

On the ride to Rochester General Hospital, Mrs. Kelly tried to cheer me up by turning around every few minutes, saying, "All will be okay, darlin'," in her thick Irish accent.

I believed her, of course. Grandma had to be okay.

A brightly colored cardinal flew into the carriage and perched beside me on the edge of the surrey, staring as if it, too, was saying, "It will be okay." The little thing's knowing eyes seemed to look straight into my soul. I reached out to touch the crimson bird, but it flew away.

As I held Grandma, I looked at the woman who had become my mother. She had fed, clothed, and dutifully cared for me when I was sick. Gram could always make me laugh and was a wonderful storyteller, two things I loved about her.

For a moment, I became lost thinking of her tales of the fairy folk who lived on the Emerald Isle, our homeland, and how these beings traveled through tunnels underneath the earth to visit the Irish in America.

When I was five, I climbed to the top of Nell's barn and immediately regretted it. I stayed up there long enough to count every missing shingle before Gram finally came outside. I called her name. She dropped the laundry and nearly fell to the ground. Uncle Peter had to climb up with Pap's rickety old ladder to peel me off the roof. I earned a spanking "for my own good," but by bedtime, Gram had softened. As she tucked me in, she giggled and said, "You know, for a moment, Helen, when I first heard you calling my name from the top of that roof, I thought the fairies were finally making contact."

I was taken from my fond memory when we went over a large bump, and Gram's head lifted from my lap, almost hitting the floor.

When the carriage jolted to a halt, Mrs. Kelly jumped down, ran into the tall brick building, and came out with two men dressed in white who helped put Gram onto a little wheeled table. The orderlies walked fast, and we did our best to keep up. I followed the squeaking table with Grandma into a cold room with a lonely crucifix on one of the walls.

The only window in the room was shut. I grew alarmed. Some classmates had said that after a person dies, a window in the room where the body lies must be open for at least two hours so the spirit can escape. I prayed that Grandma wouldn't die, but what if she did and then was unable to find the gates of Heaven?

I cried out for someone to open the window. Instead, a nurse directed me to leave the room. Mrs. Kelly met me with outstretched arms. I hesitated only momentarily, accepted the old woman's hug, and then sat on the bench with Mr. and Mrs. Kelly. When I peered down at my lap and saw what looked to be part of a carrot and maybe an onion stuck to my dress, I started to cry again.

Mrs. Kelly held me for hours until Uncle Peter and a dazed-looking Pap finally arrived. I ran to them and threw my arms around Uncle Peter.

"It was awful, Uncle Peter. I was all alone. The Kellys were kind and brought Gram here." I hoped my explanation would soften his anger about them being involved in this whole thing.

Pap came over to hug me. The sweet, sharp smell of whiskey hit me before his arms did. At that moment, I knew that while I was trying to awaken Gram, get her to the hospital, and wait with strangers, Pap had been drinking in town. I pulled away as my heart stiffened and looked up just as Uncle Peter walked into Gram's hospital room, walking right past the neighbors.

"Bob, Noreen, thank you. You can go on home now. I'm sorry for your trouble." My grandfather's words were weak yet sincere.

"No trouble at all, Tom. We were happy to help." Mr. Kelly patted my grandfather's back. I was surprised that they were as friendly as they were, knowing darn well the ruling on the Kellys in our house.

Before Mrs. Kelly walked away, she turned to me with her warm brown eyes and said, "I'm prayin' for ye, Helen."

I wanted to hug her again but, knowing better, I just stood there watching them walk down the empty hallway.

When the doctor came out of Grandma's room with a glum-looking Uncle Peter by his side, telling us that there was nothing he could do, I searched Uncle Peter's face and then Pap's, trying to make sense of the words.

Uncle Peter walked away while I held my breath, waiting for Pap to say something. Pap reached for my hand and squeezed it tight. Tears streamed down his ashen, wrinkled face.

"She is with your mother and Uncle Albert now," he said between sobs. I had to gasp for air as the lump in my throat grew.

Dear sweet Jesus. My grandmother was dead!

Uncle Peter had told me once that strong men didn't cry. Pap didn't care about nonsense like that, though. If he was happy, he laughed and smiled. If he was angry, he yelled or screamed, and today, well, today, he was sad, and he was crying loudly and without shame.

I turned to see Uncle Peter sitting on the bench, shaking his head back and forth, holding back tears.

My uncle drove Pap's carriage home while Pap moaned like a wounded animal the entire way. In between crying, I thought back to walking into Gram's hospital room to say goodbye. I saw that the window that had been closed was now open, and relief filled me, knowing Gram would make it to the pearly white gates she'd always dreamed of.

I became lightheaded, and my stomach ached when we pulled up to our house on Magnolia Street. We climbed down from the surrey and staggered to the porch. Uncle Peter held my hand.

Gram's dirty apron was squashed up in a ball in the corner. Mrs. Kelly must have known that Grandma wouldn't want people to see her with that old apron on. We walked into the house, and Sadie was sitting on the dining room chair where I had left her. My thoughts shot back to earlier that morning when Gram entered my room, and I was beyond thrilled about the day's events.

"Today is the big day," Gram had said.

Boy, was it.

The dressed-up buffet and table with all the silver and glass Grandma had been busy making shiny all week, never to be used, seemed to glare at me, while the flowers made me cringe thinking of all the times I had left similar stems at my mother's and Uncle Albert's gravestones.

I followed Pap and Uncle Peter into the kitchen. The vegetables that had covered the floor when I left were now in the roasting pan in the sink. The floor was all clean, and the goose was gone. I couldn't imagine who would have cleaned up.

Then I remembered. Guests would be arriving. I grabbed Sadie off the dining room chair and ran upstairs. I crawled into the inviting sheets and blankets with Sadie in my arms. Downstairs, I heard the big clock on the mantle in the parlor bong five times.

Uncle Peter started screaming at my grandfather about drinking today instead of being there for me and about how we could never let the Kellys into our lives, although he never offered a reason why. I heard fists pounding on the dining room table and became frightened, for I had never heard my uncle so angry.

Pap repeatedly tried apologizing, but his words were slurred, tangled up in sobs. Finally, Uncle Peter went silent. After a long moment, Pap's broken voice filled the room.

"What will I do without Mary?" he cried.

Footsteps creaked on the stairs. Uncle Peter stepped into my room, looking shaken. "Helen," he said softly, "I'll see you in the morning. Please know, I love you to the stars and back."

"Yes, Uncle Peter, and I love you past the stars." That was our usual clever exchange, one we'd come up with years ago under a starry sky.

My uncle rushed down the stairs and slammed the front door. Soon, deafening cries emerged from the kitchen, and fear filled me.

What would Pap do without Grandma?

What would I do?

TWO

October 8, 1911

I awoke to the sound of furniture shifting below and voices I didn't recognize. My head glanced out my window, and I noticed a lovely cardinal hopping from branch to branch. I got up to take a closer look.

Outside, I saw two strange men leaving our house. It took only a minute for me to remember yesterday. It hadn't been a dream.

My heart dropped.

I gathered Sadie and tiptoed to the top of the stairs, still in my nightdress. The house was darker than usual, the air heavier. We cautiously walked down into the shadowy parlor. All the curtains had been drawn. The mirrors were covered. The large clock wasn't ticking, and I realized I hadn't heard its familiar chimes since yesterday.

I pulled back the heavy curtain and saw the men outside talking to my grandfather. Then, I noticed an odd smell and stillness in the air. I froze, and a cold shiver ran up my spine. I turned around to see a large box on the floor. Inching closer, I wondered if my eyes were playing tricks on me.

There, lying in her casket, was my dear grandmother, looking as if she were off in dreamland. I screamed loud enough for the Hamiltons down the street to hear. Instantly, Uncle Peter ran to me.

"Helen, for goodness' sake!" he yelled.

"How did this happen? How did Grandma get back here?" I shouted, running to hide behind him.

"Your grandmother will be here for a few days so friends and family can say goodbye to her," he knelt down. "Helen, I'm sorry. There will be some dark days ahead."

I'm pretty sure my uncle thought I would be crying, but at the moment, I was too scared to be sad.

"Uncle Peter, why on earth would we want to have Grandma's body in the house when she is dead?" I asked, my eyes bulging.

Keeping a dead body in the house just seemed like a bad idea. I knew the story of Lazarus. What if Gram woke up and walked into my room while I was sleeping? I loved Grandma more than anything, but the thought gave me chills. I would need to put a chair in front of the door until she was gone.

"Helen, wakes are an important part of the grieving process." Uncle Peter walked over to the drapes and closed them tightly. "There are going to be a lot of people here today. Please don't be too weepy and help your Aunt Carrie in the kitchen."

But I wasn't listening anymore. My eyes were fixed on Gram's body. She wore rouge and lipstick and one of her favorite church dresses. Her Sunday Mass black veil was tucked into the coffin, just above her folded hands.

"Go and get ready for today. Put on your church clothes," my uncle said.

I couldn't stop watching, half-expecting her to move. Uncle Peter released my sweaty hand and gave me a light swat on my bottom.

"Now, go on."

I ran back up to my room to get dressed and washed up. I reached for the ceramic pail under my bed to pee, but when I lifted the lid, it was full. Grandma never let me empty the pot. I remembered all the times Pap had opened the window and tossed it out when Grandma scolded him for being lazy.

The pot was heavier than expected, and as I carried it to the window, I slipped. I stared in horror as it spilled across the wooden floor and seeped into the cracks.

On my hands and knees, mopping it up, I noticed my closet door creaking open behind me like it was inviting me in. I walked over and saw the matching dresses, one for me and one for Sadie, hanging just as they had the morning before. Maybe no one would care if we wore them today.

I got the two of us dressed and then paused in front of the large gold mirror at the base of the stairs. The dress fit just right. Sadie's too. Gram had stitched every seam with care. My hair still held curls from the salon Gram had taken me to only days ago.

Pap saw me and stepped forward, wrapping me in a firm embrace.

"You look beautiful," he said.

Then he stepped back and met my tear-filled eyes.

"Helen, you and me, we'll make it through the day. We'll make it through—" My chest became heavy as Pap's words became stuck in his throat. I knew he was trying to convince himself of this, not me.

Aunt Carrie swept in later that morning, clad in mourning black, her sobs muffled on Pap's shoulder. Uncle Will scooped me up and then offered his hand to his brother, Peter, which he ignored. Instead, Uncle Peter folded my aunt into a warm hug.

Hidden beneath the dining-room table, my favorite place to overhear adult conversation, I remembered Uncle Peter's rude comments about Aunt Carrie as she kissed my cheek. I then noticed Uncle Peter trailing her into the kitchen.

A knock sounded at the door, and I shot up the stairs out of the way. Uncle Will opened the door to Mr. Kelly, who was carrying a golden-roasted goose. I guessed it to be the same bird that rested on Gram's chest yesterday, and my stomach turned.

The Kellys were both smartly dressed in their Sunday best, no doubt expecting to join the wake. Pap stepped forward, thanked them warmly, and took the bird without inviting them in. His quiet "God be with you" drew a surprised look from my Uncle Will.

As they turned to go, Mrs. Kelly said, "Ar scáth a chéile a mhaireann na daoine."

I'd heard those Irish words before, although I didn't know what they meant. Later, Pap told me, "It is through the shelter of each other that we survive."

"Pap, why didn't you invite them in?" Uncle Will asked, puzzled.

Pap didn't answer. Uncle Will shook his head and disappeared into the kitchen. But I knew. Gram would've sat up in her casket if the Kellys had come inside.

I stepped off the stairs and took Pap's hand. He kissed me and went to the barn to check on Nell, with his head hanging low.

Gram often complained about how much Pap loved that old horse.

"You treat that horse better than you treat me!" she used to say.

Pap was good with all horses, not just Nell, and many a morning, Gram would roll her eyes at how she had been awoken in the middle of the night by some man looking for Pap to come and help with his sick horse. Pap was a spirited, kind-hearted man, an old softie, Gram would say. And although he would do anything for a person or, in his case, a horse in need, he had a problem with the drink.

"Helen, into the kitchen with you," Uncle Peter ordered, "You need to help your aunt."

I stepped into the kitchen to help, as I had been told. I intended to be polite and ask Aunt Carrie if she'd sewn her mourning dress. I knew she was a seamstress, like Gram, but she handed me an apron before I could get the words out.

"Peel potatoes, please."

"Goodness, I don't know how," I said, taken aback by her request. Gram never let me use knives.

"What? Helen, that's disgraceful." I watched as she sliced long, ribbon-like curls from the skin.

I gave it a try. After twenty potatoes, I proudly looked at the pile and untied my apron, ready to flee. My aunt glanced over at me.

"Helen, I may need more help later."

I rolled my eyes.

"Hmm," she murmured.

"Is that the dress your grandmother made you?"

I stiffened, unsure whether I was in trouble for wearing it or for not wearing black like all the ladies.

"It is, ma'am," I said, giving a curt nod.

"Helen, please call me Aunt Carrie. You know your grandmother was so excited to see you wear that dress." Tears welled in her eyes as she took my hands. "I'm very sorry,

Helen. It's not fair. Life is often not fair."

I wanted to say something kind, after all, she was trying to be nice, but Gram's old words, unrefined, uncouth, and brash, rang in my head. It seemed I wasn't supposed to like my aunt.

"Thank you," I said, quickly slipping out of the room.

Uncle Will and Aunt Carrie didn't visit often. I'd seen them only a handful of times, but I remembered how Aunt Carrie was supposed to have a baby when I was seven. Grandma said the baby died in her stomach and went to Heaven to become a cherub. I had always longed for brothers, sisters, or cousins, and the news saddened me.

The day was difficult. People came and went, whispering their goodbyes over Grandma's body. In the evening, Sadie and I hid under the dining room table. Two women were talking.

"How unfortunate she didn't get her mother's good looks," one said. "That Sadie O'Donnell, she was a stunner."

"She's still young," the other replied. "She has her mother's beautiful hair."

Goodness! They were talking about me. I ran upstairs, not caring who saw.

The kids at school often called me ugly, but Gram told me they were jealous. It was true. I was ugly.

Later, Aunt Lib—Pap's sister who only came over on special occasions—came upstairs looking for me, carrying a small gift. She didn't seem sick, yet she had lived at the state hospital ever since her sister Margaret died years ago. She always mentioned my mother through glassy eyes, then smothered me in her heavy arms and wide, soft frame, pressing me close whether I liked it or not.

I knew Aunt Lib was one of the relatives who told Gram

I needed more housekeeping chores. Because of that, I wasn't fond of her and may have accidentally told her so, once or even twice. On those occasions, Gram didn't go lightly on me.

When I saw her, I burst out crying.

"Helen, dear child," she said, engulfing me in a hug I couldn't escape.

"Thanks, Aunt Lib," I sniffled, unwrapping the gift. It was chocolate, my favorite. I popped one in my mouth, then asked, "Aunt Lib? What becomes of ugly women?"

"What? Why would you ask such a thing at a time like this?"

I'd forgotten Grandma had died. I felt guilty. "I'm sorry. It's just . . . I overheard two women say I wasn't pretty."

"That's bunk! Who would say such a thing? Why, I'll knock their socks off." She sat down beside me and took my hand.

"They didn't truly call me ugly. The lady said I didn't get my mother's good looks. Aunt Libby, why is it so important for women to be beautiful?" I wiped my wet face.

"Listen, Helen. People will try to cut you down your whole life, and they will if you let them. Would it matter if you were ugly? Would God love you any less? Would your family love you any less?"

"No, I guess not," I said.

"Don't go worrying about what folks think of your looks. You're a beautiful girl, two eyes, two legs, and a smile that lights a room. Real beauty comes from inside. Your mother had it, a light that shone through her. If you look inward, you'll have it too."

"Thanks, Aunt Lib," I sniffled.

"Why don't you go to bed? You have another long day ahead of you tomorrow."

"Will you say prayers with me like Grandma used to?" I asked.

"Certainly."

We both closed our eyes.

"May you see God's light on the path ahead
when the road you walk is dark.
May you always hear, even in your hour of sorrow, the gentle singing of the lark.
When times are hard, may hardness never turn
your heart to stone.
May you always remember when the shadows
fall, you do not walk alone."

"That's a beautiful prayer," she smiled.
"Gram taught me that," I said.
She gave me a wink. "It's a beautiful reminder, Helen, that God is always with you. Now remember, tomorrow is a new day."

The next afternoon, Sadie and I sat under the dining room table again, hidden from sight, watching everyone's feet. Uncle Will was talking to someone about Patrick Long.
I had heard that name before. *Patrick Long was my father!* I listened intently. This man told my uncle that he and Patrick's wife had just had another baby, bringing the total to four children.
"I'm happy to hear that. Patrick deserves to be happy. Nice fella," Uncle Will replied.
Nice fella? Whenever I asked Grandma about my father, she would make a face and say, "Helen, he left you as soon as your mother died, and that is all you need to know. We don't talk about your father," yet Uncle Will not only knew him but liked him. This got me wondering.
The remaining nights of the wake, I stayed up late. After Uncle Peter said the closing prayer and rosary, Aunt Carrie

would bring out beer, whiskey, and food for Pap, my uncles, and two relatives who were to stay up all night with Gram.

The idea of people staying up to watch Grandma seemed like a good idea to me, but as soon as I saw the beer and whiskey, I knew Grandma, dead or alive, was more than able to slip past two drunk men up the stairs to my bedroom while I slept. The chair in front of my door would stay.

On the final night, I sang along as Uncle Will's guitar wove through the room, and every face turned toward the music, everyone but Uncle Peter, whose chair stayed empty during those late nights. When the last chord faded, Pap blinked back tears and lifted his whiskey high.

"To Mary!

Together, we all held our glasses high.

"To Mary!" everyone shouted.

THREE

October 15, 1911

Uncle Peter took my hand and led me to Gram's casket. My unbuttoned jacket flapped open in the breeze as I staggered forward, clutching Sadie in one arm and a rose in the other. Around me, the sound of sobbing blurred with the sting of my own tears.

I kissed the rose, just like Uncle Peter said to do, and placed it gently on the lid of Grandma's new home. Pap's hand brushed mine, trembling as he cried beside me. Two more roses fell.

As I was led away, I turned back, kissed my fingers, and blew Gram one last kiss. The same way she did from my bedroom door every night.

"Goodbye, Grandma," I said, my voice barely a whisper.

"Helen, are you with us?"

Sister Mary Regina's grating voice hit me like a smack on the back of the head.

"Yes, Sister!" I said quickly, straightening in my seat and looking back at the board.

I wiped the tears, hoping no one had noticed.

That my teacher hated children was no secret. When she wasn't drilling us on arithmetic or the Bible, she was cracking a ruler across our hands for the slightest mistake. The dunce hat was the worst of it. You wore it in the corner, facing the wall, until dismissal. I glanced around at my fifteen uniformed classmates, each one stiff as a board, eyes forward, pencil in hand.

I didn't have a single friend in the room.

The thought of Gram lying dead in the parlor haunted me, and with Pap back at work, I was terrified to go home. The house would be empty.

Quiet.

Just me and Gram's ghost.

But when I trudged through the front door, ready to lock myself in my bedroom, I heard Uncle Peter calling from the kitchen. His blue eyes looked grayer than I remembered, but he wore a pleasant smile.

"I thought you could use this today," he said, handing me a peppermint stick.

Then came the real surprise.

"An old school friend of mine and his wife in Scranton have invited us for the weekend," he said. "We'll take the *Black Diamond*. It will be a train ride you'll never forget. Aunt Lib is coming to stay with Pap."

My eyes became wide. I'd never ridden on a train. Even Prudence Hamilton, the bratty girl down the street whose father owned the hardware store, had never been on a train. Wait till she found out. And skipping school, just for a day, felt like a sin and a miracle rolled into one.

When I awoke the next morning, I dressed in the outfit Gram had made for the party. I tucked my thick hair under my hat, hiding a nest of snarls I'd uncovered the night before.

I half expected a horse and buggy out front, but waiting at the curb was a sleek black Ford, gleaming in the sun. I'd never been in a car, and when the driver opened the back seat door for me I dove in eagerly with Sadie in hand. This trip was shaping up to be something truly memorable.

When the *Black Diamond* pulled into the station it had only three cars, not nearly as many as I'd imagined, but it still looked proud and majestic, like a train that had traveled over hill and dale, making passengers' dreams come true. Inside, the burgundy seats were soft and plush, and the wood walls had strange carvings, twisting creatures I'd later meet again in nightmares. The floor swirled with gold and green patterns like the cover of a beautifully illustrated fairy tale. It felt like stepping into a moving palace.

I wished Gram could see it. She would've said it smelled too much like cigars and cigarettes, but I bet she would've loved being treated so proper. I looked forward to each whistle blast as we neared the crossings, where gates came down and red lights flashed. Buggies and automobiles lined up, waiting for our train to pass. Some people waved, others gave a salute, and for a moment, it felt like we were royalty, speeding through the world like members of a king's family.

When we dined in the Pullman's elegant car, I sat up straight and crossed my ankles, just like Gram taught me to do. I wanted to make Uncle Peter proud.

Dr. and Mrs. McClatchy were waiting for us at the train station. I didn't like Dr. Brian from the moment I met him. Maybe it was his too-thin mustache, or the way he kept dabbing at his red nose with a wrinkled handkerchief, but something about him made my stomach tighten. His wife, on the other hand, was welcoming and gracious, and I immediately warmed to her.

She had a large, round belly that couldn't be hidden by the fabric of her dress, and when Dr. Brian joked about his wife's condition and mentioned that the new baby would be coming around Christmas time, I could see the sparkle in Mrs. McClatchy's green eyes. This was news to Uncle Peter, who turned all smiles and gave the soon-to-be mother a big kiss on the cheek.

Their home was grand with a fire crackling in the sitting room near the piano. A handsome cake and a shiny pie waited on the dining table. Mrs. McClatchy eagerly offered my uncle a piece of each.

Later in the evening, she impressed us with her piano skills. Uncle Peter and I were completely enchanted.

At some point, I must've drifted off on the sofa, lulled by the fire and the music and the lingering rhythm of the train. When I woke and found my throat dry, I inched toward the kitchen for a drink.

The hallway was dim, but the sound of Uncle Peter's voice and the cigar smoke creeping towards me led the way.

"And now that my mother is gone, I have another task," Uncle Peter said.

"What's that?" Dr. Brian asked.

"One of the last things I said to my sister Sadie was that I would spend the rest of my life watching Helen, guiding her to be a demure, God-fearing, Bible-following woman. I need to take care of her until she finds a husband."

It sounded like one of the men stood, so I quickly snuck back to the parlor where Mrs. McClatchy was finishing a song. I grabbed Sadie from the sofa and asked if I could go to bed.

After Mrs. McClatchy tucked me in, I sat in the dark, holding Sadie, thinking about what my uncle said: "A demure, God-fearing, Bible-following woman."

I had no idea what the word 'demure' meant, but my heart felt full knowing Uncle Peter would always protect me and keep me close to God.

The next day, Mrs. McClatchy and I stayed home, busy in the kitchen preparing dinner and making an apple pie for dessert. Later in the afternoon, when our chores were finished, Mrs. McClatchy announced she had the perfect activity to keep us entertained. She led me into her bedroom, where she pulled out her makeup and showed me some of her beautiful clothes, far more glamorous than my mother's old, moth-eaten dresses that I played with from the trunk in Gram's attic.

Mrs. McClatchy sat me down at a vanity table with a large mirror, its surface scattered with hair adornments and makeup. She picked up a brush and began working on my locks. It only took two or three strokes before the brush snagged. I anxiously awaited her scolding as she lifted my hair and discovered the tangled mess I'd been carefully hiding.

"Helen, you will have to start brushing every day. The longer you let this go, the worse it will get. You wouldn't want to have to cut your beautiful hair."

She worked patiently with a comb for several minutes, and when she was finally done, my hair was snarl-free. I felt a kinship with her. She'd been so gentle, so motherly to me.

Mrs. McClatchy dusted my face with powder, added a little rouge and red cream, and helped me into one of her gowns, pinning it to fit. The boots made me taller, and a dab of rose water behind my ears made me feel like a princess.

When I looked in the mirror, the freckles that usually dotted my face had vanished. The girl staring back looked like a young woman and a pretty one at that. Feeling regal, I descended the staircase with all the poise I could muster, my head held high as I tried not to trip in my new, grown-up clothes. But the instant Uncle Peter's eyes landed on me, my heart sank. I knew I was in trouble.

"What on earth? Go and take that makeup and those clothes off immediately!"

I turned to Mrs. McClatchy, who had worn a proud smile only moments earlier but now seemed to be fighting back the tears.

"I'm so sorry, Peter," she uttered, walking over to me and grabbing my hand. "Helen, let's get you out of these things."

As Mrs. McClatchy escorted me back to her room, the image of Dr. Brian laughing at me flickered through my mind.

"Helen, I'm sorry. I had no idea this would upset your uncle. We must be gentle with him right now. He's still grieving. Men don't cry the way women do." Her voice was sympathetic, but her watery, red eyes revealed how she truly felt.

As she smothered my face in a pleasant-smelling cream from a jar, I looked in the mirror in horror and began to sob. A clown was staring back at me with the salve, makeup, and tears blending to create a patchy mess.

How could this be? Only moments earlier, I had been beautiful! Anger, humiliation, and confusion filled me, and I stewed for the rest of the day, wondering why my uncle had done what he'd done.

At dinner that night, things felt awkward, and I was most unhappy when my uncle asked me to say Grace for the evening meal. I was still upset from earlier, but the thought of the apple pie, with that glistening baked jam on top, helped keep my spirits up.

At the end of our meal, Mrs. McClatchy stood up, holding her pregnant stomach, and said she wasn't feeling well. I saw Dr. Brian roll his eyes and lean back in his chair as she walked from the room. My uncle's face turned concerned. Mrs. McClatchy hadn't said a word during dinner, and I wondered if she was mad at my uncle.

"Time for bed!" Uncle Peter said.

It was only 7:00. Much too early for bed.

He gently grabbed me by the shoulders, urging me from my chair. "What about the apple pie?" I whined, eyeing the enticing dessert on the counter.

"You'll get as big as a house if you keep eating the way you've been, then no man will want you, and what shall I do with you?" he said with a slight chuckle. "Say Goodnight to Dr. Brian."

I did as told and walked to my room, trying mightily to push down the sting from his words.

"Go right to bed now, Helen. I'll see you in the morning. Sleep well. We have a long day tomorrow. I love you to the stars."

"Yes," I replied, avoiding my usual answer.

"I love you to the stars, Helen," he said firmly, waiting for our familiar exchange.

"I love you to the stars and back," I said, though I didn't mean it.

I closed my eyes and tried not to think about the pie, or the way Uncle Peter's eyes had gone cold, or how Mrs. McClatchy had looked like she might cry.

That night, I dreamed Grandma came to visit. Her hair looked like she'd just come from the salon, and she was smiling. At first, I was overjoyed, but then my chest tightened when I realized she had come to say goodbye.

She kissed my forehead and whispered, "Helen, you are strong and brave. You'll be okay." I reached for her, but she turned and walked away.

"Don't leave me, Grandma. Come back!" I shouted.

I woke with a start, my heart pounding. I reached for Sadie and panicked. She wasn't with me.

I feared being scolded for bothering the men if I went to fetch her, but I quickly realized I couldn't sleep without her. I decided to sneak into the parlor. Perhaps the men would be busy in the study or the kitchen.

Light from the hallway glowed beneath my bedroom door. I carefully hopped down off the bed, quietly opened the door, and tiptoed down the hallway. When I arrived in the parlor, I neither heard nor saw anyone. Sadie was sitting on the window seat where I had left her, and I ran to grab her.

Suddenly, I heard, "Why, Helen."

I nearly jumped out of my skin!

Sitting in a chair in the corner of the room was Dr. Brian, having a cocktail, reading a book. Uncle Peter was nowhere to be seen.

"I'm so sorry, Dr. Brian. I forgot my doll," I said, undoubtedly red from his discovery.

"What a nice surprise."

"Where is my uncle?" I said, worried about the inevitable reprimand that was to come.

"He needed some air and will be back shortly," he said, putting his drink and book on the table next to him as I stood, frozen in place, unsure of what to do next.

"It's okay, my dear. You and I need to get better acquainted anyway. You look lovely in your nightdress with your long hair flowing down your back. I'm reminded of how delectable you looked today, dressed in my wife's clothes. Come over here, Helen."

His last sentence was more of an order, and since I didn't want to upset anyone or get into trouble, I did as I was told. I came closer as he looked me over from head to toe. He picked me up, turned me around, and placed me on his lap. He then began to bounce me up and down.

"Do you like that?" he asked.

"Yes, sir," I lied.

His closeness to me seemed odd, but I couldn't be disrespectful or embarrass my uncle. Expressing my true feelings would most certainly backfire on me.

"I'm tired, sir, and would like to go to bed," I said respectfully.

Dr. Brian's face was so close to my ear that I could feel the heat from his breath and smell the whiskey on his lips. He made strange sounds as he bounced me up and down on his lap. His hands moved from my waist to my thighs, and I felt his hands pushing my nightdress up. I closed my eyes, held motionless, when suddenly I heard a door open.

Dr. Brian quickly threw me off his lap.

"Now grab your doll and get back to bed," he said loudly and sternly.

"Helen, what are you doing up?" My uncle demanded as he entered the room.

"I forgot Sadie and couldn't sleep without her," I said, feeling flushed and out of sorts.

"Come now. I will tuck you back in," my uncle said. "Sorry for the bother, Brian."

"No bother at all," Dr. Brian said, calmly looking at his book.

In the morning, Dr. Brian didn't join us for breakfast, which I was grateful for. We walked to St. Andrew's Church, and then Dr. Brian drove us to the train station. He acted as if nothing had happened, which made me wonder if I'd imagined the entire interaction. I was sad to say goodbye to Mrs. McClatchy. However, I hoped I would never see the doctor again.

On the train, I wrestled with saying something to Uncle Peter about Dr. Brian. Finally, I got my nerve up.

"Last night, when I went in to get my doll, Dr. Brian had me sit on his lap," I said.

"That was very nice of Dr. Brian, especially since you were supposed to be sleeping and you were bothering him." Uncle Peter continued reading.

"Well, it didn't feel the same as when I sit on your lap, or Uncle Will's, or Pap's lap. I didn't like it."

"Helen, that is because we are family. Dr. Brian is one of my best friends, and I know he cares deeply about you because you're my niece. That was all. He was trying to be nice." Uncle Peter turned from his book and looked at me with a sour face. "Is that all you can say about our wonderful weekend, young lady?"

"Uncle Peter, I had a very nice time. Thank you for taking me along—us along," I said, giving an extra squeeze to Sadie.

He smirked and asked, "And what will you say when people ask about the McClatchys?"

"They *are* nice people, and we had a wonderful time, sir." This seemed to be what he wanted to hear.

"Very good," he said. "No more strange talk, do you understand? They *are* nice people."

"Yes, Uncle Peter," I said.

The words, "no more strange talk," echoed in my head. I wanted to say more. That it felt wrong. That I didn't like it. But the way Uncle Peter sat back in his seat, arms crossed and jaw tensed, told me he wouldn't listen.

The conversation was over.

Maybe good girls weren't supposed to say when something felt bad. My stomach sank, like I'd done something wrong.

FOUR

October 15–October 31, 1911

As soon as we walked through the door back home at Magnolia Street, I was greeted with, "Take off that finery. Holiday's over, young lady. Now grab a pail and wash all the windows."

I may have strutted up to the house with a bit too much self-importance, all dressed up and fresh from the automobile ride, but Aunt Lib's tone still knocked the breath out of me. Only a week ago, she had been so lovely. Remembering it was Aunt Libby who repeatedly told Gram I needed more chores, I realized I was doomed.

I had no idea how to wash a window. And when I finished, I was certain they looked worse than before. Any warm feelings I'd started to carry for Aunt Lib at the wake were gone.

The day before Halloween, cold rain fell sideways, soaking everything. After school, Aunt Lib and I went to Main Street for errands. I was still mad about the "welcome home" she'd given me, and when she refused to buy me the chocolate candy I wanted at McGregor's, I stewed.

When we boarded the trolley, I sat seven rows behind her, plotting my revenge. I didn't tell her when it was time to get off. Poor Aunt Lib rode straight to the end of the line. She had no extra money for the return fare and had to walk all the way back in the rain.

The devil had slipped out of me, and I ran to meet her. She was drenched and shivering, her shoes soaked through.

"Aunt Lib, I am so sorry," I cried. "I don't know what got into me. Will you ever forgive me?"

She looked tired and cold, but all she said was, "Helen, that was an unkind thing to do." And we walked home together.

The next morning, Pap was waiting.

"That wasn't right, Helen," he said quietly. He never yelled or raised a hand. "You'll go to Confession."

I did. And I told Father Murphy the whole story. Well, most of it. Ten Hail Marys, three Our Fathers, and a kind act for Aunt Lib were all I needed to do to put me back in good standing with God. I'd gotten off easy. Maybe too easy.

The next day, October 31st, I came home from school to find a strange cross of twigs over the door. Inside, the house smelled of baking bread and something sweet bubbling on the stove. The table was set for more than just the three of us.

In the kitchen sat a giant pumpkin with its top cut off, and a counter covered in carrot, potato, and onion peels. Two heavy cast-iron pots simmered on the stove. Aunt Lib was happily chopping vegetables.

"Helen, I'm so glad you're home to help me," she said, pointing to apples and sticks. "Caramel is almost done. You make these, and then we'll carve the Jack-O'-Lantern. You all celebrate Samhain, right?" she asked as she diced an onion.

"Samhain?" I asked.

"Goodness. Shameful. Our ancestors celebrated Samhain for thousands of years."

"You mean Halloween, Aunt Lib."

"Helen, I know the difference."

She launched into the history, and I listened, mesmerized. The veil thinning, the spirits crossing over, the feast for the dead. She spoke like a woman who remembered these stories in her bones.

She handed me an apron. "When you're done with the caramel apples go look in your room. I hung a protective five-pointed star over your bed."

Upstairs on my bed was a witch costume she'd sewn for me, with a matching one for Sadie. A broom leaned beside it. Above the bed, an apple slice dangled from a string, and inside its browned flesh, a five-pointed star gleamed. I scratched my head, wondering how this kind of magic was always hiding in plain sight.

At dinnertime, Aunt Lib insisted that she and Pap wear apple talismans around their necks. I was dressed in my witch costume, hovering uncertainly, unsure where to sit.

What if I accidentally sat on a dead relative's lap?

Aunt Lib guided me to my chair with a wink. I looked around the table and wondered if Grandma was near. My mother? Uncle Albert? Great Aunt Margaret? What about the others whose names I'd seen in the old family Bible Gram kept under her bed?

We passed the bread and hand pies, and Pap poured cider into our cups. Aunt Lib told stories between bites, and I even managed to make them both laugh with an impression of one of Father Murphy's endless homilies. For a little while, it felt like we weren't just three people filling a quiet house. It felt like we were almost a family.

The food warmed us, the candlelight flickered, and Pap's smile returned slow and steady. I couldn't help but think, maybe Gram had found her seat at the table after all.

FIVE

November 6, 1911

Sunday came, and Aunt Lib was once again not feeling well enough to go to church. This would bring her church absences up to three. I was raised to believe you had to be dying to be excused from Sunday Mass.

Uncle Peter stepped into the kitchen after Mass while I was setting the table. I heard him ask Aunt Libby, not quietly, why she hadn't been in church again.

"Peter, there are souls far worse than mine that need saving. My time is my own."

An awkward silence followed. The clink of pots and pans was suddenly too loud.

Looking for things to discuss at dinner, I launched into a cheerful account of Samhain, our feast, the costumes, even the protective talismans Aunt Lib made. I should have noticed Pap shifting in his chair. As soon as I finished bragging about our Halloween and how much fun the three of us had, Uncle Peter got out of his chair and started wagging his finger and yelling at my poor aunt.

"Aunt Lib, you cannot come into this house and teach Helen about paganism. I will not allow this!"

Aunt Lib took a deep breath and, as calm as a warm lake breeze, said, "This is who we are, Peter. These are ancient traditions meant to be remembered, not feared. There is nothing evil about them."

"The only protection we need in life is the protection of our Lord, Jesus Christ! Not this witchcraft that you preach."

"This is not witchcraft. You don't understand it, Peter," she said, her voice steady and sure.

"Oh, I understand, all right. I understand that you don't go to church. I understand that you're filling little Helen's head with the devil's word!" he screamed as he pounded his fist on the table.

Aunt Libby got up and left the table abruptly, and Pap shouted, "Peter, I won't have you speaking to your aunt like that!"

"Pa, this is unacceptable. Completely unacceptable!" Peter shouted at the top of his lungs. With that, he grabbed his jacket and stormed out of the house.

Feeling as though I had caused this entire mess, I ran up to my room, curled up on the floor next to my door with Sadie, and cried. After that Sunday, Uncle Peter stopped coming over for dinner, and the only time I saw him was at my school or church.

In the meantime, Aunt Libby kept me busy. She taught me how to use Grandma's sewing machine, which sat in the front window of our house, how to knit on four needles—not an easy thing to master—and also how to crochet, darn socks, cook, and bake. She showed such faith in me that I felt able to do almost anything.

One night, after prayers, I asked her a question that had been weighing on me.

"Why would God take Grandma and my mother away from me?"

Her eyes shimmered, and her usually loud voice turned quiet. She reached out and tucked a strand of hair behind my ear.

"Dear, I'm not sure. But I believe those who leave us are never far. Although we may not see them, they're still here with us, loving us, supporting us, helping us whenever they're able. Dying is confusing, but love, real love, stays with us, always."

Night after night, I'd go into Aunt Lib's room, hand her my brush, and we'd talk as she shined up my hair. It seemed that Aunt Lib knew a little about everything, and I was eager to learn as much from her as possible.

I deeply enjoyed her stories and would have her repeat how Pap had bought my mother a pony and wagon for her twelfth birthday and how my mother would sneak downstairs to let her brothers in after curfew when they got locked out.

It was hard to believe that my Uncle Peter had ever broken the rules, and knowing this made me feel closer to him.

Another story was how my mother had gone to work at a knitting factory at the age of fourteen to help save for Uncle Albert's seminary education. Aunt Lib said it was Albert, not Peter, who was supposed to wear the collar until his death changed everything.

"Peter promised your grandmother on the day of Albert's funeral that he'd fulfill her dream. The family knew William wouldn't last a week at the seminary," she said with a small laugh. "Peter says being a priest is a sacrifice. I think now that you're old enough to understand, it may not have been entirely his choice."

"Everyone loved your mother, Helen, but she and Peter were especially close. In her last moments, he promised her he'd watch over you, always." Aunt Lib raised her eyebrows and shook her head slightly. "My nephew and his deathbed promises."

One night, I finally asked, "What about my father?"

She met my question with one of her own. "What do you know about him?"

"That he was so distraught after my mother died that he left a week later and no one ever heard from him again, but I know that's not true."

"What makes you say that?"

"I overheard Uncle Will at the wake. He told someone that my father has a new wife and four children."

Aunt Lib set the brush down and looked at me.

"Now that your grandmother is gone, I'll tell you something—but you must never tell Pap or your uncles. Do you promise?"

"Certainly. I won't ever tell a soul," I said firmly, believing I never would.

"Your father, Patrick, was a wonderful man. A horticulturist. He grew flowers—roses, mostly. He fought in the Spanish-American War. Brave and kind. A real gentleman. He adored your mother. You could see it in the way he looked at her." She glanced toward the window, her voice softening. "After your mother died, he brought you to your grandparents' every day and picked you up after work. He tried so hard to care for you."

"He did?" I whispered.

"He did. But one day, a few months later, your grand-mother refused to give you back. She convinced him he couldn't raise you alone. And he, grieving and overwhelmed, gave in. He didn't want to. He loved you very much."

I sat in stunned silence. Stolen? From my own father?

"Helen, your grandmother thought she was doing the right thing. She'd just lost her daughter. She was terrified he'd remarry, move away, and she'd lose you, too. And Peter, well, he never thought Patrick was good enough. I may be saying too much. I just don't want you thinking your father didn't love you."

She dabbed her eyes with a handkerchief.

"Why wouldn't he come for me?"

"He probably believes you were lost to him for good."

She pulled me close.

"I hope your grandmother won't curse me now. God rest her soul. But I couldn't go to my grave knowing you believed your father had stopped loving you."

As our bond deepened, so did my questions.

"Aunt Lib, why don't you go to church? Aren't you afraid you'll go to—" I whispered, "Hell?"

She smiled gently. "Church is good for many people, but I talk to God every day. I thank Him when I wake, and I pray for my loved ones. I don't need a building to do that."

"But the Bible says you have to go to church."

"There's wisdom in the Bible, yes. But not all of it. I've seen enough Hell on Earth to know we don't need to wait for the next life to find it."

She tickled my side, and I squirmed and giggled, then fired off another question. "Aunt Lib, what does demure mean?"

"Demure?" She smirked. "That's when a woman keeps her mouth shut. I've never been demure and never will be."

I didn't like the idea of having to keep my mouth shut.

"Can men be demure?" I asked.

"No, Helen. Being demure is only for women." She began brushing my hair firmer.

"So, men don't have to keep their mouths shut?"

"Sometimes they absolutely should," she said, "but when they do, they're called cowardly or pigeon-livered, not demure."

I wrinkled my nose. "Well, that's not fair."

"Helen," she said, "you need to speak your mind." Her face shifted, tense, almost sad. "Demure women turn into doormats. You don't want to be anyone's doormat."

"Golly, no," I said.

"Take voting, for example. A demure woman wouldn't believe she should vote. But one day, she'll hopefully learn her opinion matters just as much as any man's," Aunt Lib said.

Her words, "her opinion matters just as much as any man's," replayed in my head. I liked that kind of thinking. I certainly didn't want to be anyone's doormat. My skin grew hot as I added two and two.

"Why would Uncle Peter want me to be demure?"

Aunt Lib became silent and bit her lip.

"Best that you go off to bed now," she said, without answering.

It would be a long time before I truly understood why my uncle wanted me to be demure. But in time, I would.

The following night, I desperately wanted to know if Aunt Lib lived in the hospital because she was sick.

"Oh no, darling. Your great-grandfather took care of me. Thanks to him, I can live there the rest of my life," she said, as the brush glided across my hair.

"The rest of your life? Won't you be staying here with us?"

She smiled. Not sad, but far away. And instead of answering, she began a story.

"Your great-grandfather built a little house on his farmland for Margaret and me. We used to take your mother and uncles fishing in the creek, bake cookies, and make crafts. We made beautiful memories." Her voice softened.

"After Margaret died, I became very sad. Melancholy, they called it. The farmhouse felt too big. Life felt too big. So, your grandfather helped me move to the state hospital." She looked down at her hands. "I miss Margaret every day. I'm sorry you never knew her. She was wonderful."

I hadn't known Aunt Lib suffered from melancholy. When Grandma knew Pap wasn't listening, she'd whisper to Uncle Peter or her friends that Aunt Lib was a little batty. It broke my heart to think Grandma never understood that Aunt Libby wasn't crazy. She was just sad.

"Do you like it here, Aunt Lib?"

She pulled me close. And, like she so often did, she ignored my question.

"My dear Helen," she said softly, "I love you very much."

A few days later, after walking home from school, I entered the house and found Aunt Lib still in bed, her eyes red and swollen. She looked like she'd been crying all day. My stomach twisted imagining the worst.

She didn't sit up when I entered, just opened her arms. I rushed into them, and she held me tight, rocking me the way she used to when I missed Grandma so bad I couldn't breathe.

"Helen," she whispered, her voice ragged, "I love you so much, my little darling, but I have to leave. I'm going back to the hospital. It's where I belong."

She pulled back, put her hands gently on both sides of my face, and tried to smile, saying it was what was best. I stared at her, wanting it not to be true.

The night before, I'd heard arguing downstairs. Uncle Peter had come over, said something in a low, sharp voice, and left not long after. I'd pressed my ear to the door but couldn't make out the words. Now I thought I knew.

My throat burned. "Are you leaving because of Uncle Peter?"

Aunt Lib gave a weak laugh and stroked my hair. "Helen, you're brave. Braver than you know. Sometimes we don't feel it until we're asked to prove it."

But she hadn't answered my question.

"Uncle Peter is making you leave, isn't he?" I blurted.

This time, she didn't ignore my question. She just nodded slowly and pulled me close again. I felt her chest rise and fall in uneven waves.

"He means well," she said, her voice turning to a whisper. "But he thinks I'm not good for you. He even suggested you live with a family from his parish. Your grandfather said no. He promised me he'd keep you here, safe." She kissed the top of my head, and her tears soaked quietly into my hair.

"You can't leave me," I cried. "What will I do without you?"

We sat holding each other for a long time until our breathing evened out and our tears dried on each other's cheeks. Then Aunt Lib reached into her bedside drawer and pulled out a small black box.

"I want to leave you something," she said, placing it in my hand. I clutched it to my chest.

"Go on now," she coaxed. "Open it."

Inside was a gold band with a deep garnet, glowing red like a drop of fire.

"This was Brigid's wedding ring, my mother's mother,

your great-great-grandmother. It went to Margaret first, and when she passed, it came to me. And now to you. You're the only girl left in the family. It's yours." She took it from the box and placed it in my palm. "Brigid Hogan came over from County Clare in 1833, just fourteen years old, scared out of her wits but strong as iron. Her parents saved all year for her ship fare. She arrived with nothing but a priest's name and a prayer in her pocket."

She turned the ring over gently in my hand.

"I was told Brigid was determined and courageous, maybe a little like you. When you wear this ring, I want you to remember where you come from. You can survive anything. And may you always remember, *when the shadows fall, you do not walk alone.*"

She looked into my eyes. "Your ancestors are with you, Helen. Always guiding, guarding, and watching over you. Just ask, and they'll be there."

I slipped the ring onto the forefinger of my left hand. It fit like it had been waiting for me, for generations, maybe. I felt different with it on, as if, like magic, I was now stronger, steadier. I felt protected.

The next day, Pap and I packed Aunt Lib's trunk and rode in the surrey to the hospital in Brighton. He didn't say much. I didn't either. I think we were both afraid that if we spoke, we'd come undone.

When we arrived, nurses and staff gathered around Aunt Lib as if she were royalty returned. They laughed and cheerfully called out her name, many of them hugging her. It was clear she was deeply loved there. But I loved her more.

On the way home, I sat quietly beside Pap, the ring snug on my finger, my eyes filled with tears. I stared out the window, the trees rushing by in a blur of gray and gold. All

I wanted was to go back, to sit at the table with Gram and Aunt Libby and Pap, and pretend none of this ever happened.

But then I looked down at the ring. The garnet glinted in the afternoon light, and I remembered what Aunt Lib had told me about Brigid Hogan, who at fourteen traveled across the Atlantic Ocean to America all by herself. She left everything behind for a new tomorrow.

In my dream, Gram told me I was brave. Aunt Lib had said the same, that I could survive anything. My aunt told me not to forget where I came from and that my ancestors were with me, guiding and protecting me.

The knot that had formed in my throat didn't go away, but I sat a little straighter. I would keep going, even though I didn't know what came next.

I'd wear the ring.

And I wouldn't forget whose blood ran through my veins.

SIX

December 1911

I was angry, thinking that my aunt had been forced to leave because of my uncle's dislike for her. I never said anything to him, though, unsure of what his reaction would be. The twelve days leading up to Christmas were the most trying days of my life. Luckily, I had two things that kept me going: being good for Santa Claus and ensuring everything went smoothly so Uncle Peter wouldn't decide to send me away. The idea of being sent to live with strangers terrified me.

Being the "lady of the house" while also a fourth-grade student was challenging without any support. Grandma or Aunt Lib had kept house, made dinner, and helped me with my nightly homework. Now, I was forced to make dinner for Pap and me, clean up, complete my schoolwork by myself, get myself ready for bed, keep myself clean, and get ready for school in the morning.

I was having a grueling time keeping up with everything. Pap seemed very down and started drinking a lot after Aunt Libby left. He had promised he would care for me, but that promise had already been broken.

"Helen, I'm going out to say hi to the boys. I'll be back before long," he would say after dinner, then disappear until I was asleep.

I was afraid to ask Sister Mary Regina for help. Aside from being horridly mean, she knew my uncle. I didn't want her to think my grandfather wasn't taking good care of me. I had to ensure information like that didn't get back to Uncle Peter, and I did my darnedest to hide my melancholy from her.

Multiple times a day, I looked at great-great-grandmother Brigid's ring, turned it twice, and said Grandma's prayer. This helped a little, but wasn't enough to soothe the gnawing ache I felt. Sadly, the holiday would just be Pap and me.

On Christmas Eve, I made apple pie just like Grandma had done, thanks to Aunt Lib's training. I placed a slice on one of Grandma's delicate china dishes, along with a note for Santa listing everything I wanted for Christmas.

I asked for many things, including a shiny pair of shoes I saw in the window of B. Forman's Department Store on Clinton Street, new matching dresses for me and Sadie, a doll-size stove, games, a small piano, and pretty hair ribbons and barrettes from McGregor's.

At the top of my list, I wrote: Please bring Grandma and Aunt Lib back. I knew this wouldn't happen, but I included it anyway, figuring it couldn't hurt to ask. Next to the pie and letter, I placed Pap's present, something I had made, wrapped in fabric and tied with one of my finest hair ribbons.

I awoke early Christmas morning, buzzing with excitement I hadn't felt in months. Grandma forbade me from looking in the parlor where Santa had been, so I knew to go straight into Pap's room to wake him first. I sat on the wooden chair with Sadie on my lap next to Pap's bed, hoping to hurry him out of his slumber. As I looked around the room, I noticed Gram's nightdress still hanging in the open closet. Pap hadn't yet brought himself to take it down. My heart dropped.

I didn't want to be sad on Christmas morning. I tried to dream instead of all the wonderful things Santa may have brought me. When I couldn't stand the wait another second, I started singing "Silent Night" to wake Pap. Slowly, life returned to his unshaven face.

"I think there's an angel in my room. Who's that singing?" he said, smiling as his squinty eyes adjusted to the light. "Merry Christmas, my dear."

Pap finally got out of bed and put on his robe and slippers. Almost ready to burst, I led him downstairs into the parlor, expecting a large, green tree with many big and small presents wrapped in different colors with beautiful ribbons and bows resting beneath. My stocking, which Grandma had knitted, would be loaded with the tiniest of treasures, and there would be colorful Christmas decorations throughout the downstairs.

But that wasn't what I saw. There was no tree. Nor were there any decorations, and my stocking hanging from the stove looked very thin. On the table lay my present for Pap, along with crumbs on the plate that held the apple pie from the night before. On the chair was a small present. One little present.

I swallowed hard.

"I'm sorry, Helen. I know this isn't what you expected for

Christmas. Grandma was Christmas, you know," Pap said with a cracking voice as he walked into the kitchen to prod the coal range.

I believed in Santa Claus until I walked into that room that morning. Honestly, I did. Even though kids at school would talk and say Santa wasn't real, I never believed them.

I quickly understood Pap was telling the truth. Grandma was Christmas, and Santa Claus, and everything else special about the holiday. Not only had I lost Grandma, but I had lost Santa Claus, too. Trying desperately to not ruin the day, I grabbed the present I had made and handed it to him when he returned to the room.

"Here, Pap. I made this for you," I said, voice trembling.

Every Christmas, Grandma and I would go shopping together and get something for Pap from the two of us. This year, I looked through all of Grandma's candy recipes. She had so many tasty choices, but I decided upon pecan pralines since I had all the ingredients: molasses, butter, brown sugar, and vinegar. As Pap untied the red bow on the cloth wrapping and opened the box, a smile lit up his face.

"Wonderful!" he said, taking his time to find the best piece. "Helen, you made these?"

His smile turned to tears after eating one, and I wondered what I had done wrong. Had I mixed up the sugar and salt again?

"Pap, are they horrible?"

He laughed. Pap had a good sense of humor, and I loved him with every part of me when he wasn't drunk. "Darlin', they are most perfect. You've outdone yourself. It's only that they are so close to your grandmother's that it makes my heart a bit heavy."

Wiping the tears from his eyes, Pap handed me a small, neatly wrapped rectangular package.

"I have a little something for you also, my dear." I shook it to see if I could guess what was inside. A book, I thought. Definitely a book.

I untied the gold bow and tore through the paper to get to the prize inside, an Elsie Dinsmore book, one I hadn't read yet. I was pleased, but I couldn't help feeling let down that it might be my only gift. The thought of opening my stocking after Christmas Mass offered a flicker of hope, though not much comfort.

I got dressed for church and ran downstairs to get Pap. He was moving leisurely, and I had to hurry him along so we wouldn't be late. The children's choir would be singing "Silent Night" and "Adeste Fidelis," and I had to put on my choral cape and meet Sister Teresa and the others before the service.

After Mass, Uncle Peter kissed and hugged me and told Pap to treat me special since it was Christmas.

"I'll try to get over as soon as possible, but I have a lot of people I have to visit today. Be a good girl," my uncle said with a wave goodbye.

When we got home, we ate scones I had made with butter and homemade jelly Gram had made over the summer. My grandparents canned and pickled what they could through-out the year in anticipation of a harsh winter. Often, the snow would get so high, or the ruts in the road would freeze, that it became impossible for the carriages to reach the market.

"Pap, it's time to open my stocking!" I said, spreading a quilt on the floor, still hopeful for more gifts.

I reached into the sock, knowing that the best surprises often came in the smallest packages. I found some pepper-mints and penny candy from the store down the street and then, feeling something round and heavy at the bottom, pulled out an orange. The disappointment burned hot and sharp. I began to cry. Pap exited the room, cleaned himself up, and opened the front door.

"Helen, I'll be back soon."

I had gone to the store the day before, emptying Grandma's money jar. I bought ingredients to make chicken fricassee, mashed potatoes, turnips, and cornstarch pudding, and brought up some relishes from the basement. It wasn't the kind of Christmas dinner Grandma or even Aunt Lib would have made, but it was what I knew how to prepare. I was proud of it.

Sadie and I sat at the beautifully set table with my ironed and starched tablecloth, napkins, and Grandma's Haviland China. I even folded the napkins into triangles, just like she had shown me. We waited, but neither Pap nor Uncle Peter came home.

Our only company that day was the old clock, dinging on the half hour and the hour as we sat, waiting.

Whenever I tried to convince myself to walk over to say hello to the Kellys, the forbidden neighbors who had been so kind when Gram died, a voice in my head would yell at me, "Uncle Peter will be angry at you!"

So, Sadie and I cozied up on the itchy couch with a blanket, and I read my new Elsie Dinsmore book aloud. Finally, late in the evening, Uncle Peter showed up at the door with a bag of gifts. There was no hiding the cold dinner on the table or the missing Christmas tree and decorations, nor was there any evidence of unwrapped presents. I feared the worst, knowing it didn't reflect well on Pap.

I dove into the pile of gifts, unwrapping each one with growing delight. They were practical yet beautiful things: a new winter coat, a wool dress with an embroidered collar, a warm hat, cashmere-lined gloves, polished black boots, and a delicate set of rosary beads. Last year's coat barely buttoned, and my boots had been pinching my toes since early November.

I slipped on the new items, each piece fitting as if it had been made just for me. Then we climbed into my uncle's sleek black Ford, the one recently purchased by Immaculate Conception Church for him, Father Murphy, and Father Reilly to share.

The homes we visited were warm and festive, filled with soft lights and the scent of roasted meat and pine. Everyone greeted my uncle like royalty. They pressed expensive gifts into his hands: a gleaming silver crucifix, a thick leather Bible, a gold tie bar nestled in a velvet box. By evening's end, I was tired from smiling, not biting my nails, and saying all the right things.

When we got home, I shuddered, knowing Pap was in for it. Uncle Peter hadn't bothered to hide his anger all evening, especially about me being left alone on Christmas, of all days.

Pap slouched in his chair, an empty glass in his hand, staring off at a lit candle. Now looking more like the man I'd seen the day Grandma died. I walked over, kissed him goodnight, and caught a strong whiff of whiskey. His stare didn't change. I turned without a word and headed upstairs, knowing my bed was the best place for me.

I was beginning to see a different Pap than the one I'd known when Grandma was alive. He wouldn't have let himself go like this, not if she were still here, or if Aunt Libby still lived with us.

I climbed into bed and pulled Sadie close. Her glass eyes stared at the ceiling while I lay still, heart thudding, listening to the voices rising below. Uncle Peter's words rang out—hard and final.

"She can't stay here any longer."

I heard Pap crying. I clutched Sadie and shut my eyes tight, trying to wish away the sound. As difficult as it had

been with Pap these past three weeks, the thought of leaving
him or my home to live with strangers made me sick. Whatever a "mommy's little helper" was, I wanted no part of it.

The next day, Uncle Peter came by to deliver the news. I
begged him to let me stay. I even asked if I could live at the
rectory. That wasn't an option.

I tried to give him reasons. Pap had come home for dinner two nights in a row. He had even tucked me in and said
prayers with me. But none of that seemed to matter. Uncle
Peter's mind was made up. It was too late.

Unfortunately, the two days leading up to my departure
went quickly, and with a bag in one hand and Sadie in the
other, we left the only home I had ever known. We got into
Uncle Peter's Ford, and when I looked out the window, I
noticed the snotty Hamilton children all bundled up playing
in their front yard, several Christmas trees on the side of
the road, and smoke coming from the chimney tops of the
houses. I became weepy thinking I'd never return.

Pap hadn't said a proper goodbye to me. I didn't understand this, but as we drove away, I turned around and saw
him on the porch that frigid January morning, with no coat,
waving to me with his handkerchief, crying.

I waved back frantically until I could no longer see him
from the large backseat window, and then watched as the
road behind us disappeared. A pitiful sound left me.

From the front seat, Uncle Peter barked, "This is for your
own good. Now stop that crying."

SEVEN

Late December 1911

The Allens still had their Christmas decorations up, some wreaths, garland, and a Christmas tree. Grandma always kept decorations until January 6th, which was the Feast of the Epiphany, or as we called it, Little Christmas. Oddly, it gave me some comfort.

"You mustn't cry, Helen," my uncle demanded, handing me his handkerchief to blow my nose. "You don't want to upset the Allens. This needs to work!"

I blew my nose and patted the remaining tears from my eyes, trying to put on a happy face for these strangers who were to become my new family. I twisted my ring twice and said a little prayer as I struggled to get out of the car. Led by Uncle Peter, Sadie and I slowly moseyed up to the large front doors. My uncle rang the doorbell, something we didn't have at Magnolia Street.

A thin, mousy woman answered the door wearing a gray dress that went up to her neck and down to her wrists and ankles. She was about Aunt Carrie's age and wore her brown hair pulled back in a bun that seemed too tight.

"Hello, Father. Why this must be, Helen?" she said.

"Yes, Gertrude, this is my niece. What do you say to Mrs. Allen, Helen?" he prodded.

"Pleased to make your acquaintance, ma'am," I said with a little sniffle.

"Mr. Allen is at work and won't be home until dinner," she said. "Excuse me. Girls, oh girls, come down. Helen is here!" she called up the stairs.

Two young girls came storming down, wearing dresses that looked more like church dresses than play clothes.

"Helen, this is Madeline, and this is Catherine," she said.

Madeline, the four-year-old, smiled politely. "Nice to meet you, Helen," she said.

The six-year-old Catherine grabbed Sadie right out of my hands without asking. "Can I play with her? Please, oh, please?" she whined to her mother, petting Sadie's frilly hat.

"Sadie is mine," I said, snatching her back and holding her tight.

Mrs. Allen raised her eyebrows.

"Helen!" Uncle Peter said, his sharp tone sending a shiver up my spine. "Of course, the girls can play with your doll. Gertrude, I'm sure they'll be close friends in no time."

"I guess you can play with her, Catherine," I muttered, knowing I had no choice.

Inside, I wanted to explode. How dare she! I envisioned pushing the horrid girl to the floor as her little crocodile hands reached for my beloved doll. I bit down on the inside of my mouth, took a deep breath, and held Sadie up like Mary handing over the baby Jesus to King Herod.

"She is so pretty," said Catherine, holding Sadie close and kissing her.

"Her hair matches yours, Helen," said little Madeline sweetly while her sister touched and fussed with the bundle in her arms.

I forced a smile. Madeline, with her blond curly hair and chubby baby face, looked more like one of the cherubs painted on the walls of our church than a real child. Nothing like her sister, who looked like a miniature version of her mother.

"Let us show you two around the house," Mrs. Allen said as she walked to the kitchen. "You girls go and play with the doll in your room. Helen will be up shortly."

Fear twisted in my gut as I watched Sadie disappear from sight. I bit my nails, but Uncle Peter caught my hand and shot me a look. I said a prayer to the Virgin Mary to protect Sadie, terrified her delicate fingers would be snapped off, or her face cracked.

I tried to focus on the house: carpeted stairs, a lit fireplace in the parlor, an ornate tree with unwrapped toys beneath. The dark carved wood reminded me of the *Black Diamond*. The hanging lamps were sparkly and elegant, though not as beautiful as those on the train. The dining room had a long table, much larger than ours, framed by pink drapes and matching wallpaper. The kitchen was much larger than ours and even housed the latest range. Everything, everywhere I looked, was bigger, newer, and fancier than back home.

I went upstairs to see my room, which I expected to be at least as good as my room at Magnolia Street. However, Mrs. Allen opened the door to what seemed to be nothing more than a spacious closet. In the small box of a room stood a bed not much bigger than for a large doll, with an equally tiny table, and an oil lantern hanging from the ceiling that I wouldn't be able to reach. The room had four hooks where I was to hang all of my clothes.

"Helen, this was my sewing room until I received your uncle's call a few days ago. I decided to move my things into my bedroom. We had this sweet bed in the attic. It will fit you fine. I am happy to sew in my bedroom if it means having you here with us."

Guilt welled inside me as she spoke. She was being generous, after all. Uncle Peter put my bag on the bed, and the girls entered.

"Come, Helen. You must see my room," Catherine insisted.

Her room was grand, with a bed fit for a princess. I spotted Sadie tossed on the floor and quickly scooped her up while Catherine bragged about her toys. Madeline then led us to her room, which was just as grand. My blood simmered. I tugged on Uncle Peter's sleeve, but he ignored me.

When it was time for him to return to the rectory, panic set in. I imagined dropping to the floor and wrapping myself around his legs so he couldn't leave. But instead, I took his hand and held it tightly as we stepped out onto the porch.

"Thank you, Gertrude. Call if you need anything at all," he said.

He kissed me goodbye. I held on as long as I could, then let go, reluctantly. It took everything in me not to run after him as he got into the car and drove away.

How could he just leave me here?

I stood alone, watching his black car turn the corner. My breathing became shallow, and my tears froze on my cheeks.

"Come in, Helen, you'll catch your death." Mrs. Allen grabbed me by the shoulders and led me into the house. "You'll like it here. As your uncle said, it might take some getting used to, but you and the girls will be best friends in no time. Now go play with the girls for a bit and get better acquainted."

The next day, school started again after the holiday break, and I was expected to walk with Catherine to Immaculate Heart Conception. It was a bit farther than Magnolia Street, but if we didn't stop to dilly-dally, we could make it in twenty-five minutes. We were bundled in so many layers, we could barely move.

Mrs. Allen had told me to hold Catherine's hand the whole way there and back. I refused. I certainly didn't want people thinking she was my sister, and told Catherine to walk behind me. That didn't go over well. Catherine came home crying, and I got a good spanking on my very first day.

As time passed, my dislike for this girl only grew. Catherine delighted in getting me into trouble. On days I couldn't bring myself to hold her leprous hand because of my complete and utter dislike, I took my spankings bravely.

By the end of February, I was painfully homesick. Mrs. Allen always believed whatever story Catherine told about me, and her daughters got the best of everything. With Mr. Allen away on business trips so often, his wife spent hours locked away in her room, "resting." This left me to care for the children whenever I wasn't in school or choir practice.

Pap and Uncle Peter visited from time to time but never stayed long. Their quick appearances were small comforts in a house that never quite felt like mine. Mr. Allen seemed to come home later and later over the following months. Several trips arose, taking him out of town for weeks at a time. Those days, Mrs. Allen didn't get out of bed all day and complained about not feeling well.

One day in June, on an excursion downtown with Mrs. Allen and the girls, we were confronted by a group of women handing out flyers. One man walked by and shouted to the group, "Go back home to your husband and children." Mrs. Allen quickly directed us to cross the street, but one woman ran up to us and handed a flyer to Mrs. Allen. I believed this woman to be my neighbor from Magnolia Street, the mother of the young Kelly girl I was repeatedly told to stay away from.

Mrs. Allen mumbled, "For goodness' sake," and reluctantly took the paper, pushing it into her dress pocket.

Later that day, I asked why that man had said what he said to the women with the flyers. Mrs. Allen responded, "Women need to know their place in this world. That's all, Helen. Don't go trying to be a lion when you are just a house cat."

In July, everything got worse. Catherine promised she'd get revenge because I wouldn't let her play with Sadie. Since the awful day she nearly dropped my doll out the window, I'd been hiding Sadie in the hallway linen closet. But rushing to get dinner started, I tucked her under my bed instead.

When I came back from making dinner, I nearly collapsed at the sight. Sadie was sitting on my bed, her long curly red hair chopped to bits. She was ugly and now looked like a boy.

I stormed into Catherine's room and shoved her onto her bed, screaming that I hated her. Mrs. Allen rushed in, yanked me by the hair, pulled me over her knee, and spanked me hard. Mrs. Allen wouldn't listen to what her perfect little Catherine had done.

That night, angrier than I'd ever been, I made a terrible wish. I wished that Mrs. Allen would be punished and that Catherine would suffer. They were unholy thoughts, most certainly, and the very next morning, that devil on my shoulder must have been smiling because Mrs. Allen didn't get out of bed.

Mrs. Allen looked pale and weak, her skin clammy, her breathing shallow. She had a bad cough and said she was too tired to rise. Mr. Allen had to leave for the mill, so I stayed behind to care for her, bathing her, feeding her broth, wiping her forehead with a damp cloth.

The doctor came and left behind a bottle of medicine, but it didn't help. Within days, her breathing worsened. Her chest rattled, and she could barely speak above a whisper. The doctor returned, this time with grave news. She had pneumonia and needed to go to the hospital.

Her mother arrived from Trenton, and I did what I could to keep Madeline and Catherine fed, dressed, and out of their father's hair. Mr. Allen spent his days at the hospital, while the grandmother came and went, trying to manage what she could at the house.

A few days after Mrs. Allen entered the hospital, Mr. Allen came home looking ashen and drawn. That same day, my own cough began. I was feverish and dizzy, but I didn't say a word. I told myself to soldier through. That evening, Mr. Allen gathered us all in the parlor.

"Your mother has gone to be with the angels," he said.

I nearly keeled over. Blessed Mother Mary, I had killed her.

Catherine and Madeline began to wail. I sat frozen, my thoughts racing. I had made this happen. In a moment of fury, I had asked for this. Now it had come true.

That night in bed, I cried into my pillow and begged God to take me instead. I imagined myself descending into the underworld, certain that was where I belonged. I was wicked, and now, two girls were motherless. After experiencing Grandma's death, I knew my wish for Catherine to have a lifetime of suffering was now certain.

The next morning, upon waking, I couldn't lift my head. The days that followed were a blur. My chest ached. I coughed until I couldn't breathe. I drifted in and out of sleep, fevered and trembling. Somewhere in that haze, I heard little voices crying outside my door. Then—nothing.

When I finally awoke, I was in my old bed. Aunt Carrie, of all people, was sitting beside me, spooning broth into my mouth. I was told I nearly died and had even received Last Rites.

Grandma used to say, "Be careful what you wish for."

Aunt Carrie had taken the train from Buffalo to Rochester to nurse me back to health. Uncle Will stayed behind to work, and I later learned Uncle Peter had slept in a chair beside my bed for days while I drifted between life and death.

About three weeks after returning home, when I was stronger but still too weak to read or get out of bed, Aunt Carrie came in one morning with some news.

"I met a lovely neighbor," she said, fluffing my pillows. "Her daughter would like to come read to you. Would that be all right?"

I nodded, eager to have company. The next day, as I woke from a nap, Aunt Carrie entered the room with a girl behind her.

"Helen, this is Olive. I'll leave you two girls to get to know each other. Call me if you need anything."

She closed the door, and I opened my eyes to see someone standing there like an angel with the light from the window shining behind them. At first, I thought Olive was a boy and that I must have confused the name, but as I focused my eyes better, I could see that Olive was indeed a girl.

She was about my age, maybe older, with dark hair piled

on top of her head and held by a boy's cap. She was wearing trousers (trousers!). She had large brown eyes with thick dark lashes and lips that looked like she may have worn makeup, although I doubted this. Her cheeks were pink as if she had just run around the block, and she was a good hand taller than me.

After all the dull, tiresome time alone in bed, I was excited to see someone around the same age as me. She was the most confident, curious-looking girl I'd ever seen, and I was completely mesmerized until I looked a bit closer.

Neighbor? Why this wasn't just any neighbor.

Standing before me was the granddaughter of the dreaded Kellys, the family next door. The daughter of the woman handing out the suffrage flyers downtown. The very person I'd always been forbidden to talk to.

"Hi," she said with a smile. "I'm Olive Kelly."

EIGHT

August 1912

I stared in disbelief. So, this was Olive Kelly.

I thought back to the many times I'd caught glimpses of her visits next door. In my mind, she'd always been some sort of villain—like the ones from fairy tales. But she was much too pretty for that.

"Your aunt told my mother you've been quite ill. You almost died," she said sincerely.

I shrugged, like that wasn't a big deal.

"I'm glad you didn't. I've always wanted to meet you, and finally, here we are," she said.

Under no condition was I supposed to speak to this girl. And yet, here she was. Tall, graceful. Dressed like a boy. Moving around my room like she belonged in it. I watched her with an uneasy feeling, half hypnotized, half horrified, as she floated from shelf to shelf, touching my books, peeking into my dollhouse.

"What do you call this wamakadoo?" she asked, picking up a wand I'd made with Grandma the year before from a stick, leaves, and some feathers.

I said the strange word silently to myself. *Wamakadoo.* It was odd, but I liked the way it sounded.

"It's a fairy wand, isn't it? How marvelous," she said.

She must have gathered I was too sick to talk because she kept right on.

"I would love to go looking for fairies with you someday. Can we do that, Helen? It would be such fun foraging through the woods and finding fairy rings."

Foraging through the woods? How did she know how much I loved that? Something in me stirred. It had been so long since I'd gone looking for fairies. I didn't want Olive to be bad. I kept reminding myself that Uncle Peter must know something I didn't—that he was trying to protect me.

Olive walked over to Sadie and carefully picked her up. The Allen girls had been so horrible to Sadie, but Olive wasn't like them. She was gentle, as though she knew how special Sadie was to me.

"How pretty she is. She looks just like you, Helen, except with short hair."

Pretty?

"Confident girls cut their hair," she said. "Someday, I shall chop all mine off. I'm sure of it." She smiled and placed Sadie back beside me. "What shall we read today, Helen?" she asked, pulling off her cap. Her dark hair spilled over her shoulders like nighttime. I was spellbound.

I motioned to my bookshelf. Maybe it would be all right if she read to me for a bit. After all, I had been so lonely. And maybe Uncle Peter wouldn't visit today. Olive picked up a book titled *The Nicest Girl in the School.*

"Hmm, these all look kind of . . ." She made a face. I don't think she meant to, but I could tell she wasn't impressed. Then—"Oh look, *The Wonderful Wizard of Oz!* I'd love to read it again. The illustrations are beautiful. Don't you think, Helen?"

Aunt Lib had given me the book, and I had read it while a prisoner at the Allens. I had enjoyed it.

"Do you want me to read this to you?"

I shook my head. I didn't want to reread it, and that seemed to disappoint her.

"Maybe I can borrow it someday," she said.

Over my dead body, I thought.

"How 'bout if I run to my house and grab some of my favorites? You'll like them, I'm sure of it. I love to read. My mother teaches me, you know. I have never gone to a 'real' school like you. You go to that Parochial school, don't you?"

She spoke fast, barely stopping to breathe. I replied, "Yes," then quickly pinched myself under my bedsheets, remembering my pledge of silence.

"I'm sure we will be great friends, you and me. I'll run over and be back in a minute."

Great friends?

I'd never really had one, except for Sadie. It would be nice to have a living, breathing friend.

I cringed, imagining the kick Uncle Peter would give me if he knew what I was thinking.

"Okay," I said, then broke into a coughing fit.

Olive had that same worried look Aunt Carrie got when I couldn't breathe. She gently placed a hand on my back.

"Are you okay, Helen?"

I smiled. She certainly seemed like a nice person. Maybe Uncle Peter was wrong about her.

Grinning wide, Olive bolted down the stairs. Within seconds, Aunt Carrie was in my room.

"Is everything all right, Helen? Olive left so quickly."

"Fine," I managed. "She went . . . to get some . . . thing."

I wanted to warn her that Uncle Peter couldn't see Olive here, but I didn't have the breath.

Olive returned a moment later, a little winded, carrying three books. "Here, Helen, look at these," she said, placing them on my bed.

They were books I hadn't seen before. One had a beautiful cover showing a little girl in a garden, opening a gate with a key, *The Secret Garden*. I grabbed it and flipped through the pages.

"It's one of my absolute favorites," Olive said. "It's about a girl who finds a secret garden and a sick boy. Oh, I don't want to give it away. It's a fantastical story. You'll love it."

Fantastical?

I rolled the word around in my head like candy. I'd never heard it before, but similar to the word wamakadoo, I liked how it sounded. How it felt.

A coughing spell hit me hard, but my eyes were closed within minutes, and I was listening to *The Secret Garden*. I was so content, happier than I'd felt in ages, I forgot that Uncle Peter could possibly come by. We had just gotten to the part where Mary Lennox drinks wine and falls asleep, only to wake up and find everyone around her had died of Cholera. I nearly swallowed my tongue when the front door opened, and I heard Uncle Peter's voice.

A few minutes later, Aunt Carrie appeared in my doorway, wearing a weak smile. "Olive, thank you so much, dear, but that's all for today. Helen needs her rest."

"Aw," we both moaned.

"Helen, I hope you feel better. It was wonderful reading to

you," Olive said, gathering the books. "I'll see you tomorrow."

"Come in the morning, dear," Aunt Carrie whispered.

I suspected Uncle Peter had spoken to her, and I wondered what he'd said. She walked Olive out. Moments later, I heard Uncle Peter's footsteps on the stairs.

"Hello, my darling. How are you feeling today?" he asked, kissing my forehead.

My heart sped up. I coughed and nodded.

"Helen," he said softly, "your aunt told me the girl next door was reading to you. You know I don't like those people. I don't want her here again. It's best you don't become friends with that girl."

I wanted to tell him I was certain Olive's morals were in fine working order. That she was kind about the way she touched my doll and the way she talked about Sadie's short hair. That she liked fairies and wanted to find fairy rings with me, like Grandma and I used to. But I didn't have the strength to say it. And honestly, I wasn't sure he would have cared.

Uncle Peter grabbed my hands, held them to his face, and kissed them.

"Remember, I love you to the stars and back."

I pulled my hands away and turned to face the wall. I felt just like I had at the McClatchy's the day I played dress-up. I loved Uncle Peter and never wanted to disappoint him, but I was angry. I wanted to be friends with Olive.

"Helen," he said, "I always have your best interests at heart. Please know that. I've asked your aunt to make sure that girl doesn't come over again."

What was I supposed to do with myself? Boredom was eating me alive. I wanted to scream.

"Yes, sir," I whispered. I hated myself the moment the words came out.

He pulled out his brown rosary beads and handed me the

white ones he'd given me for Christmas. Together, we made the sign of the cross.

"In nomine Patris, et Filii, et Spiritus Sancti. Amen."

He prayed to Mother Mary to make me well, and we began the rosary. It was long. I usually didn't mind it, but today, my thoughts weren't holy. Olive hadn't been here long, but having a real friend felt nice. When the prayers ended, he kissed my hand.

"I have to run," he said. "I'll try to come back later this week. Now, you're not still cross with me, are you? Remember, I always have your best interests at heart."

He liked to remind me of that. My best interests at heart. What did it even mean? I lay on the bed with my head turned from him as he walked out of the room and down the stairs.

I heard him say to Aunt Carrie, "I know I won't need to speak to you again about this Kelly girl being over here. After all, a wild goose never reared a tame gosling."

The door closed. Then there was silence. Aunt Carrie must have gone outside with Uncle Peter.

"A wild goose never reared a tame gosling?" I had no idea what that meant. And if the Kellys were so bad, why was Pap always kind to them? It was true that Gram didn't like them, but still, it didn't add up. Everything felt muddled. I couldn't stop thinking about the Kellys. About Olive. About the things I'd been told my whole life: "Stay away from them." "They're not our kind of people."

I'd been taught all good people went to church—except Aunt Libby, that is. But somehow, her not going didn't bother me. I'd seen the Kellys at Mass. Olive, too, sitting beside her grandparents, so that couldn't be it. I hadn't met Olive's mother, though. Hmm . . . maybe she was the rotten egg. Come to think of it, I'd never seen her at church, not even once.

Aunt Carrie walked in and sat on the edge of my bed.

"Aunt . . ." I tried to speak, but a coughing fit hit, and I felt like a beached fish. The questions would have to wait.

She patted my back. "Easy, Helen. Just breathe. Stay calm."

"Olive . . ." I couldn't say anything else.

Aunt Carrie gently smoothed my blanket. "Helen, you must get your rest. Tell me later. I'll wake you for dinner."

NINE

August–Mid-October 1912

Olive broke into the house and stood in the doorway of my bedroom, staring at me with huge black eyes, smelling like the devil who had just surfaced from deep within the bowels of our outhouse. As the moonlight from the window hit her, I was shocked to see that Olive had transformed into a terrifying creature with large, sharp horns and a long, pointy tail. Dirt glistened on her red skin, and foam dripped from her mouth onto my bed. I tried to move. I tried yelling for help, but it was of no use. The words wouldn't form. She was coming for me. I was a goner.

I awoke with a jolt to hear Aunt Carrie telling Olive I wasn't up for company. When Aunt Carrie came to check on me, I asked about Olive's visit.

"I had no idea your uncle felt so strongly about the neighbors.

My goodness, he doesn't like them one bit. Best not to upset that man."

Aunt Carrie was walking about my room tidying up, and I could feel my insides start to boil. Uncle Peter didn't even know Olive, and neither did Gram. The terrifying dream came to mind, and my anger began to soften. Maybe she was evil, and they knew best. Uncle Peter was a person of great importance to God. Gram had taught me that his connection to God was more powerful than any connection the rest of us had. We needed to listen to him or risk not getting into Heaven, our life goal.

This inner back and forth continued for another minute, and my thoughts shifted to finding something to occupy myself with for the day. "What about . . ." Even with my limited speaking ability, I pushed out, ". . . the book. Did she leave it?" A brief coughing fit ensued, slowing my aunt's reply.

"I guess it wouldn't hurt. Your uncle doesn't have to know, I suppose." Aunt Carrie left my room and came back with *The Secret Garden*. She smirked and said, "Don't you go telling him and getting me into trouble, ya hear?"

The next day, I heard Olive at the door and held my breath, waiting to see what Aunt Carrie would say to her. I had read *The Secret Garden* all night and opened it as soon as I awoke, hoping to finish it so maybe Olive and I could talk about it, but I knew better.

I wanted a visitor and wanted to discuss Mary Lennox and Colin Craven. It was the most exciting book I'd ever read, and I had no one to share it with. I had hoped that today she would decide not to listen to Uncle Peter, but I couldn't blame Aunt Carrie. Like me, she didn't want to get reprimanded by him.

That evening, I asked Aunt Carrie a few questions about *The Secret Garden*, but I was still quite sick and couldn't talk for long. I wanted to know more about magic and about the robin in the story. Was the robin Colin's mother? Was the red bird I had seen several times my grandmother?

Aunt Carrie didn't know how to answer my questions and asked if she could read the book. I was thrilled to think she would do this for me. I enthusiastically handed the book to her and then found myself grinning ear to ear as we said prayers that night. When she got up from my bed, she kissed me on the tip of my nose, filling me with a sensation I had forgotten. Maybe we were starting to like each other better. The reflection of the flame from my lamp danced in her eyes, and as she reached to turn the light off, she said, "I will start reading it tonight, Helen. I will see what magic it is you speak of."

The next day, Olive came knocking at the door, and again, Aunt Carrie said, "I'm sorry, dear. Helen isn't feeling up to visitors today."

After this, Aunt Carrie came up to my room. She knew from the scowl on my face that I had heard Olive at the door. Trying to cheer me, she said, "I am quite captivated by *The Secret Garden*. I'm half-finished and at the part where Mary is about to discover who's been crying in the big mansion. How on Earth did you finish it in one night?"

"One night . . . and one day," I said with a cough.

"It is a splendid book. I haven't gotten to any magic yet, but I can see why you like the book. Mary is the name of your grandmother, for one. Mary's parents are both gone, like yours, and Mary was sent away, just as you were sent to the Allens. And then there is the bird, but I think I need to read more to understand the bird." Aunt Carrie waited to see if I would speak, but when I didn't, she said sweetly, "Helen, I've been meaning to ask you about the pretty gold ring you now wear. Pap said Aunt Libby gave it to you, that it was her grandmother's."

"That's right," I proudly said.

"You are a lucky little girl being entrusted with a family heirloom like that. Someday, you'll be able to give it to your little girl."

I noticed my aunt's faraway, darkened eyes, and it made me wonder if she would ever have a little girl of her own.

"Helen, I found a shop downtown looking for extra help with their alterations. I need to pick up a few garments and get some things at the market, but I'll return shortly."

Aunt Carrie had been gone from her home for weeks and hadn't worked since leaving Buffalo. Taking care of me was a sacrifice for her and my Uncle William in many ways, especially financially. I had heard jabby comments from Gram that my aunt and uncle didn't have much to their name.

A week went by without Olive coming to the house. Then, two weeks passed. I started to believe Olive had returned to wherever she came from, or maybe she understood we weren't allowed to be friends. Whatever the reason, she was gone. This saddened me, as I was feeling so lonely, but a part of me was glad I didn't have to worry about getting into trouble with my uncle.

After four weeks of being ill, I finally started to feel like myself again and could speak in complete sentences without coughing or shortness of breath. I was excited to get healthy and go about my life until I realized my life before all this happened was horrible! What would happen when I was no longer sick? Aunt Carrie, whom I was growing fond of, would most likely return to Buffalo, and Uncle Peter would surely place me with another family.

My gut clenched at the thought of one more person leaving me. So, I plotted to do what Colin did in *The Secret Garden*. If he could fool everyone, maybe I could too. I did feel a little guilty about lying, though.

Aunt Carrie became alarmed at my "turn for the worse" and soon called for the doctor. Dr. Langley was an older man with salt-and-pepper hair and a large, scraggly, rather unkempt-looking mustache that traveled down both sides of his plump, round face. He seemed caring enough, and I guessed most of his patients liked him. He had visited me several times when I was at my sickest, but I hadn't seen him in over a week. I was not happy to see him again.

"She has no temperature," he said as his brows wrinkled, and his pudgy blue eyes turned into slits. He grabbed his stethoscope and held it to my chest. "She has no mucus in her lungs," he proclaimed, looking relieved yet puzzled. "Glory be! I have no idea why she wouldn't be feeling well."

Then, as though a light went off in his head, he looked at Aunt Carrie.

"Helen needs fresh air and will need to start playing outside again. Fresh air is important now for her full recovery. And send her back to school one week from today."

My aunt let out a huge sigh. "Oh, thank goodness, doctor. Sorry to make you come all the way out here."

My plan was ruined. I was all better, and the doctor knew it. Aunt Carrie would return to Buffalo, and I'd go to God only knows where. Now what? I wondered.

I spent the entire evening sulking. Aunt Carrie couldn't understand what was wrong with me. When she came to tuck me into bed that night, she wanted to talk about finishing *The Secret Garden*.

"Helen, what a fascinating book. Yes, I believe the bird was Colin's mother. Do you want to tell me about the bird that visits you?" she asked.

Aunt Carrie teared up when I told her about the time in the carriage on the way to the hospital and how the bird flew down and looked right at me. I also shared how the little bird came to visit outside my window, as well as on the day of the funeral.

"I see cardinals all the time now," I told her. "It made me feel good when I read about the robin telling Mary the location of the key and the door to *The Secret Garden*. Maybe Grandma was trying to talk to me through the little bird."

"God works in mysterious ways, and why couldn't an animal or bird be some type of messenger? I think it is a lovely idea. If it gives you comfort, Helen, it is good," Aunt Carrie said.

I was on pins and needles the entire week thinking about Aunt Carrie leaving, but then a miracle happened. Uncle Will showed up at our door with three trunks, ready to move into Magnolia Street. Aunt Carrie and Uncle Will had decided to take care of Pap and me and had left their jobs and home behind in Buffalo. This was the happiest I had been in my ten years. I would now be part of a real family and wouldn't be forced to live with strangers again. Any ill will between Aunt Carrie and me was finally gone.

Due to my pneumonia, I missed the first three weeks of fifth grade. The thought of going back to school thrilled me. I was out of Sister Mary Regina's clutches and excited to meet my new teacher, a nun rumored to love children.

Sister Veronica was fond of me, and I quickly became her classroom helper. I'm sure that being Father O'Donnell's niece helped with her partiality. I loved this new role of importance. I would assist Sister Veronica with handing out papers, wiping down the boards, running errands around the school, and even singing new songs in front of the class that Uncle Will had taught me. This attention didn't help me earn more friends, though.

I continued to suffer from terrible guilt at the loss of Mrs. Allen and would awaken from frequent nightmares in a cold sweat. I feared that Aunt Carrie would run back to Buffalo, fearful I was Satan's child if I told her the truth. I missed Aunt Libby and our little talks. Unfortunately, Pap was afraid Aunt Libby would get sick if she came to visit, and Uncle Peter seemed to write her out of our lives, never even mentioning her in my presence.

Pap stopped coming home late, smelling like whiskey. He would still drink, but Aunt Carrie wouldn't take any shenanigans, and he seemed more like his old self. Uncle Will worked at one of the factories and traveled every weekend for shows, singing and playing music. Aunt Carrie asked him sometimes if he was trying to work himself to death, but Uncle Will would say, "Which would you have me give up, Carrie?" And that would be that.

It had been well over a month since I had seen Olive, but I thought of her often. One day in mid-October, she appeared as I walked home from school. Not knowing what to do, I hid behind some bushes to escape, but it was useless. She had already spied me.

Olive ran up to me, thrilled at our encounter. "Helen, you are all better! How wonderful," she said.

Olive's curly hair hung about her face. Almost a young woman of thirteen, she was getting too old for this. "People will start to speak poorly of that girl if she doesn't start pulling her locks back," I could hear my grandmother say.

Part of me was thrilled to see Olive, but the other part didn't know what to do or say. Saying nothing would have been rude, though.

"Hi, Olive," I said awkwardly.

"It was incredible. My mother and I have been helping with rallies and parades in Vermont and Massachusetts. We are suffragists, you know, my mother and I," she said with all the excitement of a child who had just come from the circus.

"A suffragist? What is that?" The minute I said it, I wanted to kick myself.

You aren't supposed to talk with her, numbskull. What if Uncle Peter or Aunt Carrie sees you conversing with her?

"Suffragists are women fighting for the right to vote. Do you know that white men have been allowed to vote since 1789, but that women are only allowed to vote in eight of the forty-eight states?" Olive said.

"Hmm," I sighed, plotting my escape. I scanned my surroundings to see if Uncle Peter would show up from a nearby tree or from around the corner to scold me.

"My mother and I met other women who are fighting so women can vote. We made banners and signs and marched through the streets. Helen, people yelled at us, and at one rally, we had tomatoes thrown at us, but we got the word out," Olive said triumphantly.

"Tomatoes? Goodness. And what word exactly are you talking about?" I asked, forgetting again that I wasn't supposed to speak to her.

"Votes for women, of course," she said.

I remembered when Aunt Libby said a demure woman wouldn't consider voting. I also recalled the time downtown when Olive's mother handed Mrs. Allen a flyer and her reaction. The handout must have been about women voting. That day, Mrs. Allen said something about trying to be a lion when you are really a house cat. Was this why Gram and Uncle Peter didn't like them? Because they were suffragists?

"Why do women need to vote, anyway?" I said, eager to

get to the bottom of this.

"Helen, many men don't think women are smart enough to vote. Some even believe that if we think too much, we won't be able to have children. Can you imagine that? You and I are certainly as smart as any boys."

By this time, Olive had me like a snapping turtle, and my thoughts of escaping faded. "Smarter, probably," I blurted out.

"Helen, women have just as much right to vote for our president as men do. We work, we are intelligent, and we have opinions. We need to fight for things important to women. Men only fight for what is important to—"

I jumped when I heard, "What are you girls talking about?" Aunt Carrie had walked up to us from the east side of Magnolia Street, holding two full bags. She wore a concerned expression along with her fashionable, long wool suit, silk gloves, and a hat adorned with a feather. I knew she was upset with me. I stood there, worried, thinking the worst.

"Here, let me help you, Mrs. O'Donnell," Olive said.

"That is very nice of you to offer to help me, Olive, but Miss Helen can take my bags. She's all better now," Aunt Carrie said as she shot me with a dirty look.

I hefted the two heavy bags she'd just hauled all the way from the trolley and wondered how on earth she'd managed it.

"And what were you girls talking about?"

"I was just telling Helen that my mother and I have been working on women's voting rights in Vermont and Massachusetts. Do you believe women should have the right to vote, Mrs. O'Donnell?"

"Lordy, Olive. You go on now," Aunt Carrie ordered.

Olive spun around with a woeful look and shuffled toward her house. We said our goodbyes.

As soon as we walked through our door with the groceries, I heard, "Helen, you know darned well what your uncle said. Why would you put me in this position?" Her usually pleasant voice held a tone I hadn't heard before.

I explained how I had tried to hide behind the bushes when I saw her. "Would you have preferred me to be rude, Aunt Carrie?"

Her tense face softened. "No. We must never be rude." And then she folded her arms as if deep in thought. "Helen, Christ probably would have done the same thing."

I knew if Christ would have done it, I would be okay. A blanket of relief fell upon me, giving me the courage to ask my aunt about something Olive had said.

"Aunt Carrie, do you think women should vote the same as men?"

My aunt looked away, then sighed. "Don't let that neighbor fill your head with rubbish. Now I know why Peter doesn't like them."

I hadn't expected that response from my aunt. I stood there, baffled. Neither of us spoke as we straightened up the kitchen.

Aunt Carrie seemed annoyed and finally said, "It seems the men are doing a fine job with voting anyway. Can't imagine I'd vote any differently from Will. Besides, with all the cooking, cleaning, and child-rearing most women do, how would we even have the time to educate ourselves on the issues?"

"Yes, ma'am. I guess there is no use in pretending we are lions when, in reality, we are just dainty house cats," I said smugly.

"My, my." Aunt Carrie closed her eyes and shook her head. "Helen, it's not a simple thing. Our church, families, and community expect certain things from us."

We stopped talking, and I helped Aunt Carrie prepare dinner. I still needed to learn more about voting. I figured I'd ask Pap later. Uncle Will was playing music at a pub outside of town tonight and wouldn't be back until much later.

"Pap, why do people vote?" I asked at dinner.

"Our Constitution says citizens of our good country have the right to vote for our leaders." Pap took a large bite of his bread.

"So, Pap, women aren't citizens?" I needed to understand why Olive and her mother were making such a fuss about this whole voting thing.

"No, women can be citizens," Pap said.

"But if women are citizens, why wouldn't they be able to vote the same as men?" I finished eating and put my fork down.

"My dear, some people think women should be able to vote the same as men, but many people are probably scared to death at the thought," he chuckled.

"Why, Pap?" I asked.

"Because men make the rules in our world, Helen." Aunt Carrie interjected, giving Pap an apologetic look as she sipped her drink.

"Carrie, what you say is true. Men do make the rules in our world." Pap patted his mustache clean. "I don't have a problem with women voting. They have just as much smarts as most men I know. Take your grandmother. God rest her soul." Pap made the sign of the cross, typical behavior when speaking about Grandma. "She was sharp as a tack."

"Pap, who will you vote for?"

"Most of the Irish in our community support Wilson. He says he'll stand up to big business."

"So, Wilson's for people like us?" I asked.

"That's the idea."

"Time to help me clean up, Missy," Aunt Carrie said, shutting down the conversation.

Pap entered the parlor and opened the *Democrat and Chronicle*, the local Rochester newspaper, while Aunt Carrie and I took care of the dinner mess.

"Helen, a word of caution, it is best not to talk about women voting in front of your Uncle Peter. The church hasn't looked favorably upon this women's voting movement, and he's made it very clear how he feels about women voting. You don't want to cross him," she said.

"Aunt Carrie, why doesn't he think women should be allowed to vote?" I asked. "Is that why he doesn't like Rosalie Kelly? Is that why Gram never liked them?"

"I'm not sure about your grandmother. May she rest in peace." My aunt quickly made the sign of the cross. "But I know your uncle has his own understanding of what makes women acceptable to God. I will leave it at that," she said.

Aunt Carrie helped me with my schoolwork, then stayed while I got ready for bed. She read to me and kissed my forehead goodnight. Ever since *The Secret Garden*, stories had become a ritual for us.

Afterward, when the room was quiet and the oil lamp burned low, questions stirred. Why would anyone march through the streets and get tomatoes thrown at them for strangers? Why risk being hated by priests, by people like Gram?

What could be worth that?

TEN

Mid–October 1912

The next day, after I got home from school, I heard a knock at the door. I ran from my bedroom and peeked out the parlor window when Aunt Carrie didn't answer.

Dear God, it was Olive. I didn't want her to know I was home, but she saw me, so I waved.

"Hi, Helen. Are you free?" she asked once the door was opened. There she stood with her long hair tucked into a knit hat, pink cheeks from the cool air, and wearing a man's sweater, her grandfather's, I assumed, to keep her warm on the chilly October day.

"Hello, Olive. I'm busy, but I'll go fetch your book for you," I said, shutting the door on her to keep her from entering the house.

Out of breath and with book in hand, I opened the

door to Olive's beaming face. The homely sweater looked almost fashionable with her outdated blue skirt, most likely a hand-me-down from her mother.

I had decided that Olive could wear anything and look swell.

Seeing her standing there reminded me of the black and white kitten that had wandered up to the front porch when I was just three or four. It was such an adorable little creature, and I picked it up and brought it into the house, thinking it could be my new friend.

"Helen, the only animals allowed in this house are dead ones, and we eat those," Gram said, much to my chagrin.

She opened the front door and shooed the frightened thing away with her broom.

I slowly handed the book to Olive, thinking about the cat, unsure whether I should shoo her away or invite her inside.

"Did you love *The Secret Garden* as much as I did?" Olive asked.

I had loved the book and wanted to talk to her about it badly, but I had a vision of being scolded. "I've gotta go now." I tried to close the door, but Olive put her foot in the doorway to stop me and pushed it back open.

"Helen, what is the matter with you? If you didn't like the book, just say so. Did you at least cry at the end?"

I tried not to be friendly or neighborly. Really, I did try, but like impossible attempts to keep the sun from rising, the words, "I cried like a baby!" spilled out.

She laughed, and then I laughed too. Part of me felt complete relief.

"When Colin's dad finally realizes he can walk . . . so beautiful. Are you sure you can't take a little stroll down the street?" Olive asked with a wide smile.

I didn't think going for a short walk with her would hurt.

I could return before Aunt Carrie noticed I was gone.

"We can go for a quick walk, I suppose." I grabbed my coat.

We walked down Magnolia Street past the Hamilton's Victorian house. Prudence was playing with her doll on the front porch, and when she saw us, she quickly ran inside. As she turned, I stuck my tongue out at her. Olive looked surprised.

"Helen, why would you do that?"

"My Lord, she is such an annoying little girl. I can't stand her." I said in a low voice. "She and her brothers . . . well, we don't get along. They've made fun of my hair and freckles since I can remember. They go to the Protestant school. Pap says it's because the Hamiltons are half-English. He doesn't like the English."

I closed my mouth and looked cautiously to my left and to my right.

Then, I glanced back at my house, willing my feet to turn, but they stayed the course.

"My grandparents don't like the English either. Tell me more about the Hamiltons. I know they own Hamilton's Hardware in town," Olive said.

A strange force kept me standing there. I knew I'd regret staying, but I pushed the thought away. I did dislike the Hamiltons, and I'd enjoy talking about them.

"I'll tell you a story. When I was six years old, Prudence, her brothers, and their cousin invited me to the rock quarry after church one summer day—"

I stopped in my tracks when I realized the story wouldn't paint me in a very good light.

The truth was, after Mass, I'd promised Gram I'd go straight to my room and change out of my church clothes while she and Pap delivered food to a sick friend. My grandparents never let me go to the quarry. Gram said it was dangerous, but Prudence talked me into it. I lost my balance while crossing a makeshift bridge and landed in neck-high water. My best shoes, dress, and hair, freshly washed and curled at the salon the day before, were drenched.

I lied to Gram about all of it to save my bottom. When she later told Mrs. Hamilton that her children had lured me to the quarry, pushed me in, and laughed at me, I'd added the laughing part to make it extra believable, Mrs. Hamilton was furious. Those kids got into so much trouble that they never wanted to play with me again.

Changing the subject, I asked, "Have you been to the quarry yet?"

"What's that?" Olive replied.

"It's an old rock quarry that's now a pond. Some of the kids from around here swim and play there. Most parents don't let their children go after a little boy drowned. Sometimes, the Hamiltons sneak down there. I don't go unless I am with an adult." I had added the last part to not appear naughty, but I noticed Olive's sour expression.

"Oh. Do you always follow the rules?" The tone of her voice and grimace made me feel babyish.

"Goodness, no!" I said, pivoting fast. "Gram said it had something to do with my red hair." That made us both laugh. "Why? How about you?"

"Heavens, if I followed all the rules, I'd never get to do anything new, different, or exciting," she said. "Speaking of hair, you've got great hair, Helen. What a gorgeous shade of red."

"That's kind of you. Yours is beautiful, too," I beamed.

By the time we reached Flint Street, we were two blocks from home. Olive reached into her pocket and held out her hand.

"Here. Butterscotch is my favorite!" she said, handing me one.

"Thanks, Olive. I love butterscotch, too." And I meant it—anything butterscotch was fine with me.

With each step, any thought of us not being friends faded. I started in on a story.

"When my grandfather's been drinking too much, he goes on and on about the dastardly deeds of the Cromwells or the importation by English devils of those damned Scotch Protestants into Ulster. He swears a lot during these rants, and Grandma gets furious—makes him go to Confession the next day to 'take the pledge,' as Pap calls it."

"Adults are funny, aren't they?" She picked up my hand, admiring my ring. "Oh, Helen, that's beautiful. Where did you get it?"

We spotted a large, cinnamon-colored tree with a blanket of fallen leaves beneath. We plopped down, awkward but happy, and I told her about Aunt Libby and the ring she left behind. We talked about not having brothers or sisters, and then she told me that she didn't have a father.

"Isn't that odd? I don't have a father, either!" I was delighted that we had this in common. "I have one, but I've never met him. Did your father die?" I asked.

"No," Olive said, picking up a leaf and studying it. "The colors in this leaf are incredible, aren't they? Look, the orange matches your hair." I assumed this topic was off-limits based on her response, but then she turned to me and said, "Can you keep a secret?"

"Of course," I said, only half believing myself.

"My mother told me something terrible on our trip. I have no one to talk to about it. You must promise you won't tell anyone if I tell you."

"I pinky-promise," I said, reaching my pinky out to hers.

I honestly didn't plan on telling anyone her secret. Secrets were a funny thing, though, and I often found that when I held on to them for too long, they made me want to explode.

"Helen, my entire life, my mother has told me my father left after I was born, but that wasn't true. She had something awful happen to her after high school. She was attacked by a boy," she said, and then, getting close to me, asked, "Do you know what rape is, Helen?"

I reluctantly shook my head no, deciding it was better to be honest than to look like a fool later.

Olive whispered, "Rape is when a man puts his thingy inside of a woman when she doesn't want him to."

"Ee-you," I said, pulling back but then getting closer again to hear more.

"You get pregnant when it goes in there, you know, and that man got my mother pregnant, with me." Olive moved away from my ear, and as I turned to her, I saw tears in her eyes.

I knew slightly what a male thingy was, but I had no idea what Olive meant when she said, "put it inside of her."

Put it where?

But I didn't want to interrupt Olive, given how upset she was.

Olive continued, "My mother didn't tell anyone, but when she found out she was going to have a baby, she had to tell her parents. She said that now that I'm getting older, I should know what happened to her."

She took another butterscotch out of her pocket and handed it to me, then got another for herself. I gladly accepted the candy and unwrapped the crinkly, gleaming paper. Holding the treat, I said, "What happened to the boy? Did he get into trouble?"

"Helen, eventually my mother told her story, but no one

believed her. She couldn't see him, it was dark." Olive shook her head. "They turned her entire story around. She was accused of being a bad person, of being immoral."

And then I understood Uncle Peter's saying: A wild goose never reared a tame gosling. He'd meant Rosalie Kelly had loose morals. She was a wild goose.

I stuffed the half-melted butterscotch into my mouth and sucked hard.

"People called my mother names for a long time, and she wasn't even allowed to go to church with my grandparents. The church doesn't welcome women who have babies when they aren't married."

"I'm sorry, Olive," I spoke carefully, trying not to choke on the candy. "Why wouldn't the Church welcome them, no matter how the baby came?"

"Because the Catholic Church doesn't like people like my mother."

Uncle Peter's face flashed before me as I nervously bit down, crunching my butterscotch.

"Helen, I know your uncle doesn't like me," she said.

Had she read my mind?

"I know why you suddenly got 'sick' after our first visit. Your uncle saw me. Sometimes I go to church with my grandparents. Your uncle smiles at everyone, but when we get to him, he turns cold. My grandparents have never said a bad word about him, but I can tell."

It all made sense now. Uncle Peter and Gram didn't like the Kellys because Rosalie was unwed and was involved in the suffrage movement.

"Helen, don't you see? My mother did nothing wrong. But because of the rape, she's been branded with an invisible scarlet letter 'A.' The Church should have tried to find the man who hurt her, not judged her."

I was still turning her words over in my head, scarlet letters and a church that turned its back, when I noticed the sky had gone amber. The sun was setting. I jumped to my feet.

"Olive, the time! I'm going to get into so much trouble!"

When I walked into the house. Aunt Carrie was waiting for me with her hands on her hips.

"And where have you been, missy? I've been worried sick about you," she yelled.

I tried to think up a story on the way home, but truth be told, I just didn't have the energy to lie.

"Ah, I—well—I—" Nothing was coming, so I figured I'd tell the truth.

"Aunt Carrie, Olive stopped by to get her book and asked me to go for a walk. I didn't want to go, really, I didn't, but I felt bad saying no. We got to talking, and I lost track of time."

"Hmm—" she said, staring at me. After a long wait, she finally spoke again. "And what else, there, girly? You forgot to say the most important thing."

I had no idea what Aunt Carrie was talking about. I just looked at her. "Ah—I—"

"That you're sorry! You should be very sorry for worrying me sick, don't you think?"

I released the deep breath I had been holding, and as I exhaled, the words "I'm sorry" floated out.

Aunt Carrie walked over to me, gave me a light tap on my bottom, and told me to go upstairs to clean up for dinner. By now, Grandma would have had me over her knee, and I'd be getting whacked so hard I wouldn't be able to sit all night. Was the punishment coming later, I wondered?

But it never came. Aunt Carrie did things differently from Grandma, and my feelings for her grew stronger daily.

When Aunt Carrie tucked me into bed that night, she asked, "So, what am I supposed to tell your uncle when he finds out you were with Olive today?"

"I don't want him to find out, Aunt Carrie," I said. "I'm afraid of what he will do."

"You think I should keep this from him?"

I felt like I had to tell her what Olive had told me. I knew it was a secret, I had even pinky-promised, but the secret, like a growing flower, was pushing right out of my mouth. It was information I didn't fully understand, and I needed help breaking it down.

Cautiously, I told her how Olive's mother had been raped. How they never knew who the man was, and that the rape was how Olive came into this world.

I told her how Rosalie Kelly hasn't been allowed into church ever since, and how she has worn an imaginary letter "A" her entire life in this city because of what happened.

"Dear Lord . . . a letter A? Helen, how do you know about that, young lady? My goodness, so much for young ears. You know what rape is, too?"

"Sort of. I'm unsure what Olive was talking about when she said the male thingy goes in there. Where does it go, Aunt Carrie?" I asked. My aunt's neck and face filled with blotchy red spots.

For the next several minutes, my poor Aunt tried teaching me about the birds and the bees, as she called it. I'm not sure who felt more awkward.

"Aunt Carrie, are you mad at me now?" I asked when she was finished.

"I'm not mad. The whole thing is rather disturbing. My heavens, way too much for a ten-year-old to know. I certainly wasn't intending to tell you how babies were made tonight," she said.

"Aunt Carrie, why would Uncle Peter or Grandma blame Rosalie Kelly for what happened? Why would they blame

Olive or the Kellys? Is this also because of their involvement with women voting?" Aunt Carrie grimaced as I continued my rant.

"The Kellys were so kind to me when Grandma died. What would I have done without them? They came over and cleaned up the vegetables on the floor, so we didn't have to do it when we got home from the hospital. Mrs. Kelly took our goose and cooked it for the people to eat at the wake. Bad people wouldn't have done any of those things, would they?"

I knew the answer. I should have asked instead why the two people I held most dear would judge good people so harshly.

"It's late. Go to bed now."

"Am I in trouble, Aunt Carrie?"

"No, Helen. You aren't in trouble. I have a lot of thinking to do. Sweet dreams."

The next day, I came home from school and found Rosalie Kelly sitting at the kitchen table with my aunt, drinking tea and eating molasses cookies. I almost thought I'd walked into the wrong house. When I saw them, I'm sure my mouth fell open.

"Helen, this is Rosalie Kelly, Olive's mother," Aunt Carrie said.

My lips parted, but the shock held the words back. Mrs. Kelly rose quickly, hand outstretched. Her smile faltered when she noticed my hesitation.

I took a breath and gathered myself. "Hello, Mrs. Kelly. It's a pleasure to make your acquaintance."

My aunt stood holding out the plate of cookies, her face lit with a big smile.

"Helen, it's wonderful finally meeting you. Olive has told me many nice things about you, but please call me Rosalie," she said.

Children didn't call adults by their first names, and Rosalie Kelly was never allowed in our house. Yet, here she was, in my kitchen, giggling and chatting with my aunt like they'd known each other for years, telling me to call her Rosalie.

I didn't know what to think. But somehow, it felt right. Like maybe the world was finally trying to fix itself.

That evening, when Aunt Carrie tucked me into bed, she told me she was rethinking what Uncle Peter told her about the neighbors.

"Helen, as far as I can tell, the Kellys are fine people. Maybe you and I could have a secret between us. Would that be all right?

"What would that be, Aunt Carrie?" I asked, over the moon, just thinking she might share a secret with me.

"I like Rosalie Kelly, and you seem to like Olive Kelly. Maybe we don't have to let Uncle Peter know we are friendly with them. We won't lie. We just won't share that information. Okay?" Aunt Carrie asked.

"Okay, Aunt Carrie. Here, let's pinky-promise to seal the deal."

I held out my pinky to hers, and Aunt Carrie and I had our first secret that night.

ELEVEN

November 1912

Uncle Peter would only come over for short visits since my recovery. He and Uncle Will seemed constantly at odds and could not agree on something as straightforward as the weather. The tension between them made everyone uneasy.

One night, I overheard a distraught Uncle Will rant to Aunt Carrie.

"Peter would rather Helen live with strangers than us. We'll never meet up to his standards."

One day in early November, a couple of weeks after Olive told me about her mother's rape, I showed Olive the rock quarry. Olive was at her grandparents' house more frequently due to her mother's involvement with the suffragists, and we began to see each other whenever possible.

While there, I picked up a rock, a good skipping stone,

and rubbed the flat surface. Olive had never skipped rocks before and hadn't the slightest idea about the art of stone skipping. A confident aura washed over me at the thought of teaching Olive something new. I flicked the stone in my hand, and it skipped three times across the pond's surface. Not my best, but not bad, I thought.

"Nice, Helen. Let me try," she said.

Olive reached down, quickly found the perfect stone, and flicked it across the water. It skipped four times. This pretty much summed up our relationship: whatever I could do, Olive could do better.

As Olive and I searched for fairies and skipped stones with me guiding her to all my secret places, a quiet, sisterly warmth began to stir in me. It was unfamiliar, like something I'd always longed for but never known.

"Olive, you and I are sorta the same. You know—how we both don't know our fathers."

I wanted so badly for her to see it, too. That we belonged to the same imaginary club. My stone fluttered across the water, and I bent down to find another.

"I guess we sorta are," she replied with a crooked smile as a slight breeze rustled her hair.

"My Aunt Libby, the one who gave me the ring, told me a secret before she left. Do you promise not to tell anyone?" I asked.

"Of course," Olive said.

She held out her pinky, and the two of us intertwined our fingers, pledging secrecy as we had before. I told Olive how my grandmother had stolen me from my very own father, how I had always been told he left me after my mother died, and how he had a new family.

"How sad for you, Helen, losing your father all over again."

I hadn't thought of it that way, "losing my father all over again." A tightness grasped my throat, but the chill from the overcast November day numbed me enough that I kept talking. Olive was a good listener, and I had so much inside of me that needed to come out.

"Aunt Lib says it's okay for him to have a new life. I don't understand how he could just forget about me, though. Aunt Libby said he loved me so much, and she was certain he still did."

My throat felt dry, and my words started feeling choked. To avoid crying, I walked away, busying myself with looking for more skipping stones.

"Helen, my grandparents told me that the mother in the last home you were at died from the same pneumonia that made you so sick. That must have been really scary for you."

An awkward silence passed over us.

"You, okay?" she asked softly while folding a leaf into an odd shape.

I swallowed. I knew I could trust her.

"Staying with the Allens was difficult. I hated it. While I was there, I . . . well—" I almost revealed how I killed Mrs. Allen. But caught myself.

"What? What is it, Helen?"

"Well, it's not important, and you may not like me anymore if I tell you," I laughed nervously.

"Just tell me, silly."

"I . . . may have. . . well, I think I . . . I'm just going to say it. I may have killed Mrs. Allen." A huge sigh escaped me just as Olive released a loud gasp.

"What?" Fear filled Olive's pretty face. "What are you saying, Helen?"

"Those girls, her daughters, were so horrible to me, and when they cut Sadie's hair, dear Lord, I cursed them that night. I think I placed a hex on all of them. Mrs. Allen always sided with her girls. And Catherine, why did she have to have everything, even Sadie? It wasn't fair."

I wondered what I was doing. It had been so hard for me to find a friend, and here I was, convincing Olive I was a soulless person by telling her the worst thing I'd ever done.

"Tell me more," she said, her brows pinched with worry.

"Olive, I'm certain that is why their mother died. I called up something dark that day, something ugly. And it made her sick."

I started to cry. Olive grabbed me by the shoulders and hugged me. It felt good to be held, and I closed my eyes, letting the tears pour out.

"It's absurd for you to think you killed their mother, although, for a second, you had me. People can't just wish for something bad to happen, and then it does. If that were so, don't you think there would be utter chaos in the world?"

"Olive, I'm a bad person for thinking such wicked thoughts." I cried loudly and looked around to make sure we were still alone.

"Oh, Helen, they were vile children who weren't raised properly. I'm sorry about the entire dreadful experience."

Unable to stop the flood of tears, I paused to catch my breath, then surprised myself when I shouted,

"Mrs. Allen left me! Just like my parents. Just like Grandma. Just like Aunt Libby! I just wanted her to love me!" I broke into sobs. "What's wrong with me, Olive?"

She pulled me close.

"My dear Helen, you're going to be okay. You need to know—you're just as broken as the rest of us. It might look different, but we all carry something."

Olive reassured me that day that none of it, Mrs. Allen's death or the others who had left, was my fault. Older and wiser, she gently nudged me out of my sorrow and reminded me how to begin again.

Together, we started gathering a treasure trove of secrets, mighty ones, sure to get someone into trouble if ever told. And just like that, the cloud I'd been living under since Grandma died began to lift.

I had a best friend now.

At the beginning of December, Rosalie Kelly asked Aunt Carrie to attend a suffrage meeting in town. As different as they were, the two shared a sisterly kinship.

Many nights, after working long shifts at the textile mill, Uncle Will would go into town to play music. But this particular Wednesday, he and Pap were both home. I was in bed reading when I heard Rosalie Kelly's name come up downstairs. I crept to the top of the stairs to listen.

"Pa, I'm worried Rosalie's putting strange notions into Carrie's head," Uncle Will said. "I'm not sure where this suffrage movement is headed. What do you think about it?"

"William, Carrie will be fine," Pap said. "Your mother and my sisters taught me years ago that women are pigheaded and stronger than hell. Best to give 'em what they want."

There was a long pause, followed by the sound of glasses being refilled. The scent of Uncle Will's cigarette drifted up the stairs.

"What do you think of the Kellys, Pa?" Uncle Will asked. "Carrie says Mother didn't like them. Peter thinks lowly of them. Now Carrie and Helen have gotten friendly with the Kellys, and I don't know how I feel about it. And I didn't realize Olive didn't have a father. Did you know that?"

"Son, there've been rumors about that poor woman for years."

"Carrie says Rosalie was raped after high school. Doesn't know who the father is."

"Oh, boy. I hadn't heard that," Pap said.

"Carrie says folks here have treated her like junkyard dogs. Including Peter." He hesitated, then added quietly, "She is different. Acts a little like a man."

"She's never been coy or dainty," Pap said. "But that's no reason for your brother to judge her."

He went on, "Let's be clear, whatever Peter says, I've always thought the Kellys were decent, hardworking Irish. Your mother, God rest her soul, and Mrs. Kelly were even friendly until Olive was born. It troubled me when Peter convinced your mother that they weren't our type. Said good Christians would question our morals if we kept their company. Something about status in the community." Pap chuckled.

"It makes sense," Uncle Will said. "Peter thinks women come in one model: pretty, demure, and penitent. Rosalie's none of those. She's a sinner in his eyes and the leader of a movement the church has never supported. Definitely a woman who doesn't know her place."

The front door creaked open. Aunt Carrie was home. I raced back to bed and yanked the covers up to my chin, pretending to be asleep.

When she came through my door, something followed her in, something electric. The room felt different.

"Helen, are you awake?"

I opened my eyes, squinting like I'd just been stirred from a deep sleep. "How was the meeting?" I asked, stifling a pretend yawn.

She sat on the edge of my bed, her eyes brighter than usual, almost teary.

"It was incredible," she whispered. "I learned things I never knew. I met women fighting to change our future. Women who believe we deserve freedom, liberty, and equality just like men."

She reached for my hand.

"Helen," she said, smiling through her tears, "I'm a suffragist now."

Even though I didn't yet grasp the full weight of her words, they settled inside me, deep in my bones, like something sacred. I could never have predicted just how much they'd change everything for her and for me.

TWELVE

December 3–December 10, 1912

As I walked home from school, Olive ran towards me, holding a piece of paper.

"Helen, Helen! I won the writing contest!"

"For goodness' sake, Olive, you're going to freeze to death," I said. Her coat was wide open, and she wore neither a hat nor mittens. "What writing contest?"

"Look, it's all right here!" she said, handing me a typed, official-looking letter from the office of Anna Howard Shaw, president of NAWSA, the National American Women's Suffrage Association. "I didn't think I'd win, but I won. I actually won!"

"By golly, Olive." I thought of all the times Olive had outshone me, and felt my fingers tighten on the crisp paper.

"My mother, a group of suffragists, and I will walk from

New York City to Albany over Christmas to push the cause. Then, when we arrive at Governor Sulzer's inauguration, I will recite my poem. I'll be on the same stage as the governor! Helen, isn't it fantabulous?" she squealed.

"I'm so happy for you," I said, trying to hide the envious twitch in my eyes.

The suffragists were in the paper almost every week, and now Olive's poem would be part of that very noise that seemed to be changing the world.

Olive and Rosalie had their march from New York City to Albany all set. Everything was all planned, that is, until the day Olive and I went sledding.

One Saturday, shortly after Olive got the news, I looked out my window to see that about six inches of snow had fallen. It looked like a perfect day for sledding. I got bundled in my long underwear and put everything on I could find to keep me warm, including two flannel petticoats and my usual long stockings fastened to my underwear. I topped it off with a heavy wool skirt and a thick sweater that Aunt Libby had recently knitted me. By the time I put on my wool coat, I could barely move, and a vision of a stuffed pillow came to mind as I walked over to fetch Olive. When she came down to the door in her snow clothes, my eyes widened, and my eyebrows raised.

"Not fair! Why do you get to dress like a boy, and I can't?"

Overhearing me, her mother came out of the kitchen giggling.

"Helen, practicality must be the driving force behind women's fashion. It's ridiculous what they have us wearing. A friend from Poland gave me these winter clothes when her son outgrew them. They certainly make more sense than wearing a skirt to play in the snow, don't they?"

Rosalie Kelly was strong, outspoken, and someone who came up with her own ideas, not the ones she was told to have. With each interaction I had with her, I learned that this suffragist didn't have a demure bone in her body. Any hope that Uncle Peter would reconsider his disapproval of her diminished.

Olive and I decided to go where all the neighborhood kids gathered, about five blocks away. When we arrived, some children were hitching onto the back of the trucks on their sleds without the drivers knowing. I was surprised when I saw Connor and Sean Hamilton sneaking up behind an unsuspecting truck, wrapping a short rope around the bumper, and sliding down the road.

Connor Hamilton was the oldest in the ninth grade, Sean was a year older than me in sixth grade, Prudence was a year younger and in the fourth grade, and little Liam was in the second grade. Our dislike for each other was mutual, and any chance we got to be nasty to each other, we were.

Without their bratty sister Prudence to squeal on them, the boys had decided to have a day of risky fun. When they spotted Olive and me, they did everything possible to reel us in, most likely to get us to participate so we wouldn't be able to blabber about them being "bad boys."

"Bet you scaredy cats won't do this. You're both too chicken." Connor and Sean squawked at us. "Bok, bok, bok."

They walked back up the street and were ready to get another ride. They hopped onto their sled, a much better sled, I might add, than what Olive and I had, and hitched onto the back end of a passing truck.

"Eat your hearts out!" they screamed.

When they walked back up the street after untying their sleds at the lower block, they yelled to us, "Chicken. Bok, bok, bok! Girls are chickens. You're too scared!"

"We aren't chickens. We aren't!" I shouted, trying my best to protect our honor. "Come on, Olive. Let's show them. They can't talk to us like that!"

"Have you ever done this before?" Olive asked.

"Sure, I've done it many times," I lied. "It's fun. I promise."

"I'm not sure this is a good idea," Olive said.

"We'll let go as soon as we get to the next street," I pleaded.

I went over to the boys and, in a cheeky tone, said, "We'll need to borrow this," grabbed their rope, and walked back to Olive.

We waited for the next truck, hopped on our frail old sled, and looped the rope around the bumper of a grocery delivery truck. The driver must've seen us because he stopped short after only a few feet. We shot forward and slid under his vehicle, landing hard on the icy road.

I heard Olive scream.

I saw the driver's feet. He yelled for us to come out from under his truck. We squirmed out like worms, and I was the first one the man saw. He pulled me up from the ground, grabbed me by my snow-covered arm, and started wagging his finger at me.

In my side vision, I could see the boys laughing. Realizing Olive was still on the ground, I looked down to find her crying, struggling to get up. When the man looked down at Olive's beautiful face, with her crimson lips and cheeks and frozen tears on her eyelashes, his voice softened, and his anger disappeared.

"Let me help you, young lady," he offered.

"I think I hurt my ankle," Olive said. "I can't walk on it."

"You kids live around here?" the man asked.

"Yes, sir," Olive replied.

"Hop in. Let's get you home." The man helped Olive into his truck, and as I walked behind them, I turned to see the

Hamilton boys. Their laughter had turned into silence. I stuck my tongue out at them and hopped up into the seat.

On the way to our neighborhood, the man scolded us for what seemed longer than one of Father Murphy's homilies and lectured that he would tell our parents. If I'd known all this, I'd never have gotten into his vehicle. However, with Olive's ankle in a bad way, I guessed it was payback for our stupidity—well, maybe my stupidity.

When we pulled up to Olive's house, the man got our sled out of his truck, helped Olive out of his vehicle, and assisted her up the stairs to her grandparents' home. A very annoyed Mr. Kelly answered while I tried to slither away, but the truck driver grabbed me by the arm before I could escape.

"Not so quick, kid. Where do you live?"

Cornered, I pointed next door.

Aunt Carrie opened the door with a look that said more than any scolding could. Once again, I didn't get a spanking, something I greatly appreciated with my new caretakers, but as punishment, I had to go to Confession and was banned from seeing Olive for a week. That felt like ten years in best friend time.

Olive's ankle was broken, and now the plan for her to walk from New York City to Albany with the suffragists was foiled. Olive had said it was just bad luck. But I knew better. I had ruined everything.

THIRTEEN

December 11–December 25, 1912

THE CARDINAL

Cardinal, Cardinal with lovely red feathers
Bringing me joy in all seasons of weather
Though a favorite of hers
Now a favorite of mine
Is it her that I see
Or a bird on the vine?
Oh, bird on the vine
What is it you say?
I'll leave you not ever
I'm with you each day.

—Olive Kelly, Christmas 1912

December had always been my favorite month before Grandma died. My memories were filled with joy: decorating the house, baking treats, buying gifts.

Aunt Carrie, ever thoughtful, asked what I wanted for Christmas, so I gave her a long list of presents, and of everything that had to happen to make it feel like it used to. I was hopeful this Christmas could be just as merry as the ones with Grandma, and Aunt Carrie seemed determined to make that happen.

Rosalie had secured three round-trip train tickets to Albany, all of which were paid for by the suffrage committee.

"We simply cannot allow Olive to miss the opportunity of a lifetime!" Aunt Carrie declared, determined to make things right, knowing I was partly to blame.

She would take Olive and me to Albany so Olive could recite her prize-winning poem at the governor's inauguration. I had no idea how she planned to make it work with Pap, Uncle Will, and especially Uncle Peter, but Aunt Carrie had given Rosalie her word. There was no turning back.

The Christmas tree and decorations had gone up early, bringing a comfort I couldn't quite explain. I loved shopping for presents with Aunt Carrie, just like I had with Grandma—small, useful gifts for Uncle Will, Uncle Peter, and Pap. On those trips, I'd pause at the toy store windows, dreaming of the fancy things I knew better than to ask for. As I grew, I learned what Christmas could and couldn't bring.

After weeks of preparation, Uncle Peter would join us for dinner on Christmas Eve and Christmas Day. I hadn't seen much of him since Aunt Carrie and Uncle Will moved in. We would've liked to invite the Kellys over, especially with Rosalie off hiking from New York City to Albany during the holiday, but that was out of the question with Uncle Peter staying both days.

I brought gingerbread cookies to the Kellys and gave Olive her gift, a linen handkerchief with her name stitched in needlepoint. In return, she gave me a beautiful poem about cardinals.

Back home, I helped Aunt Carrie with the Christmas feast of fish, vegetables, potatoes, apple pie, and her beloved fruitcake. She told me she'd made that "fussy" cake every year since childhood. Preparations had started in October, and every week since, we'd gone into the "special" closet, grabbed the rum Pap bought, and poured a full cup over the waiting loaf. I was certain the cake was thoroughly drunk by now, and I couldn't help but wonder what would happen to us when we finally ate it.

Before dinner, Aunt Carrie went upstairs to change into her new dress, the one she'd been sewing for weeks for the New Year's Eve party in Albany. I couldn't wait to see it. I slipped into my prettiest church dress and changed Sadie into the red velvet gown Grandma had made a few Christmases ago.

We waited in the parlor by the tree, the lights twinkling softly. When Aunt Carrie cleared her throat at the bottom of the stairs, almost as if announcing her arrival, I turned and gasped.

"Mercy me!" I blurted.

I hadn't realized how beautiful she was until that moment. She looked like one of the women in the fashion magazines she sometimes flipped through at the newsstand. A deep pink ribbon crowned her head in a neat bow, matching the sash cinched at her tiny waist. Her long brown hair was curled and loosely pinned. The pale pink dress, with its rounded neckline and soft pleats, floated to her ankles, revealing white shoes with little purple bows. She'd dabbed on rouge and lipstick and even stained her nails pink. When the men saw her, they all drew in a breath, even Uncle Peter.

The fish was cooked to perfection, but the real show was yet to come: the cake. Aunt Carrie lit a match and touched it to the top, calling it a flambé. For a moment, I thought the whole house might catch fire. But when the flames died down, what remained was nothing short of a masterpiece.

Around eight o'clock, there was a knock at the door. Uncle Will jumped up and hurried to answer, with Aunt Carrie close behind. I heard voices in the foyer, introductions, and laughter, and peeked out to see who had arrived.

To my surprise, two well-dressed Black couples stood in the entryway. The men held instrument cases, and the women carried platters wrapped in cloth and tied with bows.

"Everyone," Uncle Will said cheerfully, "I'd like you to meet two of my bandmates and their lovely wives. This is Jay Bolder, who plays cornet, and his wife, Ruth, and Freddy Hadder, who plays trumpet, and his wife, Ethel."

We had never had Black guests in our home before, and I was excited to meet Uncle Will's friends and sing carols with them. Pap and Uncle Peter greeted the men politely and shook their hands, but when Aunt Carrie led the women into the kitchen, Uncle Peter suddenly announced he had other visits to make that evening. He went straight to the closet for his coat and hat. Uncle Will's jaw tightened.

"Please thank Carrie for dinner . . . nice meeting you, gentlemen. I'll see you all at Christmas Mass tomorrow, I'm certain," Uncle Peter said, trying to sound light.

He looked caught off guard when Mr. Hadder replied warmly, "Never missed a day in my life, Father! But we're Baptists. We attend The First Baptist Church on Fitzhugh Street."

"Oh, of course," Uncle Peter said, his smile slipping.

"Willy tells us you're a preacher," Mr. Hadder added, trying to keep the conversation going.

Uncle Peter forced another phoney smile.

"Yes. Immaculate Conception. Merry Christmas." He buttoned his coat, tipped his hat to the room, and added, "Will, Pap, gentlemen. Good night." He kissed me on the forehead, then walked out without saying goodbye to Aunt Carrie or the women in the kitchen. This was behavior I'd never seen before.

After he left, the music began. Uncle Will played his guitar while Mr. Bolder and Mr. Hadder brought the room to life with their horns. We all sang carols, and I was thrilled when everyone complimented my voice.

Aunt Carrie and the musicians' wives stayed in the kitchen talking for most of the night. I later found out that my aunt had invited them to a suffrage meeting after the trip to Albany.

Before I retired for the evening, we put my stocking on the fireplace mantle and a smaller one that Aunt Carrie had thoughtfully made for Sadie. Although I knew Santa wasn't real after last year, part of me wasn't ready to say goodbye to the jolly old man just yet. It seemed to me that Santa stood for so much more than just presents. I cut a piece of apple pie and put it on the table near the Christmas tree.

I awoke to a warm house filled with the sweet smell of scones. I quickly climbed out of bed, pulled on my robe and slippers, and ran into Pap's room, shouting for him to wake up. Uncle Will's bed was empty as he was already at the mill.

I waited anxiously, nearly bursting with excitement. Finally, Pap came out dressed for the day, and we headed downstairs together. A radiant Aunt Carrie, already in her church clothes, greeted us in the foyer.

My mouth fell open when we entered the parlor. An ornately decorated tree stood surrounded by a dozen or so colorfully wrapped packages. The pie I'd left out was gone, and the stocking hung heavy on the mantel. I ran to Aunt Carrie and hugged her tight, struggling not to cry. I knew she had done all of this.

I unwrapped present after present, stunned to find everything on my Christmas list: a new church dress, one for Sadie with a matching hat, the little purse from Chromwells, books, games, and a pair of lovely black shoes I hadn't even asked for.

Afterward, we went to Christmas Mass, where Uncle Will met up with us. I sang in the choir, and then we said hello to Uncle Peter. I never looked forward to visiting the cemetery, and I didn't want to go on this perfect Christmas Day. The morning had been so cheerful, and I knew how heavy my heart would feel once we passed through the cemetery gate.

We trudged through the snow, found Grandma's tombstone, and placed six lit candles for her. One from each of us, including Aunt Libby. Upon leaving, a bright red cardinal appeared on a nearby snow-encrusted branch. It sang a quick song and flew off into a neighboring tree. Aunt Carrie and I smiled at each other. I was certain Gram was saying hello, just like the poem stated that Olive gave me for Christmas.

Back at home, after breakfast, I opened my stocking. Inside was a tortoiseshell comb, Old Maid cards, lavender water, candies, and warm new mittens. Then Aunt Carrie reappeared, holding a large box.

"You'll need this for New Year's Eve. There'll be a fancy party that night," she said, her face glowing.

I held the box tightly, imagining what might be inside. I looked around the room at the tree, the presents, Pap, my beautiful aunt, and my eyes welled up. Pap must have felt whatever I was feeling, too, for when I caught eyes with him, I saw they were glassy.

"Go ahead. Open it," Pap said, wiping away a tear.

Inside was an ivory-and-rose dress, elegant and finely stitched, with matching pantaloons Aunt Carrie had lovingly sewn. I could hardly believe my eyes. It looked like something a princess might wear to a winter ball.

Later, Pap, Uncle Will, and I headed to the state hospital to see Aunt Lib, whose increasingly poor health made visiting us at Magnolia Street difficult. She had decorated a small tree in her room with red and green hand-knitted ornaments. Beneath it, on a tiny red cloth skirt, sat a present with my name written so large I could see it from the doorway.

Aunt Lib was draped in her typical black garb and looked tired. It saddened me when she had difficulty getting to her feet from her rocker. Pap and Uncle Will rushed to her side.

"Now, boys, I'm fine. I've gotten along splendidly without a man in my life for the last sixty-five—or is it sixty-six years?" she teased, glancing upward as if confused. Pap and Uncle Will shook their heads back and forth, wearing faint smiles. Aunt Lib kissed them each on the cheek, then moved toward me, smothering me in a firm embrace.

"Now tell me all about yourself. How is my favorite young woman faring?"

"I'm very well, Aunt Libby. I'm happy," I said, surprising even myself with the realization. Uncle Will and Pap's faces lit up.

"I finally have everything I've ever wanted," I whispered.

"And what's that, my dear?" Aunt Lib whispered back.

"A real family. And a best friend," I said softly, just for her. I held back the tears at the mere realization.

Aunt Lib's thin upper lip all but disappeared as she grinned from ear to ear. She pulled me into another hug, then nodded toward the tree. "Go on. Get your present."

I crawled underneath and retrieved the small package with my name on the tag. Inside was a hand-knitted throw, sure to keep me warm on chilly nights. I threw my arms around her and kissed her cheek. I settled onto a small footstool beside her, while Pap and Uncle Will sat on folding chairs a young man in a medical uniform had brought in. Aunt Lib took my hand gently in hers.

"Still biting your fingernails, I see?" she teased, giggling. Then her eyes drifted to the gold ring on my finger. "I'm glad Brigid's treating you well."

She stared at me for a moment, her eyes glossy. Something inside me turned. I wrapped my arms around her familiar shoulders and gave her a squeeze. Our visit wouldn't be long, so I did my best to cheer her up and maybe cheer myself up, too.

I told her about the brave women we'd met, suffragists fighting for the vote, and about Olive and how Aunt Carrie and I had joined the cause. But just as I began to tell her about our upcoming trip, Uncle Will cut in.

"Helen, I think that's enough," he said, with a quiet edge.

Aunt Lib looked from me to Uncle Will. "How does Peter feel about all this?"

Uncle Will cleared his throat. "Peter doesn't know."

She shook her head slowly. "You all need to be careful. This whole thing could be a powder keg. Peter's a funny egg. But I'm proud of Carrie and of you, Helen, for your bravery."

Pap leaned forward, his voice low. "Elizabeth, I have no problem with the girls voting. But hiding it from Peter? That's another story. He'll find out eventually, and when he does—well, that powder keg might just blow."

Uncle Will sat up straighter. "It's none of Peter's business what we do or believe. I'm tired of walking on eggshells just to keep him calm."

Aunt Lib let out a heavy sigh. "William, you and Peter have been at odds ever since Albert died. Don't let old wounds stand in the way of Helen's happiness. Please, tread lightly."

"I'm not afraid of Peter," Uncle Will said, his voice sharp. "I'm proud of the girls. The world is changing all around him, and he can't stop it."

Pap frowned and shook his head. "The world may be changing, yes. But Peter can stop Helen from being a part of it."

Aunt Lib looked at me, her expression softening. "This isn't the time or place for all this," she said quietly.

Before we left, Aunt Lib told me that, although she wasn't as spry as she used to be, she still wanted to help the suffragists. That pleased me more than I could say. I couldn't wait to tell Aunt Carrie.

Aunt Libby was now one of us.

I didn't know what Pap and Uncle Will would tell Uncle Peter when he discovered Aunt Carrie and I weren't home on New Year's Day, but I trusted the grown-ups would handle it. I was going to be part of history and "rub elbows," a term I had heard Aunt Carrie use with Uncle Will when referring to highfalutin' people.

When we returned home, Uncle Peter walked out of the kitchen wearing an apron over his ankle-length black cassock.

"You certainly couldn't have been helping out in the kitchen, brother," Uncle Will scoffed.

Uncle Peter swung Uncle Will a scornful glance and then looked at me. "Helen, darling, I have an extra special present for you that I think you will be quite happy about. Gather everyone, and then you can open it." He said, gesturing to the treasure under the tree.

I waited for people to gather around and picked up the large present. I shook it and sized it up, trying to decide what might be inside. Within seconds, the green silk ribbon was ripped off, and the gleaming red paper was shredded.

Before me was a doll with long red hair, dressed in a majestic blue velvet gown that matched her eyes. The resemblance to how Sadie looked when I first opened her four years ago was unmistakable.

"A doll?" I asked, confused.

"You can toss out your old doll with the short hair now. Look how pretty your new doll is," he said.

"Uncle Peter, I'd never get rid of Sadie because she is old and ugly!" I snapped, insulted.

How could he think, even for a moment, that I'd trade Sadie in for a newer, prettier version?

"Peter, isn't she lovely? Helen will have so much fun dressing her," Aunt Carrie said, trying to smooth over my outburst. I knew she was trying to avoid a blow-up. "Helen, isn't she pretty?" she prodded.

"Thank you, Uncle Peter," was all I could muster. I picked up my new doll, brought her to my room, and stuck her under the bed in her box.

After eating our Christmas dinner, the adults exchanged gifts. The room became silent when Uncle Peter handed Aunt Carrie a small box wrapped in exquisite paper, topped with a large bow.

"Peter, how beautiful it looks. I almost don't want to unwrap it," she said.

"Go on now. I promise it won't do you any good to just look at it." Uncle Peter teased.

A delicately etched glass bottle filled with perfume was inside. Aunt Carrie lifted it from the box and turned it in her hands, studying the intricate design. When she realized what it was, a smile slowly spread across her face.

"Peter, this was too much," she said softly. "You shouldn't have."

"Don't be silly. You married my brother. Consider it a consolation gift."

Uncle Will didn't find this funny and gave his brother a cutting glare.

Aunt Carrie opened the handsome bottle and brought it to me. The heavenly liquid smelled like a million roses, and I was sure I'd never enjoyed anything as fragrant. Aunt Carrie dabbled a little behind her ears and on her wrists and walked up to Uncle Will.

"What do you think, darling?" Uncle Will's eyes closed in delight, taking in the lovely aroma. Then his eyes quickly opened, and an ugly frown covered his face.

"Wasn't that nice of my brother," Uncle Will said sarcastically. "Here, Carrie, open my present. The girl at the store did a fine job wrapping it." A competitive flicker filled his eyes as he handed the expertly wrapped box to my aunt.

Inside was an expensive-looking evening bag covered in tiny pearls and colorful beads that my aunt had admired for weeks in the store window of B. Foreman Co.

"William, thank you, thank you! I can't wait to wear this for . . . well, it'll be a thrill when I can wear it."

I could tell Aunt Carrie had nearly slipped, mentioning New Year's Eve, but caught herself just in time.

That night, after bedtime prayers, Aunt Carrie asked, "Dear, did you have a nice day?"

"Nice day? It was fantastical!" I said.

"Fantastical, aye? What was your favorite part?" she asked with a smirk.

My heart was too full for just one answer.

"All of it! I loved all of it. You made Christmas special again," I said. "I've already forgotten last Christmas."

Most nights, Aunt Carrie would kiss me goodnight on my forehead, but that night, I longed to be held as Gram would often do. I reached out and held her. When she realized my firm grip, she seemed to relax and hugged me back tightly. When we pulled apart, we were both giddy.

"Do you really think it's okay for us to go to Albany?" I asked.

"Helen, I believe we owe it to women everywhere, not to mention Olive, to be there. Those people and the governor need to hear Olive's impactful words. It will all work out."

That night, I fell asleep dreaming of Albany, surrounded by suffragists. I didn't yet understand that hoping everything would work out was its own kind of dream.

FOURTEEN

December 30–December 31, 1912

We were already running late when we reached the station. Olive hobbled beside us on her crutches, grimacing with every step, while Aunt Carrie moved through the crowd like she owned it—her new blue wool coat cinched perfectly at the waist, a fur scarf at her neck, and her hat pinned just so. Not a hair was out of place.

Olive and I had dressed in our best clothes, having passed Aunt Carrie's morning inspection. I was beginning to understand just how important appearance was to her.

"You want people thinking you come from good families, don't you?" she had said, smoothing the collar of my coat.

Olive, polite as ever, never argued with adults, especially my lovely aunt, but I knew she found the whole thing ridiculous. Pretending to be someone you weren't, as if class meant anything at all when women couldn't even vote.

As we boarded the train, I noticed the other passengers slouched in their seats, holiday-weary, their bags stuffed with leftover gifts. We weren't headed home like they were. We were headed into something bigger.

We arrived in Albany just before sunset. Rosalie met us at the station, limping toward us with open arms. She'd gotten into town on the 29th, still recovering from the thirteen-day march from New York City.

"Goodness, you made it!" she called, her voice bright despite the fatigue in her steps.

"Momma! I missed you so much!" Olive shuffled toward her, nearly losing a crutch in the rush.

Rosalie's tired face became radiant. "And how have you been handling all this walking, my girl?"

"I'm fine, Momma. Just fine." They clasped hands, their eyes locked, and then tenderly embraced each other.

In that instant, I realized no one had ever looked at me that way, and it saddened me, thinking no one ever would. That was the look only a mother gave to her child.

Rosalie turned to Aunt Carrie and beamed. "Why, ladies, we're all here together in Albany. What could be better?"

Aunt Carrie hugged her. "Rosalie, how did it all go?"

"Oh, you don't want to see my feet," Rosalie laughed. "Blisters, bruises . . . lost both big toenails. On day ten, we marched through snow so thick we couldn't feel our legs. Someone said women are born walking uphill. I think they were right."

Just two weeks earlier, on December 16th, Rosalie had left New York City with twenty-five women from NAWSA bound for Albany on foot. They'd worn union suits under heavy wool skirts, cloaks, sweaters, and mittens—dressed for sleet, snow, and public judgment. Rosalie said some on the committee had disapproved of their men's boots, but she'd insisted practicality came before appearances.

Slung over their shoulders were knapsacks inscribed with the words "Votes for Women," filled with literature to share and some personal supplies for the journey. Some carried walking sticks, American flags, or signs they raised to passersby. As they all proudly headed north out of the city, they shouted, "First aid is all right for our bruises small, but nothing will cure us but votes for all!"

Along the way, they stayed with supporters who offered food and shelter. Rosalie had arranged many of the stops herself. Their journey would end with a grand New Year's Eve party in Albany, followed by Olive's poem reading at the governor's inauguration the next morning. We would be staying with Mrs. Maeve LaFay, a wealthy widow and major suffrage donor. According to Rosalie, her mansion was the most elegant in the city, and we were to be on our absolute best behavior.

Aunt Carrie and I walked ahead while Olive and Rosalie inched toward the shiny silver Rolls-Royce waiting just outside the station. Rufus, our driver, shooed away a crowd of wide-eyed men with a wave.

None of us had ever seen a car like it, long-nosed, sleek, with a polished black top and wheels that looked more like art than tires.

Aunt Carrie took the front seat with her bag on her lap. The rest of us squeezed into the back, Olive's crutches poking our knees as we settled in. Rufus glanced at Aunt Carrie and struck up a conversation. I noticed men often did. The way she straightened her posture and offered a quick smile told me she didn't mind one bit.

"You ever seen a Rolls-Royce before, Miss?" he asked in an accent I couldn't place.

I later found out that Rufus was from Boston.

"No, sir. I never have," she replied.

"This here is one of the finest automobiles ever created. It's the Silver Ghost," he said.

Instead of letting Rosalie tell us about her thirteen-day journey, Rufus became chatty and insisted on center stage, telling us about every building or neighborhood we passed. I decided that the smooth-talking man was definitely trying to impress my aunt.

"Speaking of ghosts, beautiful house it is, the LaFay home. It has quite a history, though. Any locals will tell ya that it's haunted. Betcha girls will like that," he said with a chuckle.

"Haunted? Honestly, Sir. Don't scare the girls, please," my aunt said.

Rosalie nudged me and whispered, "Don't worry. It's just a story."

"It's known by all the locals, ma'am. Lady Maeve's twelve-year-old son, Frederick, died tragically from a faulty gas pipe not long after movin' into the home in 1892, and then Mr. LaFay dropped dead outside the home in 1904. Both their spirits still live there and have been seen by many a guest."

"You *are* serious?" Rosalie asked as though maybe she had thought he was teasing before. Olive and I looked at each other, our ears perked.

"Yes. It was very sad when that young boy died, and so unfortunate when Mr. LaFay passed. He was a fine gentleman, well respected, and a very successful businessman." He spoke spritely, and I suspected he had told this story more than just a few times.

"Do you all believe in ghosts?"

The three of us in the back looked at each other. I was

anxious to hear everyone's answer. Aunt Carrie spoke first.

"God would never allow that. Souls either go to Heaven, Purgatory, or that other place."

"You mean Hell?" Rufus announced, seemingly proud that he knew the answer.

"Rufus, please. We don't speak such vulgar words in front of the girls," Aunt Carrie scolded.

Rosalie spoke up. "Oh, anything is possible. There are many things we don't understand."

"I think the idea of ghosts is rather comforting. If someone I loved died, I hope they'd come to visit me after they passed," Olive said. "Helen, what about you?"

"Gram and Aunt Libby believe in ghosts. They are smart ladies, so I guess it's possible. Tell us more, sir," I said. Aunt Carrie turned around, giving me a dirty look.

"It's been said that when young people come to the castle to stay, Frederick LaFay comes out to play." Olives and my eyes became the size of dinner plates, and I got goosebumps all over my arms.

"Rufus. That's enough," Aunt Carrie said.

"Just some good fodder for ghost stories for you ladies," Rufus added.

Olive and I pinched each other in disbelief when we arrived at a majestic gray stone castle that was three stories high.

Large, inviting Christmas wreaths hung on the brown, curved double doors, and a turret climbed on one side of the castle like in a fairy tale. I could see three porches from the road and counted ten windows across the front of the house. I was confident that we were about to add to the memorable experiences of our lives, although I could never have guessed how memorable they would be.

A man in a suit and a bowtie answered the door and

invited us in. A bit hesitant yet exhilarated at the thought of seeing a real ghost, we stepped into the grand foyer. Mrs. LaFay came down the stairs and greeted us with genuine warmth. She showered Olive with compliments about winning the contest and spent the rest of our visit bragging to anyone who'd listen.

The house was a bit gloomy, hung full of moody art, rich dark furniture, colorful rugs, brown wood every-where, even on the ceiling. A double staircase, too many fireplaces to count, and best of all: electricity and plumbing. Turning lights on with a flick of a switch felt like magic. The bathroom had a real faucet, a flushing toilet, and a bathtub.

Olive and I would be sharing one of the eleven bed-rooms in the house. Ours had a fireplace, a bed large enough for five people, and an elegant green jewel-tone sofa that Rosalie gestured towards.

"Here is a 'fainting sofa' for us to faint upon when things get too difficult, girls," she said. "Society tries to make us feel so weak. Rubbish, I tell you. You're only weak if you believe you are!" she exclaimed in Rosalie fashion.

That night, after we rolled each other's hair into curls for tomorrow's big event, Aunt Carrie and Rosalie tucked us in and went to their rooms. Olive fell asleep quickly. I lay there staring up at the pressed metal ceiling, thinking about what Rufus had said in the car.

Every creak I heard became a ghost flying around our room for its nightly haunt. I stared at the ceiling for hours until sleep finally came.

In the middle of the night, I was hurled out of dream-land by three loud knocks on our headboard. I froze, afraid to move, and then, suddenly, I felt something grab my toes. Trying not to scream and wake the entire house, I frantically shook Olive awake.

"Olive! It's Frederick! He's in our room!" I whispered, trembling.

I gathered all my nerve and jumped up to turn the light switch on. Olive shielded her eyes with her pillow as I searched every corner of the room. To my dismay, nothing was out of place.

"Helen, you imagined it. Just go back to sleep." Olive peeled off the blankets, hopped out of bed, and turned the lamp off.

I forced Olive to sleep on my side of the bed that night and propped up my pillows so that I could stand guard until morning, scouring the room for ghosts. All night long, my eyes went back and forth, back and forth, like a spectator at a tennis match.

When I saw glimmers of the sun coming in through the sides of the drapes hours later, I praised God's good name.

"We made it to the morning, dear sweet Jesus!" I said loud enough for Olive to hear.

"Helen, go back to bed!" I was glad that at least one of us wouldn't be falling asleep at the big New Year's Eve party that night.

FIFTEEN

New Year's Eve, 1912

The second I buckled the last strap around my ankle, I jumped up and pranced around the room, eagerly showing off my new shoes and dress to Olive. The dress hung loosely below my waist, the prettiest I'd ever worn, and large bows held back our curly locks.

"Olive, I wonder if he thinks I look pretty," I said as I twirled around, looking at myself in the mirror.

"Who thinks you look pretty?" Olive asked, a confused look on her face.

"Why, Frederick, of course," I chuckled.

"Mercy, Helen O'Donnell!" Olive scowled.

"At least he knows we can look better than we did last night!"

We both laughed at the thought.

"Helen, do you think I look all right? Is my dress okay?" Olive asked. "I hate that I still have this brace on my ankle. I just want to run and walk normally again."

Olive's dress was one of her mother's old ones, lovingly altered by her grandmother for the occasion.

"You look fine, Olive. You could wear a gunny sack and still be the most beautiful girl anywhere you went," I said truthfully.

My aunt floated out of her bedroom looking as pretty as a picture and wearing the perfume Uncle Peter had gifted her, which almost caused a fight between my two uncles. I'd remember that alluring smell anywhere. Her new beaded purse, which Uncle Will had given her at Christmas, dangled from one hand, and a strand of faux pearls hung around her elegant, long neck. I had seen the necklace on her dresser once and asked about it.

She said pearls were too expensive, but in the dark, no one could tell the difference if one acted as though they deserved costly things. Whether the pearls were genuine or not, Aunt Carrie reminded me of an actress playing her part on stage, ready to be who she wanted to be.

I must confess that I was disappointed but not surprised when Rosalie stepped out of her room, donning an unflattering dress and wearing her hiking boots. Rosalie and Aunt Carrie were complete opposites in the fashion department.

My aunt thought it was essential to dress the part as she knew people were always judging how women presented themselves. Rosalie, on the other hand, didn't seem to care a bit. She didn't even wear a stitch of makeup. I thought about what she'd said the day Olive and I went sledding.

"Helen, practicality must be the driving force behind women's fashion."

I had heard Uncle Will refer to Rosalie as manly. My

family believed that women and girls should look feminine. I knew this from the countless comments from the men, Grandma, and even my own aunt. Looking feminine meant wearing the correct clothes, wearing one's hair the acceptable way, not being too plump, and, when old enough, wearing a little makeup to brighten one's face. However, wearing too much makeup could bring about gossip or rude comments.

Olive mentioned that when she asked her mother about makeup, Rosalie told her it was more important to be respected for one's brain, not one's looks. I liked this thought, as apparently I hadn't been blessed by God in terms of attractiveness, but it did make me wonder. After all, Olive had both brains and beauty. Could it hurt to have both?

The band was playing a heavenly waltz when we started down the stairs, and I envisioned grabbing Olive and running to the dance floor to swing her around. I remembered that Olive was injured and concluded that this wouldn't be the type of party that Pap and Grandma would put on. Everyone looked very serious. It reminded me a little of Sunday Mass.

Many attendees were hikers who proudly wore their casual attire, including men's boots like Rosalie's, and a button with an attached ribbon that read, "I Walked NYC–Albany 12.16.12." The other female guests, women who weren't the walking type for whatever reason, were bedecked in exquisite dresses and accompanied by men who wore top hats and tails, along with shiny shoes and canes. These were the "elite" of Albany, Rosalie had said, who had contributed financially in some way to the suffrage movement in New York State.

I was so mesmerized by the extraordinary dresses and servants walking around with sumptuous fare that it took me a moment to notice the long food table in the parlor. When we walked into the room, Aunt Carrie took one look at my mouth dangling open and quietly said, "Make sure you eat like a lady, Helen. Remember, ladies, don't eat much."

Eat like a lady? But I wanted to try everything!

I took one look at Olive, and we knew what we had to do without speaking a word. We waited until Olive's mother and my aunt were in the other room and then darted toward the food table. The spread began with smoked fish, freshly baked rolls, tiny potatoes, various meat options, salads, and a selection of cheeses. After that came several varieties of the most perfect, ripe fruit I'd ever seen. Next came an entire section devoted to gorgeous desserts. Tiny pink-frosted squares that seemed to call my name, and little bowls of chocolate pudding I wanted to tip straight into my mouth. A maid with white hair serving the food gave us a piercing stare, making me wonder if she could read our minds.

"Helen, let's just start with hot chocolate," Olive said. "We can come back."

"Really?" I replied, disappointed.

We politely asked the maid if we could have hot chocolate, and when she poured the steaming sweet drink from a glistening silver pitcher into our dainty cups, we watched in great anticipation. I took one sip and noticed a massive bowl of whipped cream hiding behind some glimmering frosted treats, begging to be devoured. We thanked the maid, and when she turned, I grabbed the spoon and scooped up as many tablespoons as would fit into my teacup. Olive frowned at me, and the maid turned around and saw my cup overloaded with cream about to dribble over the sides.

"You girls need to run along now," she said with raised brows.

I took a big sip to avoid spilling my drink, then followed Olive to the stairs, where we sat down. I took another sip. Knowing I probably had a big white mustache on my upper lip, I glanced at Olive, hoping to make her laugh.

"Seriously, Helen, we need to act respectable," she said. "We don't want to embarrass my mother. Remember, we're guests here."

"I'm sorry. Of course, Olive. I'll try harder," I said, taking a ladylike sip from my cup.

I noticed she'd pulled out a small notebook and was scribbling in it.

"What's that for?" I asked.

"Helen, I want to remember everything," she said. "I'm going to write about it for the NAWSA newsletter. My mother said it would be appreciated."

I finished my hot chocolate and went to put my cup down on a nearby marble table. My aunt's voice could be heard. I motioned to Olive, and we listened from around the corner.

"Rosalie, I don't know why it would matter what color their skin is. They are women, too, aren't they? They're fighting just like we are. Why wouldn't we be unified in this fight? You know, all women together?"

Olive and I turned to each other with startled looks.

"Carrie, you don't understand. The NAWSA is a national organization, and many members in the South feel that fraternizing with Black women is harming our chances of winning the vote. We are trying to distance ourselves from them."

"So, when you say our chances, you are referring to white women only? Shouldn't this be the time to win the vote for all women?" Aunt Carrie said.

"At this point, we don't want to do anything that could take the vote away from us. We've been fighting for too long and are so close! You don't understand, Carrie. You have just gotten involved in this fight. This battle has been going on since the first Women's Rights Convention at Seneca Falls in 1848 and even before that."

"Rosalie, yes, I am new to this, but I disagree with NAW-SA's strategy. I believe that together we are stronger, not weaker."

"It's not my decision, Carrie. It's best if your Black friends go to the Negro branch of the Political Equality Club, headed by Sarah Mulrooney Ruhlin in Rochester. We, unfortunately, are fighting this battle divided."

"I would have thought that you, of all people, would be fighting harder for the Black women's vote. You, who have been judged and discriminated against since your rape," Aunt Carrie whispered, but Olive and I knew what she said and looked at each other.

I stood and walked around the corner, hoping to change the conversation.

"Helen!" Aunt Carrie exclaimed, surprised.

Olive trailed behind me, and the two of us, well-trained spies of sorts, talked as if we had no idea what the two women were discussing.

"Did you try the hot chocolate yet, Aunt Carrie? Oh my, it's divine! You must," I said.

"Girls, are you getting on okay?" Rosalie asked.

"Yes, ma'am," we both responded.

"Carrie, I need to speak with some friends. Can I leave you with the girls for a few minutes?" Rosalie asked.

"Of course," Aunt Carrie said.

I grabbed my aunt's hand. "You need to see what's on the food table."

The three of us walked over to where the maid with the white hair was. I met her penetrating eyes with a smile, knowing I was now protected with an adult shield. Olive and I watched my aunt gingerly put a few pieces of food, including two oysters, onto a small plate.

She casually put a raw oyster into her mouth, and her

cheery expression turned to one of complete distress. Her pale skin took on a greenish tint, and she nervously looked around to see who was watching her. She caught my eye, quickly put her plate down, and walked away, trying to appear calm.

Olive and I followed secretly behind her and hid behind a plant, curious where she was going. She stopped, looked around, opened her exquisite evening bag, and spat the oyster into it. Olive and I laughed so hard that Aunt Carrie heard us and came marching over.

"If you girls ever tell a soul," she whispered with a scowl that turned into a smirk.

As we all were having a hefty laugh, Aunt Carrie added, "That was the most disgusting thing I have ever tasted in my entire life. It was slimy, for goodness' sake; slippery, actually. How could anyone eat those?"

"Well, I'm not going to try them," I said, wiggling in disgust. The same dance I did when I saw a big spider.

Olive, all business now, stepped in, "Excuse me, Mrs. O'Donnell. I'm writing a story about this event for the NAW-SA newsletter, and I think it would be wise to get some quotes from a few attendees. May I take Helen to meet some people?" She pulled a paper and a pencil from her pocket, ready to work.

"Will you be okay, Aunt Carrie?" I asked, thinking that if she and Rosalie were at odds, she might want company.

"I'm going in to listen to the band play," she said. "You girls go on. I'll be fine."

My aunt walked off, and we trotted past the food table again. My favorite place of the evening. While the white-haired maid was busy helping a guest, I seized the moment, grabbed a sticky pink cake, and pushed it into my mouth as quickly as I could.

"Helen, stop!" Olive scolded, turning around just as I closed my mouth to hide the evidence.

We entered a large room full of people, and Olive confidently approached an elderly woman standing alone.

"I'd like to introduce myself. My name is Olive Kelly, and this is my friend, Helen O'Donnell. Rosalie Kelly from Rochester is my mother."

The woman's purple dress was adorned with feathers, lace, and colorful beads, and was a masterpiece of sorts. Now this was a woman who wasn't afraid to be seen.

"Of course, I know your mother. She's done so much for our movement in the Rochester area. How wonderful that you and your friend came out for this. I'm Mrs. Van Damme," she said, holding out her hand.

"My mother was one of the founders of the New York State Woman Suffrage Association in Saratoga Springs decades ago. I was seven when I attended my first suffrage event with her."

Olive and I watched as she spooned her last oyster into her mouth. Then she said, "Go fetch me some more oysters, Helen, won't you please? They're simply marvelous."

"Yes, ma'am." I did everything possible to avoid Olive's eyes, certain I would lose my composure. I marched over to the table purposefully, put several of the unsavory things on a plate without being bothered by the maid, and headed back to Mrs. Van Damme and Olive.

"Thank you, dear. I was just telling Olive I saw Elizabeth Cady Stanton speak when I was a young girl. That event was life-changing for me. She said men and women were created equal. We were entitled to equality in politics, religion, morals, education, family, and work. Frederick Douglass was even there."

Mrs. Van Damme's hands were moving back and forth

very theatrically. She told her story while Olive and I watched her spoon one unappetizing oyster after the other into her mouth.

"Do you both know who Frederick Douglass was?"

I had never heard of him and shook my head. Olive, of course, knew who he was, which made me feel brainless, a frequent occurrence when I was with her.

"Olive, why don't you tell Helen who Frederick Douglass was?"

"Helen, he was a writer, one of the greatest orators of our time, and an escaped slave who endured horrible treatment. He lived in Rochester for two decades and founded a newspaper in the mid-to-late 19th century. He fought his entire life to abolish slavery and for the voting rights of Blacks and women. He died in 1895." Olive recited this as though she had memorized it from a book. The Rosalie Kelly Homeschool for Social Justice, I smirked to myself.

"Nice, Olive. Yes, Douglass was an incredible speaker. If he hadn't attended the first women's convention, the Declaration of Sentiments Elizabeth Cady Stanton promoted might never have passed. That's been the movement's backbone ever since.

"I never knew that," I said. "But . . . why aren't Black and white women united in the fight for the vote?"

"Helen—!" Olive nudged me sharply, maybe knowing something I didn't. But Mrs. Van Damme didn't seem offended. In fact, she nodded thoughtfully.

"Helen, the NAWSA is headed toward becoming the NAWWSA—National American White-Woman Suffrage Association. It's not just Black women—Asians, anyone 'not white enough' are being sidelined. I disagree with it. For years, we fought side by side. It's a tragedy."

"I don't think it's right," I said, glancing at Olive.

But this time, she didn't scold me.

Mrs. Van Damme reached out and took my hand. Her expression became somber.

"Girls, here it is sixty-four years later, and only a few women have the right to vote. We've been asking for a basic right of any female citizen for the past sixty-four years. I thought we would win this battle in my lifetime, but I'm growing old, and now I'm tired. I pass the torch on to you, young ladies. You will be responsible for bringing us to the finish line. Helen, if you can get the vote for Blacks, whites, and every other female citizen, then by golly, do it."

She looked right into my eyes, and for a moment, I really felt like she had passed a torch on to me. I could almost feel it burning inside my heart.

Something about her words made me pause and see the movement in a different light. Sixty-four years. Before the Civil War. How had they kept going? I finally understood why Rosalie, Olive, and the hikers marched through blisters and snow. If it didn't happen in their lifetime, it would be up to girls like us.

The band started playing one of my favorite songs, "Let Me Call You Sweetheart," and I ran into the grand parlor to hear it better. A smile crept onto my face as a jolly, grandfatherly man grabbed Aunt Carrie's hand and spun her onto the dance floor.

She sparkled. I noticed several men watching her as she giggled, letting the old man spin her around again and again. Just then, Rosalie appeared beside me with Olive and two of the hikers.

"Looks like your aunt's having a swell time," Rosalie said.

"I do believe so," I said.

"Carrie!" Rosalie waved her hand.

Aunt Carrie left the dance floor, to the evident disappointment of her partner, and joined us.

"This is my dear friend, Carrie O'Donnell, and her niece, Helen, and I believe you may know my daughter Olive," Rosalie said to two women from New York who were very active in NAWSA.

I was so relieved to hear Rosalie call my aunt, her dear friend, that the stiffness in my shoulders quietly unwound.

"Olive, of course, we've met before. Congratulations on winning the poetry contest. I'm thrilled to hear you speak tomorrow. Remember, you speak for us all," Ida Craft said.

Mrs. Craft was a small woman with a round face and a receding chin. Her wire-rimmed glasses and serious nature reminded me slightly of Sister Mary Regina from last year.

"Yes, ma'am. I'm honored to have been selected from over a hundred entries. I'm nervous, of course, but after what my mother and the hikers have just done, my nerves feel like nothing," Olive said, sounding far older than her years.

She was so polished, poised in a way I wasn't sure I'd ever be.

Jessie Stubbs, an attractive woman with kind eyes and well-defined cheekbones, said, "We were so sorry to hear about your ankle. How are you managing?"

"Very well, ma'am. Getting on just fine. Thank you for asking."

"You know I used to be a nurse when I lived in Chicago before my husband died, but now I attend Columbia in the city where I am studying Philanthropy. What do you girls want to be when you grow up?" she asked.

What do I want to be? The question surprised me. My mother worked in a mill, and my grandmother and aunt were seamstresses. I assumed I would be a mother and a seamstress too.

But something told me that wasn't the answer these women were hoping for.

"I'm not sure, ma'am, but I like to help the sick," Olive replied.

"Maybe someday you will be a doctor," Miss Craft said. Have you ever considered becoming a doctor who helps women? God knows we need doctors who understand us." The women all nodded their heads in agreement. I noticed Olive stand up a bit taller from the corner of my eye.

"I never thought of that, ma'am, but I'd like that," Olive said.

"Helen, what about you?" asked Mrs. Stubbs.

I wasn't about to say seamstress when Olive might become a doctor. I had an audience, and I played it up a bit.

"Maybe I'll go to Columbia someday. I could become a teacher," I said, like it was something I'd always dreamed of.

The truth was, I'd never even heard of Columbia before tonight.

"Helen, that would be wonderful," Aunt Carrie replied.

"Teaching is noble," Mrs. Stubbs added. "But why stop there? Why not be a professor?"

"Helen, you're certainly smart enough," Aunt Carrie said.

I blinked at the surprise in her voice.

"Carrie, what do you do with the NAWSA?" Ida Craft asked.

"Miss Craft, I'm new to Rochester and have been attending meetings and learning as much as possible.

"Wonderful!" Miss Craft gave an approving nod.

"Carrie, I'm happy that you are here. The movement needs smart, classy women like you," Mrs. Stubbs said.

Soon after, we were told to retire for the night. Olive had to be at her best for the inauguration parade. Rosalie wasn't taking any chances. I'd never stayed up for the stroke of midnight on New Year's Eve, and I was disappointed. I thought I'd get to hear the bewitching chime ushering in 1913. But that wasn't going to happen.

To be honest, I was petrified to sleep in our room again tonight. Everyone had looked at me oddly at breakfast when I asked the maid for an apple. I sliced it, revealed the five-pointed star inside, and hung the pieces with my hair ribbons over our bed, hoping to keep Frederick, or any other ghost, away!

But even with that fear, my mind was racing. I kept thinking about the hikers. About Mrs. Van Damme. About Ida Craft and Jessie Stubbs. I could feel that burn inside me, ignited by Mrs. Van Damme. And Jessie Stubbs had only made that fire hotter.

And then the thought came to me. Those women believe I can be a professor someday. What if they're right?

SIXTEEN

January 1–January 7, 1913

SONGBIRDS

Existing beautifully and with grace,
A beacon in the land of the free.
Her frailty only an illusion
She carries strength and dignity.

We should bow down to her courage,
For fighting year after year,
Decades of steady trudging
For all that she holds dear.

She brings a future of fairness,
Asking only for justice due
Reaching for the stars and stripes,
Our flag—red, white, and blue.

Pain and suffering unequaled by many
In her decades-long quest for light,
Hope held close beneath her wings,
Beating bold and bright.

A tomorrow where we sing together,
In perfect harmony
One destiny, one people, one nation,
For the world, for all to see.

Grandmother, sister, and brother
Rise up from where you are.
Stand tall and sing together,
For your daughters.
For us all.

—Olive Kelly, 1913

The apple talismans Aunt Lib had taught me about must have worked because our last evening sleeping in the LaFay Castle was ghost-free. When I awoke the next morning and saw the light of day peeking in through the shades, a breath of quiet gratitude escaped me. The young lad had apparently not been able to say goodbye to us.

"Thanks, Aunt Lib," I said aloud.

Aunt Carrie had gotten me up early to get dressed and out the door for New Year's Day Mass, a holy day. I looked at myself in the mirror, all bundled for the walk down to St. Francis of Assisi Church. Me—suffragist and future professor. My grin stretched wide, my freckles scattering across my face. I had never been excited about my future. I didn't have to work in a hot, crowded mill or sew clothes like most women I knew. Their work was important, but it wasn't what I wanted. Not anymore. I wanted to teach women to be leaders among their families and communities. I was filled with a sense of purpose. I would study hard, earn good grades, attend college, and make a positive impact on the world.

Albany, like Rochester, was cold and snowy in January, and today, January 1, 1913, was no exception. Rosalie distributed white robes and light green silk sashes, donning the anthem, "Votes For Women." Many suffragists held signs such as "Liberty and Equality for Women Too!" "Votes for Women," and "In the Kitchen AND the Voting Booth!" We all took our positions, standing in rows; some suffragists were atop horses. Excitement coursed through my veins.

I looked at Aunt Carrie, and she grabbed my hand.

"Helen, we are making history. I am certain!"

I thought Uncle Peter would fall over if he knew where Aunt Carrie and I were, and I wondered if my grandmother and my mother would approve.

When Governor Sulzer came out, Olive was introduced

by Ida Craft, whom we had spoken with at the party the night before.

"Governor, we congratulate you on your inauguration as Governor of this fine Empire State. As you know, we are fighting for the right to vote, just like our male citizen counterparts.

We now ask that you kindly lend your ear to the winning poem, written by twelve-year-old Olive Kelly from Rochester, New York. May we have everyone's respect and attention for this young girl, who arrived by train, with a broken ankle, to be here today?"

Ida Craft looked to the governor, and when he nodded, she turned and motioned for Olive, who limped forward on her crutches, to come up to the platform.

Many in the crowd clapped and cheered, though a few jeers rang out as well. But Olive didn't let it faze her. She walked with the confidence of Joan of Arc, and when she reached the stand, Miss Craft handed her a bullhorn. Leaning lightly against the podium, Olive recited her poem from memory, her voice steady, mature, with just the proper pauses and stops.

"Good morning, and congratulations, Governor Sulzer. It is a great privilege to speak before you all today. First, I would like to thank my mother and all the hikers who walked instead of celebrating Christmas with their families this year, showing that we won't stop until we get the vote!

The audience applauded.

"Someone asked me earlier why I wrote my poem about songbirds. I've been lucky enough to be surrounded by songbirds my entire life. My mother, my grandmother, all of the suffragists, many of you here today, and the lot of you who don't even know you are songbirds yet." Olive cleared her throat, studied the crowd for a moment, then started her poem.

A pin could have dropped as the twenty-five walkers from New York City looked on approvingly, and thousands of others listened intently.

I had never been prouder or more moved.

Or so envious of anyone.

> *". . . Grandmother, sister, and brother*
> *Rise up from where you are.*
> *Stand tall and sing together,*
> *For your daughters.*
> *For us all."*

Hundreds of women sitting in the stands stood proudly with the encouragement of Olive's final words. From their hesitant expressions, many realized they were supporters of the suffrage movement for the first time. I saw one woman standing to my left, her hand on her round, pregnant belly, and the other holding the hand of a little girl who couldn't have been older than five.

At that moment, I believed that future generations would never give up this fight. I thought back to Mrs. Allen, who said house cats shouldn't pretend to be lions. I now knew a brigade of determined house cats was mightier than the roar of any ferocious lion.

When a couple of dozen men in the audience stood, more than a few individuals could be seen wiping tears from their eyes, my aunt and me included. It began with one brave soul and then spread like wildfire. Husbands, fathers, and sons rose to stand next to their women, who stood proudly. The supporters who didn't have seats and were already standing clapped their hands. I knew the power of that moment would stay with me for a lifetime.

Everyone applauded, even Governor Sulzer. He walked

over to Olive, shook her hand, and thanked her for her passion and the inspiring words she had shared. By the end of the event, dozens of people had approached to congratulate her, each one eager to meet the beautiful twelve-year-old suffragist from Rochester.

It was becoming increasingly difficult to conceal the jealousy I felt over the attention Olive was receiving. I scolded myself for being so petty. She was my best friend, after all, and best friends weren't supposed to be jealous of each other. Maybe if I'd just been able to stand next to her, just for a moment on stage, I would've felt better.

I did my best to stuff away my unholy thoughts.

We left right after the event, plenty cold from standing outside for two hours, and hurried to catch our train. Rufus was waiting for us on a side road and brought us back to the LaFay Castle so we could say our goodbyes and collect our things. I made sure to grab the apple talismans, as forgetting those would have sparked quite a conversation in the house and possibly prevented a future invitation back.

As we were leaving, I saw a dark shadow in the window when I looked up at the castle one last time. When I blinked, it was gone. Part of me thinks it was the maid, the sun, or my mind playing tricks on me, but the other part thinks it was the ghost of Frederick LaFay coming to say goodbye.

"Did Frederick come to visit you?" Rufus asked as we drove away.

I told the man my story, and he laughed. "Told you so."

The car was crowded on the train ride home, and we couldn't sit together. I sat with Aunt Carrie, and Olive sat with her mother.

"I'm not sure what Pap and Uncle Will said about

New Year's Day to your uncle. I don't want you to lie if he asks you, but best not to offer information about the trip. Understood?" Aunt Carrie said.

"Understood," I said.

Mr. Kelly awaited us when the train arrived at Bragdon Station in Rochester. When we got home, without hesitation, Aunt Carrie asked Uncle Will about the day with Peter.

"Strange thing, maybe an act of God, but he called us to say he wasn't feeling well and wouldn't be coming over. You missed a big one, Carrie. Maybe God took pity on you," Uncle Peter told her.

Phew! We wouldn't be in trouble with Uncle Peter.

We shared our exciting stories around the hot stove, and I told Pap and Uncle Will that I would be a college professor someday. They both laughed. Pap said, "Helen, you would make a marvelous professor." Uncle Will said, "Helen, you are a smart girl. If any woman could be a college professor, why not you?"

Aunt Carrie seemed different when she tucked me in for the night. She sat up taller and more confident. Holding my hand, she said, "I didn't know what to expect this weekend. We took a chance to do a good deed for the Kellys, which paid off. We were part of history. When you have children, you can tell them all about it."

"Aunt Carrie? What if I decide not to have children? Is that okay? Does every woman have to be a mother?" I asked.

"Being a mother is one of the most important jobs on the planet. Don't let all this career talk make you think that being a mother isn't important. Those lucky enough to be chosen as mothers must take that role very seriously. It must always come first." She tucked the quilt across my legs.

"If you can't do that, then don't have children, but maybe you could do both, teach and be a mother. Just marry a good man. You need a special, forward-thinking husband for that to work." She leaned down, pressed a kiss to my forehead, and headed to the door.

"Good night, Aunt Carrie!"

I badly wanted to say, "I love you," but Aunt Carrie had to say it first, and she never had.

The next day was a school day. We were all invited to share about our holiday, and I was excited to brag about my weekend. I spoke about the Governor's inauguration, the fancy party at the LaFay Castle, and how I had met the hikers who walked from New York City to Albany. Sister Veronica asked many questions. Her last question made me realize I had made a huge mistake.

"Helen, your uncle is pleased with all this?"

"Oh, um—"

How foolish I was. The nuns adored my uncle and were always trying to win his favor, chatting him up with small talk. He would most definitely hear about this story.

"Why, of course," I lied and instantly wanted to smack myself.

"How lovely," Sister Veronica said sincerely, making me wonder where she stood on the movement.

I was restless for the next few days, worried about what would come next. I struggled to sleep or eat my meals. This was going to be bad. I just knew it. During the day, when I was home, I kept looking out the windows to see if Uncle Peter had finally learned of my trip. Would today be the day? I kept asking myself?

Finally, three days after my fifth-grade "share," Uncle Peter came knocking. Holy Father, save us, I prayed when I saw him. Like a soldier deserting his regiment, I ran up the stairs and hid at the top, careful not to be seen. Aunt

Carrie would have to fight this battle alone.

"Carrie? Is Will here?" Uncle Peter asked in an angry tone.

"No, Peter. You know he works until five, but you can wait for him. Come right in. Is everything okay?" she asked calmly.

They walked into the parlor, and Aunt Carrie offered him a drink. Wasting no time, Uncle Peter curtly responded with, "Carrie, I'm going to ask a simple question. Was Helen in Albany for the governor's inauguration?"

Aunt Carrie hesitated momentarily and, as if summoning her courage, said, "Why, yes, she was. She had an opportunity to be a part of history, and I thought it would be good for her."

"You did, did you? And how would Helen have gotten there? Did you take her?" he asked in a piercing tone.

"Yes, Peter. Olive Kelly won a writing contest and was to recite her piece at the Governor's inauguration. However, she broke her ankle and couldn't go with her mother. Without us taking her, she wouldn't have been able to recite her winning poem. It would have been a shame."

"Carrie, those people are a disgrace to God. I thought I made it clear that Helen was not to consort with the Kellys. How could you allow this?" he barked.

"What do you mean . . . a disgrace to God?" My aunt asked.

"God wants women at home where they belong, listening and obeying their husbands. It's in the scriptures! Men must provide for their families, protect their families, and support their country, which includes voting for politicians who will serve in office. Woman's duty is to take care of their husbands and bear their children. This is God's will!" There was a short pause from my uncle's rant, and then, with a thunderous voice, he yelled, "Rosalie Kelly is a floozy and a follower of Satan. How could you?"

My aunt was silent, and I knew her neck was probably

bright red with large spots by now. I ran down the stairs, ready to defend her.

"Uncle Peter, Olive is my very best friend. She's a good girl, not wicked like you say!" Then I cried, "Rosalie Kelly is a fine mother, and I don't care what you think! You're wrong about them. You're just plain wrong!

Uncle Peter grabbed me, threw me over his knee, and began whacking me with the vengeance of Genghis Khan while Aunt Carrie and I both screamed.

"You will never talk to me like that again, young lady. Do you hear me?" he shouted as he paddled my rear. "You will respect me!"

"Peter, you stop that! It was all my fault, not Helen's. Stop spanking her!" my aunt cried out.

"Why, I should spank you, too!" Uncle Peter growled as Uncle Will rushed into the house.

"What in Sam Hill is going on here?" Uncle Will yelled.

Uncle Peter stopped spanking me, and I ran to Aunt Carrie, terrified. I had never seen Uncle Peter so angry, and he had never hit me.

"I will not be made a fool of. I will not have Helen raised by a bunch of immoral heathens. I will never forgive either of you for your utter disregard for Helen's Christian upbringing. Taking Helen to Albany without my permission and allowing her to become friends with that Kelly girl . . . Will, how could you have allowed this?" Uncle Peter's words boomed through the room.

"Peter, I will not have you beating Helen or disrespecting me or my wife. Who are you to speak to us this way, and what gives you the right to judge the Kellys as you do?" Uncle Will snapped.

"Will, you are a weak man . . . can't even keep your wife in line. Why on earth did I think you could take care of my Helen?"

"Why, you son of a—" Uncle Will said, sharply cut off by Aunt Carrie.

"Will!" she shouted to stop the curse words from being spoken.

"You walk around here thinking you are Jesus Christ himself, and you're not," Uncle Will said, slamming his hand down on one of the tables.

"If you ask me, your wife needs to know her place!" Uncle Peter bellowed.

This enraged Uncle Will, and he ran over and grabbed Uncle Peter by his jacket, screaming, "You bastard!"

Suddenly, Pap walked into the room.

"I don't know what the hell is going on here, but this is my house, and it will stop! Do you boys hear me?" he roared. I had never seen Pap so mad and thought his anger might kill him.

The room became silent, and Pap regained his composure. "Now, Peter, you go on home, and we can talk about this later when people have had time to simmer down," Pap firmly said.

Aunt Carrie ran to her room, and I was left to explain what happened. I felt responsible, knowing none of this would have happened if I hadn't convinced Olive to hitch onto that truck that snowy day.

"Uncle Will, I'm so sorry. I shared about my trip at school. It was foolish of me. I should have realized it would get back to Uncle Peter," I sobbed.

"Go to your room, Helen. This wasn't your fault, but we are all eating in our rooms tonight," Uncle Will said.

I ran upstairs and climbed onto my bed, hugging Sadie close.

You're an idiot, Helen!

I wondered if Uncle Will and Aunt Carrie would want to get rid of me now or leave me and move back to Buffalo. Why did I have to open my big, fat mouth? I twirled the ring Aunt Libby had given me and said the prayer Grandma had taught:

May you see God's light on the path ahead
when the road you walk is dark.

May you always hear, even in your hour of sorrow, the gentle singing of the lark.

When times are hard, may hardness never turn your heart to stone.

May you always remember when the shadows fall, you do not walk alone.

This prayer always made me feel better, and I pleaded with Grandma and my mother to help make things right.

Uncle Will brought soup and bread up to me, and after eating, I heard Pap and Uncle Will arguing. I wanted to know what was being said, so I hid at the top of the stairs. I was surprised when Aunt Carrie came out of her room and joined me. Instead of ushering me back or reprimanding me, she put her finger to her lips, and together we listened.

"Pa, I will not let Peter control us or tell us what to do or who to be friends with," Uncle Will said. "He accused me of being unable to keep Carrie in line or care for Helen appropriately. Who the hell does he think he is?"

"William, Peter can be pig-headed and stubborn. He has always been the one in the family who thinks he knows what is best for everyone. I don't know how you will do it, but you must fix this. I won't have my only two surviving children feuding."

My aunt motioned for me to quietly go back to my room. She came in and closed the door.

"Helen, this isn't your fault. The adults will figure it out, and everything will be fine. I don't want you worrying about this."

Her words didn't comfort me. A big moan left me as I crumbled onto my bed.

"Aunt Carrie, I'm so sorry. It's my fault. All of it. It was wrong for me to have shared about my trip with my class. I was trying to be a showoff."

She sat on the bed and held my hand.

"Helen, going to Albany was part of God's plan for you. For us. We learned and experienced things over those two days that we never would have otherwise. Regarding sharing with your class, sometimes we let our pride get in the way. You learned that it doesn't bring good things."

SEVENTEEN

January 28–January 29, 1913

Winter had taken full hold of Rochester, and Aunt Carrie and I had stopped hiding our friendships with the Kellys. The fight was still fresh in everyone's mind, like a bruise that hadn't even begun to fade. When I asked Aunt Carrie where things stood, she just said, "Don't mind yourself in adult business. It'll all work out."

I wasn't so sure.

At least school gave me something else to think about. As soon as Olive had her brace removed, she started meeting me outside Immaculate Conception to walk me home each afternoon.

One of the first days she came to get me, there was a big blizzard, and the snow had the perfect amount of moisture for good packing. Some classmates started building a snowman in front of the school. We weren't allowed to dilly-dally on school property after dismissal, and Brother Francis yelled from the porch, "Get on home!"

Olive was standing across the street, waiting for me patiently. We had only walked a short way on Edinburgh Street before we heard the Hamiltons on the other side of the road.

"Stay over there so you don't give us cooties," Sean screamed at us.

Prudence chimed in, "You girls are contagious! Stay on your side of the street!"

I shouted back, "Go home to your mama and da—"

A snowball struck me fast, leaving me with a mouthful of snow, courtesy of Sean. As I wiped my face, Connor let fly another snowball, this one grazing Olive's head.

She picked up some snow, formed a nicely shaped ball, and threw it with a force that seemed to be powered by God Almighty. I wasn't sure what to expect when Olive threw that ball, but she threw as good as any boy. I should have known from her rock-skipping talent.

I don't know who was more surprised when Connor got hit right in the head, me or him. I didn't throw as well as Olive, but I threw all right for a girl, at least better than Prudence, who threw like a complete ninny.

Soon, an all-out snowball fight ensued, and when we arrived at John Street, we were outnumbered by Prudence and her three brothers and were forced to run home. By the time we arrived at Magnolia Street, we were cold, wet, and humiliated. We ran into my house, where Aunt Carrie was at the window sewing a dress for one of the wealthy women in town.

"What do we have here?" she asked.

"Aunt Carrie, the Hamilton children just battered us with snowballs. They're so mean!" I cried.

"I'm sorry to hear that." She smiled, her needle still moving as she sewed.

"Mrs. O'Donnell, we have to show them!" Olive said, breathless but fired up. "We need a plan."

My aunt chuckled. "Go get out of those wet clothes before you both catch your death."

I started shaking snow from my coat, ready to do exactly that and curl up by the stove where it was warm and safe.

"Helen! Mrs. O'Donnell!" Olive's voice cut through the room like a blade. "We have to go back out. We can't just run away."

I went still, thinking of Olive's words.

The truth was, I didn't want to go back out, not with the Hamiltons laughing behind our backs. Part of me never wanted to show my face again.

But Olive stood her ground. "We can't let them scare us," she said, her voice steady now. "We have to be courageous—face people like that head-on."

Aunt Carrie let her needle pause. Her eyes flicked from Olive to me, then back again.

"We need a better plan this time," Olive went on. "What if we go back and make piles of snowballs? We'll stockpile them along the way home. Then, tomorrow we'll be ready. We'll have a good offense," Olive said like a general rallying her troops before battle.

She started bouncing on her toes, excited by her own idea. Unlike me, Olive didn't just feel things. She acted. She thought ahead. She believed in the next move.

"Goodness, Olive," Aunt Carrie said with a crooked smile, "what does a good offense even look like?"

I was glad she asked because I hadn't the faintest idea.

"It means we're prepared. It means we catch them off guard," Olive said.

I looked at Aunt Carrie. Her hands went quiet, and the needle stilled in her lap. She was thinking. I liked the plan. More than that, I wanted to be brave like Olive.

"Aunt Carrie? Can I go back out? Please?" I begged.

"Look at you both. You're soaking wet."

"Please, Aunt Carrie. I'll do extra chores. I promise. Please!"

She sighed and set her sewing aside. "Hmm. I am sick and tired of hearing about those Hamilton children being bullies. Go on, then, but be back before dark, you hear? And Olive, tell your mother you'll be late. I don't want her giving me the devil if you miss dinner."

Even though we were as wet as drowned weasels, we bundled back up and charged outside like true warriors. We spent the rest of the afternoon packing snowballs and hiding them behind trees and fences, building our arsenal.

We were cold and soaked. But we had a good offense.

Sitting in my 5th-grade classroom at Immaculate Conception the next day, I couldn't take my eyes off the clock and kept imagining the look on the Hamilton children's faces when they saw we were ready for them. When the dismissal bell finally struck, I ran to get dressed in my winter garb and flew out of the building to find Olive waiting for me.

When we started walking home and came upon the Hamiltons, Connor wasted no time in calling us "pigeon-livered," saying we were dead meat. That was all Olive needed to jump into action.

"Helen, Stop One!" she commanded.

We both ran, which made the Hamiltons think we were running home. "Chickens, bok, bok, bok!" They yelled like they had on the day of the sledding accident. Little did they know they were about to get pummeled by two girls.

We loaded our arms, and when they got within striking distance, we started hurling snowballs at them, which seemed to shock them. Olive and I were outnumbered, but our snowballs stung badly when they hit. They had thawed out a little during the day and were now more like ice balls. It wasn't long before Prudence took her younger brother Liam's hand and ran home crying.

Then, we just had Sean and Connor to deal with. We exhausted our first pile of snowballs, and Olive instructed me to go to Stop Two. Again, we ran, and the boys thought we were running home, but huzzah! We had even more ammunition at Stop Two. We threw those ice balls until they were all gone and ran to Stop Three to continue our unstoppable juggernaut, a great word Olive taught me.

We kept it up all the way to Stop Six on Magnolia Street, ducking, shouting, and laughing until our legs ached and our gloves were drenched.

By the time the four of us reached my house, we were so worn out we collapsed in a heap on the porch, breathless and laughing heartily. The war was over. And though no one surrendered, something shifted. We weren't friends, but we were no longer enemies.

EIGHTEEN

February 1–February 15, 1913

Weeks after my uncles' fight, I realized I hadn't seen Uncle Peter at the house. I also noticed that Aunt Carrie and Uncle Will had started arguing. Aunt Carrie seemed angry at him. I finally got up the nerve to ask her at bedtime, "Are you and Uncle Will all right? Something feels different between you two."

She took a little while to answer, and I thought I saw tears in her eyes. "We just have many things going on right now. It's nothing for you to bother yourself about."

About two weeks later, Aunt Carrie and Uncle Will sat me down one night for a huge surprise. My father would be in town on business and wanted to visit.

My father? Why on earth is my father coming to visit after all these years?

Part of me wanted to finally meet this man, but part of me was angry he hadn't contacted me sooner. Aunt Carrie and Uncle Will continued to clash, and I wondered if my father's visit had something to do with it.

I counted down the days until my father's arrival. Every evening, I stared in my mirror, wondering what he would think of me. Seven days passed, and then my father was expected after dinner.

I didn't know what to do with myself and fussed with my hair that my aunt had rolled in rags the night before, retied the bow on my dress, and bit the nails on my right hand down to the skin.

"Sadie, we must 'act like ladies' as Grandma would say. No talking unless spoken to, no talking too loud, no nail-biting, be cheery, sit straight, no—." I heard a knock at the door, and my stomach churned. Oh boy, this is it. The moment I'd been waiting for, for years.

I sat on my bed, listening for my cue to come down.

"Helen, your father is here!" Aunt Carrie shouted.

I picked Sadie up and started walking down the stairs. There, at the entryway with Uncle Will and Aunt Carrie, stood a tall man. He had the same shape face as me, the same odd nose, the same long skinny frame, and the same lips. Why he looked just like me. I looked like him! The only similarities between my beautiful mother and me were our hair and eye color.

So, this was Patrick Long. My father.

Aunt Carrie had already taken his winter coat, and his wet boots were by the door. He wore a three-piece suit with a pocket watch that gleamed in the foyer's light and held a shiny package in his hand, presumably a gift for me. A faint, crooked smile filled his face when he saw me at the bottom of the stairs. It comforted me oddly when he twirled one side of his mustache anxiously. He wasn't handsome like my uncles, but something was dashing about the way he stood there.

Holding onto the railing, afraid to let go, I stood for a moment, staring into his dark brown eyes. Last time I saw those eyes, I was only a few months old. Logically, I shouldn't have remembered them, but somehow I did. I didn't want to breathe, move, or speak for fear I'd wake myself up and discover it was just a dream.

This was my father, my real father!

"Helen, my darling," he said.

He ran to me and kneeled down, smothering me in kisses. I felt his chilled arms around me and his warm tears on my face. I wondered if my heart, which I was certain everyone in the room could hear, would jump right out of my body as I melted in his embrace.

Since learning at Grandma's wake that my father was still out there, somewhere, I had imagined this moment. In my mind, I always cried, but my tears weren't budging. When we finally broke apart, he looked at me carefully, as if examining my every feature.

He was probably thinking I was an ugly girl, nothing like my mother. I broke the uncomfortable silence with the words, "Hello, Father," unsure how that word would roll off my tongue. Aside from talking to a priest, it was the first time I had ever addressed anyone with it. In the many times I'd imagined meeting my father, I sometimes called him Father, but more often, I wouldn't call him anything because I was so angry at him for not being in my life. Today, "Father" just slipped out of my mouth.

"Here you are, a young woman of ten years, almost eleven. Your birthday is coming right up," he said, looking into my eyes.

My father remembered my birthday. So many birthdays

apart. So many birthdays, wondering why he left me. My heart became heavy. I tried not to cry. Instead, I nervously blurted out, "Is it very cold outside?" And then felt silly. Of course, it was very cold outside. I knew from my walk home from school.

He chuckled and responded, "Why, yes, it is. I took a carriage over, and I'm still thawing out." This made me laugh, which helped ease the tears that were about to come.

Aunt Carrie directed us into the parlor, where I introduced my father to Sadie.

"You named your doll after your mother? Oh—" He became speechless, and tears welled in his eyes. He cleared his throat and sat down on the itchy horsetail hair sofa. He twirled his mustache and looked around. "I remember this old sofa . . ." He couldn't finish his sentence, and we all sat quietly, waiting.

"Helen, I am so sorry about the loss of your grandmother. I'm so sorry I wasn't there for you. It was wrong. I should have come sooner . . . I should have come sooner." He sobbed. "I was afraid . . ." Loud whimpers came from him, making my stuck tears come gushing out.

"Oh, Father!" I dropped Sadie onto one of the parlor chairs and rushed over to him, putting my arms around him.

"Helen, losing your mother was the worst thing that ever happened to me. I wanted to keep you. I wanted to keep you so badly, but I had nothing to offer you. Can you ever forgive me?" He kissed my head and embraced me firmly.

I reached for him as we both cried. I didn't want to say it was all right, because it wasn't, so I said nothing.

My father pulled a handkerchief from his coat pocket and handed it to me, while my uncle took the one from his own jacket and passed it to my father. Uncle Will gently patted his back, trying to comfort him.

"Patrick, the important thing is that you are here now," Uncle Will said.

After the tears stopped, my father handed me the gift he brought. I was thrilled to find a game I had heard some children talk about at school, Pirate and Traveler.

"Can we play?" I asked everyone.

"That seems like a good idea," Aunt Carrie said, possibly relieved we had moved past the tear-filled introductions.

Uncle Will and Aunt Carrie sat in the two chairs across from my father and me. My father read the directions, and we placed our wooden pawns at the home port in South Africa to start. Next, we all drew a red scorecard that told us our destination.

We needed to complete ten trips to become pirates and fight for the "pirate booty." My first stop was Bombay, India. I spun the spinner, which landed on ten, then moved my traveler ten spots along the route toward my destination. Everyone was enjoying getting to our locations and learning about the "booty" at each place.

My father asked me simple questions about school and friends, I suppose, to better get to know me. He told me he had married a wonderful woman, and they had four children. Benjamin was seven, Robert was five, Shauna was three, and John was two.

"Helen, you would love your half-siblings. They are wonderful children," he said. "And your stepmother is a kind, gentle person."

Half-siblings? Stepmother? I was surprised when he said these things.

I had siblings, siblings I'd never met. And a stepmother! I knew all this, but when he took out a photograph and showed me the family, all the air seemed to leave me.

I felt faint.

I should be in that picture! How different my life would be. I could have had a "real," normal family if Grandma hadn't taken me away from my father and pushed him out of town.

Why was he so weak? Why did he listen to her? And why isn't he blaming Grandma? He didn't even mention the theft. I was positive Aunt Libby wouldn't have lied about this.

With tears streaming, I angrily got up and ran to my bedroom. I could hear Aunt Carrie running up the stairs behind me.

I flung myself onto my bed. My aunt came in and closed the door.

"It's okay, Helen. You have every right to be upset," she said. "But your father has come a long way. Let's dry your eyes off and walk back down to him with your chin up to say goodbye."

After a few minutes, I did as Aunt Carrie said and dried my tears. When we came downstairs, Aunt Carrie held me close and explained that this was a lot of new information for a young girl, and she recommended that we try again some other time.

Uncle Will gave her a disappointed look, and as I stared at the unfinished game sprawled across the table, I became ashamed at my outburst. Would I ever see him again after behaving so poorly?

"We'll all have to become pirates some other night," my father said. "Helen, I didn't mean to upset you. Can I see you before I leave, and can we try again?" he asked.

"Yes, Father. I'd like that very much," I said, sniffling.

He smiled.

"How long are you here?" I asked.

"A few more days," he said, reaching for the coat Aunt Carrie held.

Uncle Will and my father pulled on their winter coats, bracing for the cold ride to the inn. As they were leaving, the old clock chimed in the parlor. My father glanced at his pocket watch and buttoned his coat.

"That old clock," he said, shaking his head.

For a second, I thought he might cry again—but he didn't.

The thought of him leaving hit me hard. People I loved always seemed to go. And he had already left me once.

I threw my arms around him and cried, "I will see you again, won't I?"

"Of course, Helen. If you want to," he said, holding me tight.

"I'd like that, Father," I sobbed.

He took my hands in his and kissed them.

"Good night, my darling. I'll look forward to our next visit."

NINETEEN

February 15–February 17, 1913

When Aunt Carrie tucked me into bed that night, my head was spinning, and my eyes burned from crying.

"You poor darling," she whispered, brushing the hair from my forehead. "This was a difficult evening. Are you all right with him coming to say goodbye before he leaves?"

"Most certainly," I said quickly. "I didn't mean to storm off like a crybaby. I just—" I paused. "I hope he doesn't think I'm bratty now."

Aunt Carrie reached for Sadie on my dresser and tucked her in beside me, just like Gram used to.

"It was a big night. He knew that, Helen. You had every right to cry."

"He looks like me, doesn't he?" I asked, feeling both proud and strange about it.

"Yes, Helen," she said with a soft smirk. "There's no deny-ing the family resemblance."

"I wonder if he thinks I'm ugly," I whispered, hoping she'd say something to prove me wrong.

"What a silly thing to say. I saw the way he looked at you—you're the most beautiful girl in the world to him."

She stopped suddenly, and when I looked up, her eyes had that far-off, glassy look again.

"Time for prayers," she said quickly, catching my gaze.

As I whispered my usual prayers, I asked God to watch over my father and my new half-siblings. Aunt Carrie didn't stay to read me a story like she usually did. She left right after prayers. That wasn't like her. But then, she hadn't quite seemed herself lately.

The next day, Olive came to pick me up from school. I told her I didn't want to run into the Hamiltons and that I desperately needed to talk to her. We ran to South Fitzhugh Street and turned left onto Hubbell, a route we never took. Everyone said the whole street was haunted by the orphanage fire of 1901 that killed twenty-six children and two adults. Gram always said it was the worst tragedy Rochester had ever seen. But today, I was willing to brave a few ghosts if it meant getting last night off my chest.

I told Olive about my father and the photo he'd shown me of his family.

"What he did was wrong, Helen. He shouldn't have left you. He could've taken you back from your grandparents," she snapped. "You are his child, after all. Fathers are sup-posed to be there."

I was surprised by her outrage. Olive didn't have much patience for men, and any chance she got to pick them apart with her fine-tooth comb, she did.

"He better not be coming around now to take you away from us."

"That's ridiculous! If my father had wanted me, he would've come long before now," I said.

When I got home, the smell of something delicious drifted from the kitchen. Aunt Carrie, in her apron, was cooking up a feast, her face and neck blotchy.

"Aunt Carrie, is everything all right?"

"Your father will be coming for dinner tonight. Better get your homework out of the way now," she said, without looking up.

"He's coming tonight?" I asked, spotting a loaf of fresh bread and a perfect berry pie on the counter. I couldn't help feeling excited.

"Yes, your uncle Will invited him."

"That's wonderful . . . right?"

"Yes, Helen. It's all so wonderful," she said, though her tone wasn't entirely convincing.

By the looks of it, she'd been cooking all day. Was she annoyed to throw together a proper dinner on such short notice?

"Why don't you head to your room, do your homework, and dress for dinner. You'll want to look nice for your father."

"Are you sure you don't need help?"

"No, I'll be fine. Run along, Helen."

I nodded and left the kitchen, trying not to think too hard about the tightness in her smile.

Uncle Will and Pap arrived home earlier than usual. I ran downstairs, eager to show off my Sunday dress and the braid Olive had just taught me.

"Well, don't you look beautiful," Pap said, touching the braid lightly. "You look like one of the Indian girls who sometimes come into town."

"Do you like it? Olive taught me," I said, beaming.

"I love it . . . and I love you." He pulled me into a hug. "My dear Helen." A heavy breath left him.

"Pap, rough day at work?" I asked, sensing something was off.

"A bit more than usual, dear," he said, his voice quieter than before.

"Pap, is it okay that my father's coming for dinner? Grandma didn't seem to like him."

I watched his face closely, searching for unspoken answers.

"Helen, your father is a good man. Your grandmother, God rest her soul, knew that, too," he said, making the sign of the cross, "I'll leave it at that."

I turned to Uncle Will, who was slipping off his coat.

"Uncle Will, thank you for inviting him," I said.

He gave me a thoughtful look. "What do you think of him, Helen?"

"He seems swell," I said.

"I've always liked Patrick," he replied. "Such a kind man. Wouldn't hurt a soul."

"Although . . . I am curious why he never came before."

I started to put my finger in my mouth to bite my nail but stopped myself.

"Helen, you heard your father last night," Uncle Will said, a bit too quickly. "He didn't think he could give you the life you deserved back then."

Before I could respond, a knock came at the door. Uncle Will glanced at Pap, then at me, and stepped forward to open it. Pap was sweating. When had they last seen each other? Pap had helped Gram take me away. Was this going to be awkward?

Uncle Will opened the door. My father stepped inside. He and Pap froze. Then, suddenly, they embraced.

Pap's eyes shimmered. He blinked hard, fighting back tears.

"Tom. Nice to see you," my father said quietly.

They pulled apart. Pap shook his head, too choked up to speak. That small exchange said everything. Pap regretted what he'd done. And my father had forgiven him.

Then my father turned to me, lifted me off the ground, and spun me in a circle.

"How's my little angel?" he asked.

"I'm good, Father. It's nice to see you again."

As we walked into the dining room, we passed a picture of my mother on the wall, one that my father likely hadn't noticed the day before.

"Glory be," he said, bringing a hand to his mouth. He stopped and stared, twirling his mustache. "She was so beautiful. Too young to die."

He pulled out a handkerchief, dabbed his eyes, then blew his nose.

"You have hair just like hers," he said softly.

"My best friend, Olive, taught me how to braid it. Do you like it, Father?" I asked, eager to please.

He took my hair in his hand gently, pretending to inspect it. "Quite impressive, Helen."

We all sat down for dinner and thanked Aunt Carrie for the lovely meal. My father spoke of his work as a horticulturist at the Cleveland Botanical Garden and how he was often invited to speak to garden clubs across the state, even to teach at local schools.

When he said that, I almost told him I wanted to be a professor someday, but I wasn't sure how he'd react, so I stayed quiet and folded my hands in my lap, trying to look demure.

I'd never heard of a horticulturist before. The idea that my father created beautiful gardens amazed me. He'd even produced new varieties of roses by grafting them together. To me, that seemed magical.

Aunt Carrie was setting the apple pie on the table when my father said, "I know the children would love you, Helen."

"That's kind of you to say, Father," I replied, daintily dabbing the corner of my mouth like Aunt Carrie had taught me.

"Oh yes, Helen is great with children," Uncle Will added.

I thought I saw Aunt Carrie shoot him a look, but it was gone in an instant.

I couldn't recall Uncle Will ever seeing me with children, but I accepted the compliment and gave him a smile.

"Cleveland's a wonderful place," my father continued. "Parks, good schools. We love it there."

He set his fork down and looked around the table.

"I'm very happy for you, Father," I said, our eyes locking.

"Helen, Dorothy, and I would like nothing more than for you to come live with us in Cleveland," he said. "I promise, you'd be very happy there."

I nearly fell off my chair. Sadie slipped from my hands and hit the floor.

"What?" I whispered.

"Helen, you're my daughter. I want you to live with us, Dorothy and I both do."

Tears welled in his brown eyes as he stared at me.

"It nearly broke my heart to leave you after your mother died. But I thought it was best. I left because I loved you—if that makes any sense. I had nothing to give you then. But now . . . I do. You'd have a new mother, and brothers, and a sister."

I looked around the table—Aunt Carrie, Pap, Uncle Will. No one said a word. Had they all known he was going to ask me this tonight?

Pap hung his head. Uncle Will looked like a puppy on the edge of his seat. Aunt Carrie's face was unreadable. And my father—he looked like he was holding his breath.

"I . . . I don't know what to say, Father. I mean, Magnolia Street is my home," I said quietly.

"Helen, we'll come to visit," Uncle Will said, his voice calm and sure. "Your father is a fine man. He loves you very much."

I looked toward Aunt Carrie. Her skin had begun to blotch. Without a word, she pushed back her chair and disappeared into the kitchen.

That's when the doubt crept in. She hadn't told him I would stay. She hadn't come to my rescue. Do they want me to go with him? Maybe they've had enough after everything with Uncle Peter. Maybe they want their quiet lives in Buffalo back. Am I supposed to say yes?

Then Pap spoke faintly, but with a finality that left me stunned.

"Helen, your father loves you very much. Maybe it would be best."

I felt like the girl on the trapeze at the circus. The one who'd just let go, suspended in midair, waiting for someone to catch her.

"I . . . I'm not sure," I stammered. "I love you, Father. I really do. I just don't know. There's Pap . . . Aunt Carrie and Uncle Will . . . Uncle Peter, my best friend, Aunt Libby . . . my school. How could I leave them?"

My father nodded. "I understand. How about this, I'll come back tomorrow evening after dinner. That'll give you some time to think. Would that be all right?"

"I . . ." The words caught in my throat.

"Yes, Patrick," Uncle Will said, stepping in. "Come back tomorrow. We'll talk it through tonight."

Move away from Rochester? This was my home. How could I leave now, especially when I didn't want to? Why hadn't my father come for me when I was younger, when I would've said yes in a heartbeat? I didn't know whether to cry or be angry.

I reflected on the past month. Maybe I wasn't lovable. Maybe, like everyone else I'd ever loved, Aunt Carrie and Uncle Will would leave me, too. Was I a wretched girl? Had I caused Mrs. Allen's death? Olive said I hadn't, but . . . what if I had? God knew the truth, and maybe this was my punishment. It all made sense now. Aunt Carrie had been acting strange because she wanted to get rid of me.

That night, when she came in to tuck me into bed, she sat beside me and said,

"Helen, your father loves you very much. And you'd have siblings. I don't know if I can ever give you that."

Tears welled up in my eyes. Aunt Carrie rubbed my back, but it didn't help.

"It's okay, Helen," she whispered. "It'll take some getting used to, I'm sure. But I think you'll be happy . . . in time."

"What about Olive? What about Pap? What about you?" I burst out.

Her neck flushed crimson.

"I'm not feeling well, Helen. I'm going to bed early tonight."

She left without turning down my lamp, without prayers, without a story. She left when all I needed was for her to say I could stay. That I didn't have to leave. That she and Uncle Will wanted me. That Magnolia Street was my home and always would be. But the longer I lay there, the clearer it became. I wasn't wanted.

I would go with my father, because that's what they needed. Perhaps it was what my mother and Grandma wanted, too. I was devastated, torn clean in two.

I longed to speak to Aunt Libby. She would know what to do. But she was too far away. I couldn't get to her.

Muffled voices echoed through the walls. What were they saying about me? Hot tears spilled as I imagined the worst—that they thought I was a horrid little girl.

I needed Olive. But I'd have to wait until tomorrow.

The next morning, I sat at my desk in a complete fog, unable to see the road ahead. I couldn't eat my lunch, so I slipped away to the church where the afternoon service was being held. Part of me hoped I might see Uncle Peter, though I was still mad at him for spanking me.

The church was nearly empty. A few people sat scattered across the pews. I slipped into the back row and knelt as Father Reilly began Mass. It was always in Latin. The rhythm of the words lulled me, like a song.

I found myself twirling my ring and thinking of my brave great-great-grandmother Brigid. She must have been terrified, coming to America at such a young age.

I closed my eyes and whispered Grandma's prayer. When I opened them, my gaze settled on the statue of the Virgin Mary. Surely, the Mother of God would help me. I prayed to her softly and urgently, begging for help.

Back in the classroom, the clock hands barely moved. I waited for the bell, waited for Olive. At dismissal, I ran to her, crying.

"Come on," I said. "Let's take Hubbell Street. I don't want the Hamiltons to see me crying."

We scurried down South Fitzhugh Street, and when we were out of earshot from anyone, Olive turned to me and asked, "Helen, what's wrong?"

"Olive, it's my father. He wants me to move to Cleveland to live with him. I don't want to leave my home!" I sobbed.

"I had a feeling about this," she said. "Your family is here. You can't leave."

"After what happened with Uncle Peter and the Albany trip, I think Aunt Carrie and Uncle Will want me to go with him. He's coming tonight for my answer. Olive, what am I supposed to do?"

"That is simply despicable, putting that decision on you. I absolutely don't want you to go. You belong here—with me, with everyone who loves you. How dare your father think he can just saunter in after ten years and take you from your life!"

"Shhh, keep your voice down, Olive. It's not that easy. I don't even know if they want me anymore."

"Helen, your aunt and uncle love you very much. That is just silly talk."

"I wouldn't blame them, not after what happened with Uncle Peter. I can't believe I was foolish enough to tell Sister Veronica. What was I thinking?"

"Helen, you can't go. Under no condition can you go to Cleveland!" Olive shouted.

And whether with the help of my great-great-grand-mother Brigid or the Virgin Mary herself, that evening, Uncle Peter turned up at the house, storming in like thunder. He hadn't been over since the big fight, but there he was, furious about my father taking me away.

Pap must have told him what was happening. And just like that, I became a firm believer in help from above. When my poor father arrived, he didn't even have time to take his boots or coat off because Uncle Peter was waiting there for him, ready to pounce like a tiger.

"Pat, Helen won't be going with you now or ever. Rochester is her home, and here she'll stay," he shouted.

My father looked startled. He turned to Uncle Will, like he'd expected him to speak.

"But . . . Will—" he began.

Uncle Will didn't say anything. He just looked down, hanging his head.

Then my father turned to me. "Helen, what do you want, my dear? This should be your decision."

I felt completely torn. Part of me knew my life was here and that leaving would destroy me, but it seemed clear Aunt Carrie and Uncle Will didn't want me anymore. The other part whispered that my father was a stand-up man, and I couldn't hurt him. I wanted to fly straight to the moon, away from it all. I didn't want to be forced to choose.

I kept saying, "Ah—well—," while twirling my ring.

Finally, Aunt Carrie broke the silence for me.

"Helen, I love you very much. You have a home here with us!"

A huge sigh of relief washed over me. I ran to her. "Really?"

"I love you like my own daughter," she said firmly.

We both started crying as we hugged. By the time our tears dried, I noticed that Uncle Peter's scowl had turned into something like relief.

"I love you, too! I want to stay here," I sobbed.

I craved Aunt Carrie's love desperately, especially right now. I hugged her tightly, feeling a new heavenly sensation that filled me from head to toe. My Aunt Carrie loved me! But within seconds, I came out of my fairy tale and realized I was in a room of eyes watching me.

Pap had tears brimming. Uncle Will looked angry for some reason, and my father, well, when I looked at him, I wanted to curl up into a ball and fall to the floor.

I walked over to him and said, "Father, I am happy here. I love you, but I don't want to go."

It was like someone had sucker-punched the poor man.

His face went pale, and he looked as if all the air had been knocked out of him. That crushed me. I stood there, not knowing what to do. Then I walked back to Aunt Carrie and took her hand.

My father paused for a long while as we all waited to see what he would do next.

"I'll be going then," he said quietly. "Please keep in touch with me, Helen. I will write often and will wait in great anticipation until I see you again, my love. May I kiss you goodbye?"

His voice quavered as he struggled to get the last words out.

I ran to him with open arms, desperate to ease his pain.

"Father, I love you. I'm so sorry."

We looked into each other's tear-filled eyes. Then he raised my hands to his face and kissed them ever so slowly, like he was trying to savor the moment.

He gave us all a nod, then turned to Uncle Will.

"Will." My father said, his brow furrowed, his voice now tight with anger.

Then he tipped his hat specifically to my Uncle Will and walked out the door.

TWENTY

March 1–March 3, 1913

I stuck my finger for the third time on a stubborn "R." "Why can't we just say, 'Votes for Women' and skip all this embroidery?" I grumbled. Aunt Carrie didn't even look up.

"Because Helen. This stitch will march, even if you can't."

For the past month, Aunt Carrie, Aunt Libby, and I had been busy sewing twelve purple, white, and gold sashes, the colors of the suffrage movement. We embroidered "Rochester, NY" on the front and "Votes for Women" on the back.

Aunt Carrie's words, that our stitches would march, did little to ease my envy of Olive, who would be marching at the Capitol without me. I fussed and complained until she promised to bring me back a souvenir. Something to prove she'd thought of me while she was off making history.

It took plenty of convincing for Aunt Carrie to get Uncle

Will to agree to the trip, but eventually, he relented. After the Albany fiasco, it was decided I should stay home with Uncle Will and Pap.

Alice Paul was the coordinator of the Washington, D.C. parade, an important event to push forward the idea of amending the Constitution so all women across the country could vote. A massive show of support for the movement was expected on March 3rd, the day before Woodrow Wilson's inaugural parade at the Capitol.

Ms. Paul had been arrested several times and jailed on three occasions for her civil disobedience and window-breaking. She was force-fed for weeks while in prison during a hunger strike. Although Aunt Carrie disapproved of Alice Paul's radical past as an English suffragette, Rosalie convinced my aunt that Ms. Paul's intentions now focused on being a peaceful American suffragist.

Several wealthy backers in the area, supporters of the late hometown heroine Susan B. Anthony, covered the train fare for the local suffragists, believing that broader representation from around the country would strengthen the cause. The suffragists would take the evening train the night before. They'd attend the march and return that same evening, arriving home early Sunday morning, in time for church.

The morning after Aunt Carrie left, I was surprised to find Uncle Will in the kitchen, frying bacon and eggs. I hadn't known he could cook. The three of us, Uncle Will, Pap, and I, ate together, and then, without a word about chores or choir, Uncle Will took me sledding down Creek's Hill while Pap stayed home with the newspaper. Aunt Carrie would never have allowed this, but Uncle Will was in charge that day, and I didn't ask twice.

Uncle Will had never taken me sledding before, and the thought of skipping choir and spending time with him, just the two of us, sent a thrill through me. We bundled up, borrowed an extra sled from the Kellys, and set off for Sycamore Grove. We went up and down the hill, again and again, until we were breathless and spent, our faces red with cold and laughter.

As we sat at the table eating soup, still thawing, Uncle Will leaned back in his chair and said, "Helen, a very special singer is performing with our band tonight. I'd like you to hear her. Would you like to come see me perform?"

Pap lowered his newspaper at once.

"Will, if Peter or Carrie finds out, all the demons in blazes will be let loose. You can't take a child to a club like that."

"Why not, Pa? Peter will never find out, and don't worry about Carrie. I will take care of Carrie. Serves her right for leaving me," he joked. "I want you to come too. I know you would enjoy hearing Mamie sing."

"You sure there, Will? I'm happy to stay home with Helen." Pap slicked back his white hair, unsettled.

"Pap, Helen will be fine. Seeing Mamie Johns is something special I want both of you to experience," Uncle Will said.

"I would love to go," I burst out, unable to keep still. I was already imagining how Olive's face would look when I told her what I had done while she was off in Washington.

"You've met Freddy Hadder and Jay. Their wives, Ruth and Ethel, are at the march with Carrie," my uncle said.

"All right, Will. I don't want to be around when Carrie finds out, though, and I certainly don't want to be around if Peter ever finds out." Pap's forehead wrinkled up as he shook his head.

Pap turned to me. "This'll be a long night, Helen. You'll have to stay awake. It's way past your bedtime."

"I can do it, Pap!" I yelled.

"Helen, best not to mention this to your aunt. Let me do that." Uncle Will winked.

"I understand, Uncle Will," I said. "Mum's the word."

Of course, I knew Aunt Carrie never would have let me go. I ran to my room and began dressing in layers, just as Uncle Will had told me to. Two pairs of wool stockings, a heavy sweater under my winter coat, and my thickest scarf and mittens to keep me warm.

"Clubs get very warm, but the ride over will be cold," he'd warned.

Uncle Will came down the stairs at nine o'clock, looking handsome, wearing his suit and tie. I was melting from being a bit over-eager to attend the club. Sitting in the kitchen with the stove on was too much, and the heat caused me to struggle to stay awake, but nothing was going to get in the way of my going to see Uncle Will perform.

We took the carriage out into the cold March night. The snow from the day before had been cleared, and the roads were smooth. Uncle Will was relieved as frozen rivets in the road could snap a horse's leg or wreck a wagon wheel. The ride to the east side of Rochester wasn't long, but the air was cold and biting. When we arrived at The Grotto, we tied up Nell behind the building and covered her with every blanket we had. Pap promised to check on her through the night, and I knew he would.

We entered through the back door, where a handful of men stood smoking and talking in low voices. The air smelled thick, and the club was dark. I could barely see. Smoke and the smell of sweet liquor and beer filled my senses. When my eyes finally adjusted, I was surprised to find we were only three of a handful of white folks in the club. I wasn't used to seeing so many Black people in one place, and I quickly felt like an outsider. I grabbed my uncle's sleeve. Dozens of smartly dressed Black men and women, some Indians too, were talking loudly, all holding drinks. Some women wore colorful dresses that looked more like costumes, and I became mesmerized, feeling like this was part of the evening's entertainment.

My uncle had me by the hand as we pushed through the crowd with Pap closely behind me. I noticed some people became quiet as we passed through with three or four disapproving glares, mostly from women, directed at my uncle. I thought about my aunt and Uncle Peter and wondered if this was a bad idea. What would they do if they found out I had been to a club? Pap walked over to the bar as Uncle Will and I worked our way to the stage.

"Well, well, if it isn't the fabulous Will O'Donnell." A tall, broad-shouldered man in a striped suit called from the stage, a brass horn dangling from his fingers.

Uncle Will grinned. "Good evening to you, too, Kid," he shouted above the loud voices.

The man's teeth flashed white against his dark skin as he walked over and bent slightly toward me. "And who's this little lady?"

"Helen, my niece," Uncle Will said, placing a hand gently on my shoulder. "Helen, meet Mr. Cory."

"Hello, Mr. Cory. You're the trombone player," I said, trying to sound older than I was.

Kid raised an eyebrow. "That's right, sweetheart. But you can call me Kid."

"Yes, sir—Mr. Kid," I said, a little unsure. I wasn't used to calling grown-ups by their first names.

He let out a deep laugh. "I like this one. Smart and polite."

Another voice chimed in from the side. "She's the songbird from Christmas."

I turned and beamed at Jay Bolder, remembering his easy grin. "Hi, Mr. Bolder!"

He leaned on the bar, swirling his drink. "So, you're skipping bedtime for a night of jazz and debauchery? Your aunt know about this?"

"She most certainly does not," Uncle Will interjected before I could answer. "And I'd appreciate it if that remained our little secret."

Jay smirked. "Your secret's safe with me, but . . ." he whispered something into my uncle's ear that I was unable to hear.

"She'll be fine, Jay," my uncle responded.

"Mr. Bolder what is debauchery?" I asked.

The men laughed.

"Nothing you will experience tonight, my dear," my uncle said.

Kid tapped his trombone with a knuckle. "Well, you're certainly in for a treat, Miss Helen."

Those who weren't sipping drinks were smoking cigars or cigarettes, and the room had a cloud of smoke that lingered on the low ceiling. I found a spot under my grandfather's table and made a cozy seat for myself with the winter clothes I had finally peeled off. Mr. Hadder handed me a birch beer, and I eagerly awaited the music.

Soon, the instruments started playing. Jay Hadder was on cornet, Kid Cory on trumpet, my uncle on stand-up bass, and John Lamb, an Irish friend of my uncle's, was playing the piano. I had entered a new, fantastical world. As the first notes were played, my ears perked up at the unfamiliar sound. Soon, a ripple of energy went through the room like a powerful ocean wave.

The music, a cross between blues and ragtime, Uncle Will had said, had a complex beat unlike anything I had ever heard, and the rhythm made people get up and dance.

I wanted to dance, but instead kept tempo with a bounce of my foot. Aunt Carrie and Uncle Will had practiced the waltz in the house a few times, but this was fast, beautiful, quick dancing with twirls, swirls, and dips where partners got close, very close. Dancers were chest to chest, and my cheeks heated when I saw some couples kissing. This was deep, passionate kissing I'd never seen before. I knew Aunt Carrie and Grandma wouldn't have approved of this.

Midway through the show, a beautiful woman with skin the color of molasses walked to the stage to sing with the band, making the crowd go wild. Mamie Johns wore a long green dress, accentuating her womanly curves. Every note she sang filled my head with fairy dust, the only way I could describe her voice, making me feel things inside that I'd never felt. Her voice was pure magic.

Maybe I could be a professor during the day and a singer at night, I thought to myself.

I tried to stay awake until the end, but eventually, sleep overcame me. Pap woke me after midnight, and Uncle Will carried me out to the carriage, bundling me in all the blankets. The ride home was quiet. My eyes drifted closed again, the music still lingering somewhere behind them.

Uncle Will told me once that music was the great unifier. That it didn't matter what color a person's skin was, only what kind of soul they had. I think he meant that music could bring people together, if they'd let it.

It made me wonder why white folks seemed so afraid of people with darker skin. The people in that club weren't any different from anybody else. Not better. Not worse. Just people.

It bothered me how folks got judged for things they couldn't help. I knew what that felt like. I got teased for my red hair and freckles, like I'd picked them out on purpose.

But those things weren't me. And being white didn't say who I was. There was more to me than what people could see. I had a soul. That's what we were taught in catechism. We all had one. Aunt Libby said some animals even do.

The sisters at school said we were all made in God's image. That He loved each of us just the same. But it didn't feel that way, not the way Uncle Peter talked about the Kellys, or how folks spoke about the colored girls who cleaned the church steps, or the Indians who came into town, or the fact that women couldn't even vote. And sometimes, the way the shopkeepers looked at the Irish, like we didn't quite belong. I was old enough now to see it.

A dull ache, or maybe it was an emptiness, settled in my stomach. It was uncomfortable, and it was growing. But then I realized that it wasn't in my stomach at all. It was in my heart.

And maybe I'd never be old enough to understand why the world wasn't fair.

TWENTY-ONE

March 4, 1913

I was brushing my hair, still half-asleep, when Aunt Carrie came running down the stairs at 8:45, one boot on, the other in her hand. She must've arrived early that morning while I was still in bed.

"Wait! Wait! I'll only be a minute!" she shouted.

I had fifteen minutes to get to church. I'd be late for choir, and Sister Teresa would be furious. I tried to hurry Aunt Carrie along. Two minutes later, we were in the back of the carriage with blankets across our laps, the same ones that had covered Nell and me last night at The Grotto. I hadn't seen Uncle Will and Aunt Carrie speak yet.

Did she know?

We took off down the street, Pap focused on getting us to church on time. Nothing was worse than walking into Mass late. "If Christ could die on that cross for your sins, the least you can do is get to Mass on time," I could hear Gram say.

"Helen, part of me wishes you had been there, but the other part is so relieved you weren't," Aunt Carrie said, tugging on her boot. "Some of the men were horrible. It was shocking. But overall, life-changing."

Her mood was far too cheerful. I was confident she didn't know about our night out.

"Why? What did the men do?" I asked.

"We were in rows of four at the beginning of the parade, and before we knew it, thousands of people, mostly men, were crossing the barriers and started to squash us into a single file. I was spit at, called a floozy, and told to get home and go back to my children. And those were the nice things the men said to me." Aunt Carrie chuckled.

"Carrie, honestly. Really?" Uncle Will asked from the front seat.

"Aunt Carrie, what is a floozy?" I asked. I had heard the word before, although I didn't remember where, but I had no idea what it meant.

"Heavens! It isn't a nice word. It is demeaning and instantly makes women immoral, whether they are or not. Don't ever use it, Helen," she said sternly.

"Okay, Aunt Carrie, I won't. Why were they so horrible to you all?" I asked.

"Many of the unkind men seemed to be drunk, and the parade was some kind of spectacle to them. They threw their cigarettes, their cigars, and their foul words at us, but we kept marching. We didn't cave." Aunt Carrie said with her chin held high.

"Goodness, Aunt Carrie," I said, surprised at the sound of it all.

"I can't believe you would put yourself through that,"

Uncle Will yelled to her from the front seat.

"It was an empowering experience for us all, and I'm glad I went," Aunt Carrie shouted.

When we finally arrived at Immaculate Conception Church, Aunt Carrie turned to me and whispered, "Women are stronger together. Don't ever forget that, Helen. So often, we are petty towards other women, but this gets us nowhere as a group. We must support each other—"

"Come on, ladies!" Uncle Will said as he helped us down from the carriage. As soon as her two feet were on solid ground, Aunt Carrie wrapped her hair up, tucked her long brown locks into her hat, affixed her hatpin, and kissed Uncle Will quickly on the lips.

"Before we walk into church," Uncle Will said, guiding her toward the stone steps, "there's something I ought to tell you."

Ah, here it comes, I thought, placing my lace veil over my head as I walked into church.

"I took Helen to the club last night."

He paused a second, then added with a shrug, "We heard Mamie Johns."

He kissed her cheek and pushed the heavy door open before she could reply.

Uncle Will was strategic like that. While he mostly supported women's voting rights and Aunt Carrie's involvement, he had his ways of letting her know when he thought she was doing too much. This was one of those times.

As we walked into the church, I glanced at Aunt Carrie and saw her lovely face wilt. I hurried up the stairs to the choir room, grabbed my cape, and slipped into my seat by the edge of the balcony. Luckily, Sister Teresa hadn't seen me come in late.

I looked down at the pew where my aunt, uncle, and Pap sat. A woman in front of them turned and shushed Aunt

Carrie and Uncle Will. During Mass, Aunt Carrie never took her eyes off the altar, though Uncle Will kept glancing at her, trying to catch her eye. I was certain she was boiling inside. Maybe that's why he said what he did just as we walked into church, hoping that an hour and a half of holiness would cool her down.

When we arrived, I was certain everyone hoped Father Murphy wouldn't be giving one of his lengthy sermons. And the moment he stood, I couldn't help myself. I let out a little groan, to which Sister Teresa cleared her throat and gave me a disapproving stare.

"Cain let Satan into his heart. Even the smallest drop of Satan's evil can rot a soul, eating away at what goodness remains until love itself is gone. This is the devil's plan. Jealousy is the road to eternal damnation!"

That was the last thing I remember hearing before Sister Teresa's sharp nudge and icy glare jolted me awake.

"Helen, it's time to kneel," she said with a scowl, pointing to the hard, wooden ledge reserved for the Mass's dozens of reverent kneeling moments.

We saw Uncle Peter as we usually did when the service was over. Many people were waiting in a long line to see the handsome, young priest, mostly women, old and young. I watched as he shook all their hands, giving kisses on the cheek to only a select few. When we finally got up to see him, he didn't seem happy to see my aunt and uncle.

"Hi, Pa," he said, shaking Pap's hand. "How are you doing today?"

"Tip top, son, and you? he replied.

"Will, Carrie—hello," Uncle Peter said, without looking into their faces, and then turned to me, "Hello, darling, how are you?"

I was still annoyed at Uncle Peter for spanking me for

going to Albany, but I reminded myself that he was the person who had saved me from having to move to Cleveland with my father.

"When are you coming over next?" I asked him.

"I will try to get over soon. I promise." This was the same response I heard several times over the past few months.

We headed towards the burial grounds and approached the large wrought iron gate doors, a border for the dead and the living that silently proclaimed, "This is ours" and "That is yours."

After Grandma died, I began holding my breath as I entered, a superstitious ritual I started after hearing some of the kids talk in school about the cemetery. My disdain for this place had only grown over the years as it continued to claim new residents from beloved family members.

Most people would get lost in the cemetery, but it was a familiar place for me. I'd been there roughly five hundred times by now. The numerous tall monuments, stately angels with swords guarding their dead, and crosses, everywhere. I would work on my arithmetic skills by adding and subtracting the dates on the stones and be reminded how cruel life could be.

Walkways had been shoveled for us, but many tombstones were still covered in snow, the poor graves, as I would call them. Small and flat, they would get buried in winter, and I often wondered how those people could visit their loved ones with them hidden like they were. We walked until an older woman appeared wearing a long battleship-gray coat and a large hat. I recognized her as one of Grandma's friends, Mrs. Byrne, who had been to the house before.

"Good morning, O'Donnells and Thomas. How are you, kind sir?" She said, looking at my grandfather.

"I am doing fine, Myrtle, and the family?"

"Roger has developed a cold. He's home in bed. He'll be sorry he missed you," she said.

As soon as Mrs. Byrne said it, I had to control myself from smirking.

Mr. Byrne hated going to church. Everyone in our church community knew this, as gossip spread like spilled milk. Each Sunday, the congregation would look to see if Mrs. Byrne was alone again. Grandma frequently talked about Mr. Byrne's poor soul on the way home from Mass and was sure to mention him to her Sunday visitors.

Most people I knew didn't trust those who didn't belong to a church. I had often heard that businesses in town with a non-church-going owner wouldn't be patronized or that children of parents who didn't attend church couldn't be played with.

We said our goodbyes to Mrs. Byrne and walked on until we reached familiar names—Grams, my mother's, and Uncle Albert's cemetery neighbors. Baby O'Dowd (1895), Colleen O'Dowd (1874–1897), Annabelle Rose Walsh (1862–1901), and Frank Walsh (1850–1889). We never knew any of them, but they all shared the same dirt in death. I hoped they were friends in Heaven.

We walked until I saw Sadie Long—Loving Wife, Daughter, and Mother (1879–1903). A white marble tombstone, with a graceful angel holding a child chiseled into it, an image I'd always imagined was my mother and me.

Next to my mother was Uncle Albert's granite tombstone, which read: Albert O'Donnell—Loving Son and Brother (1885–1902). To the left of Albert was a tombstone larger than the others that said Mary Collins O'Donnell—Loving Wife (1853–1911), and right under it was written, Thomas William O'Donnell—Loving Husband (1848—).

I thought it odd to have tombstones with the names of

the still-living, but Pap told us he wanted things to be easy for us when he passed away.

I stared at Grandma's tombstone and caught a faint whiff of the perfume she wore on special occasions.

Was I imagining it?

Memories of our Sunday "visitors" drifted in—how her friends would coax Pap into fetching a pail of beer from the pub and pour me a tiny mugful. I'd sit in my little rocker, sipping and listening to stories, mostly about people from church. Stories Gram called gossip.

Her bright, sparkling eyes and soft smile came to mind, and soon I was wiping away the torrent that had started. I couldn't understand how she could be under the snow now, sharing the cold ground with worms and bugs.

It gave me some comfort knowing she was with my mother and Uncle Albert. I imagined the three of them dancing together in the heavenly realm, but the tears wouldn't stop.

When Olive came over after breakfast, she was all smiles, holding the wrapped souvenir she'd brought back for me. I was jumping up and down, thrilled at the thought of a memento from the parade.

"Oh, what is it? What is it?" I repeated until it was finally in my hands.

I gingerly unwrapped the handkerchief, tied with one of Olive's lovely silk hair ribbons. A sharp, sour smell hit me.

It was a half-smoked cigar.

"Disgusting! Why, you—!" I shrieked as we both flopped onto the floor in fits of laughter.

"Well, you asked for a souvenir! Some crotchety old man threw it at me. I stopped, picked it up, and carried that stinky thing in my handkerchief for the entire march just so I could bring it home to you."

"I suppose I should thank you for the stinky cigar, then?" I giggled.

"Now tell me everything! I want to hear all about it."

I jumped onto my bed so ecstatically that I thought I'd break it, then quickly sat down.

"It's a majestic city. So many people, Helen. I've never seen such crowds," she said, grabbing a brush and running it through my hair.

"Tell me more, Olive. What was it like?"

"There are beautiful buildings, with details from Egypt, Rome, Greece, all the places I've loved reading about. Tall columns, domes, flat roofs. The White House is grand, with a big front lawn and gigantic pillars."

I closed my eyes, imagining it, as she kept brushing.

"We held flags and banners. There were women from all over, even from countries where women already had the right to vote. One of the organizers from New York, Inez Milholland, led the march on horseback. I didn't see her myself, but they say she looked like Joan of Arc, with her crown and white cape. Women held signs representing every state. It was incredible."

"Don't stop! Tell me more," I said as she started braiding.

"We sat on the train with some of your Aunt Carrie's Black friends who were attending the march," Olive said, tugging gently at a knot in my hair. "But they weren't allowed to march with us. They had to walk at the back with the other Black suffragists. Your aunt was furious, so the entire Rochester group marched at the back with them."

"Goodness, she didn't tell me that," I said, standing up. "That's awful. They couldn't even march with their own state?"

"No. It was ridiculous. The day ended with a silent play, featuring women in armor and children in white. Oh! And we met a group of women who walked 250 miles from New

York City. Can you believe that? Through the cold, through towns and snow. They are incredible."

Her eyes widened. "And I forgot the mice! Some boys let loose dozens of them, trying to scare us. But we didn't flinch. We just kept marching. I didn't see them, thank goodness!"

"Go on," I said.

"We started as a wide group, but people kept squeezing us until we were forced to march single file. So many rude men. Heavens to Betsy. Taunting, howling, and even tripping us. One girl had a cigarette put out on her face. The things they said . . . " She shook her head. "I've never been so proud to be a woman, and so frightened, all at once."

"I don't understand why anyone would do those things," I said.

"My mother says men are threatened. They fear losing their power, their control over us."

"Tell me more, Olive."

"Helen, the march was scary. Some men spat in the faces of the marchers. The police just laughed and didn't help. The Virginia cavalry had to come in to protect us. Even though it was hard, we kept marching. We remembered why we came."

I sat still, my braid half-finished, her hands resting gently on my shoulders. I didn't know what to say. Part of me wanted to cry, and the other wanted to scream.

"I wish I'd been there," I said. "Even with the mice. Even with the spitting."

Olive gave my shoulder a squeeze.

"We marched for a brighter future. Our future, Helen. And someday, all women will vote for the president of the United States. I promise. After seeing those women in Washington, I know the suffragists won't accept anything less."

TWENTY-TWO

September 1–October 22, 1913

It started with Aunt Carrie leaving the table. Quietly at first, with just a hand to her stomach. Then one morning, I found her behind the outhouse, bent over in the grass. I ran back inside, arms crossed, bracing for the worst.

When she came through the kitchen door, I asked, "Are you dying? Please tell me. I can take it."

What she told me instead would change everything.

"Helen, you can't tell anyone," she said softly. "I don't want to get my hopes up. The last time was so terrible. But . . . I'm pregnant."

A frail smile lit her pale face.

"What? My goodness!" I clapped my hands, unable to hide my excitement.

"Now, Helen, this is our secret. Do you understand?

I'm not ready to tell anyone . . . just in case."

"Aunt Carrie, I won't tell anyone."

In my mind, though, I figured surely Olive didn't count. I ran straight to her house after finding out, bursting with Aunt Carrie's news.

A few weeks later, Aunt Carrie told Uncle Will and Pap. However, the rule was clear: no one was to speak of the baby until he or she was safely born. After losing a pregnancy and watching so many women in our community, even in our own family, die in childbirth, Aunt Carrie believed it was bad luck to count chickens, or babies, before they hatched.

Officially, the baby would be my cousin. But to me, I was gaining a brother or sister. I delighted in the thought of the baby arriving in the spring. I made lists of names, imagined games we'd play, and pictured tiny cotton outfits. In my mind, I would teach my new sibling to walk, talk, read, and write. I had big plans to be the best sister in the world. Uncle Peter and Aunt Libby wouldn't be told until Aunt Carrie's bump made secrecy impossible.

That summer had already deepened my bond with Olive, Aunt Carrie, and Uncle Will. I had never been happier. For the first time, I truly felt part of a real family, one like the kids at school had.

The idea of moving to Cleveland to live with my father had long been buried, never spoken of again. Until one of his beautifully written letters arrived, inviting me to visit for the summer. He was eager for me to meet his new wife and my half-siblings. Though I loved him, I knew in my heart, I wasn't ready for more.

As summer faded and school approached, I found comfort in knowing Sister Teresa, my chorus leader, would be my new teacher. She reminded me of Sister Veronica from the year before, calm, kind, and never one to use the paddle or dunce hat. It felt like another small blessing, the kind that reminded me how safe and steady life had become.

One day, around this time, I was walking home behind the Hamiltons. Their dog, Harlequin, came bounding toward them, tail wagging, as they reached Magnolia Street.

It all happened so fast. A car came speeding around the corner. The wet leaves on the road made it impossible to stop in time. The automobile slid forward and struck Harlequin just as she leaped across the street.

The driver jumped out of his Ford, pale and trembling.

We screamed and ran toward Harlequin, who was lying motionless in a pool of blood. For a terrifying moment, we thought she was dead. But as we drew closer, we saw her side rising and falling. She was still alive, though badly hurt.

"I'm so sorry! I couldn't stop in time!" the driver moaned, bending over the dog.

Olive had been sitting on her porch, waiting for me to come home. The moment she heard the screeching tires and our screams, she came running.

Like a drill sergeant, she rattled off orders.

"Helen, get my grandmother! Sean and Liam—clean rags! Prudence, hot water! And if anyone has an old blanket, bring that too! I'll stay with Harlequin."

To my surprise, Sean, Liam, and even Prudence sprinted toward their house. I wasn't sure they'd actually do what Olive said, but they did.

I bolted into Olive's house without knocking, shouting for Mrs. Kelly. She was already on her feet, having heard the commotion, and sprang into action the moment I asked for a blanket.

Together we hurried down the street, where Olive and the driver were crouched beside Harlequin.

Mrs. Kelly took one look and shook her head.

"Hmm. We'll need to clean her off if I'm to see what's the matta. Here's a blanket. Shall we move 'er?" she asked.

"Yes, Nana. Maybe over there," Olive said, pointing to a soft bed of leaves near the walking path.

Mrs. Kelly and Olive slid the blanket beneath Harlequin and gently lifted her off the road. I stood frozen, amazed by their quick thinking. I hadn't the foggiest idea what to do.

Just then, the Hamilton children returned with their mother, a basin of hot water, and clean rags, just as Olive had asked. Olive began cleaning up the blood.

"Nice, Olive. Get this spot 'ere," Mrs. Kelly directed.

While Olive worked, her grandmother stood by, praising and guiding her. The rest of us just watched, hoping for good news. The blood didn't seem to bother Olive. As she dabbed at the mess, calm and focused, she looked like a surgeon. It reminded me of that day at LaFay Castle when she said she wanted to be a doctor.

Once the wounds were clean, Mrs. Kelly leaned in for a closer look.

"We'll need a doctor to stitch her up. I know Doc Young has worked on dogs and cats," she said. "Helen, is your aunt home so I can use your telephone?"

"Yes, of course, ma'am," I said eagerly, relieved to finally be of some help. We got up and hurried to my house.

"Aunt Carrie! Aunt Carrie, come quick!" I shouted as I burst through the door. "The Hamilton's dog was hit by a car. We need to call Doc Young!"

The doctor arrived in no time, his black bag in hand, already ministering to poor Harlequin. The driver had left, but before doing so, he pulled a few bills from a thick wad in his coat pocket, enough to cover treatment. Mrs. Hamilton had arrived by then, too.

"Oh my, what do we have here?" Doc Young asked as he knelt beside the dog.

"She was running to greet us," Prudence cried. "A man in a Ford . . . he couldn't stop in time."

Sean looked over at his little brother, who was sobbing, "Stop being a baby, Liam," Sean snapped, making Liam drop his head. With the doctor now there, Sean seemed to feel the need to show that boys didn't cry—at least not in public.

"Who was the smart one who got the hot water and rags?" the doctor asked.

"That was Olive, Doc," I said, glancing proudly at my friend.

"Good thinking, young lady," he nodded.

He gently examined Harlequin, now just a heavy, limp mass of damp fur. After shaving around the injury, he dabbed the area with a pungent liquid.

"She's one lucky dog," he said. "Only a broken leg. She'll need some stitches."

He set the bone, then reached into his bag for a splint, needle, and thread. Like hemming fabric, he carefully stitched the wound. Olive held Harlequin's head the whole time, keeping her calm and still.

"See that right there, young lady?" Doc Young said, pointing to one of the stitches as he looked at Olive. "Watch how I tie this knot. Want to try the last one?"

"Yes, doctor!" Olive beamed, excitement practically radiating off her.

It was too much for me. I had to get in on the spotlight.

"Can I do one, too?" I asked.

"Not this time," Doc Young said gently.

Once again, Olive was center stage. We all watched as she tied the knot.

"Ah, would ye look at that?" Mrs. Kelly murmured, her smile wide and proud.

"What do you think, Doc?" Olive asked, still holding the thread.

"Nice job, young lady. Maybe someday you can be a nurse," he said.

"Or a doctor, sir!" Olive replied, chin high.

That made both Mrs. Kelly and the doctor laugh.

"Maybe so. If you girls get to voting someday, who knows what opportunities lie ahead."

"Doctor, will she make it?" Sean interrupted.

"She has a good chance, son. She'll need rest and fluids. Sugar water for the first couple of days. And keep her from licking the wound. No playing. She's got to stay calm and heal."

"Doctor, if you ever need help in your office, I'd love to learn more about what you do," Olive said. "I'm a good student, sir."

Doc Young glanced at Mrs. Kelly. "If it's all right with your grandmother, it's fine with me. Come by my office next Wednesday after your studies."

"Yes, sir!" Olive said, nearly jumping with joy.

After Harlequin's accident, Olive and I started playing more with the Hamilton children, who now clearly had a new level of respect for us, especially Dr. Olive. Surprisingly, we soon became good friends. Although I use the phrase 'good friends' generously in regards to Prudence. We could now walk home on the same side of the street, laughing, joking, and playing games.

A few weeks later, Olive and I were invited to a sleepover. The main event: a Ouija board, which Michael, the oldest Hamilton brother, had recently acquired.

Their dormitory-style bedroom had four narrow beds, two on each side of the room, perfect for launching ourselves from mattress to mattress. The evening began with a massive candy binge. We pooled everything we'd bought earlier and ate until we lay sprawled on the floor, groaning and giggling, too full to move.

Next came the pillow fights, whacking shoulders, ankles, and arms until feathers and laughter filled the air.

Then Connor suggested that we play the game "Questions and Commands." When it was Olive's turn, she chose a question. Connor didn't even pause. The words lept out of his mouth before anyone could stop them.

"Do you have a father?"

The room went still. Olive hesitated, and I held my breath, waiting.

"My father died when I was two, before I ever knew him," she said.

The Hamilton's faces fell. They offered their condolences, long and solemn. Olive had fooled them completely. She glanced at me, and our eyes met for just a second.

Then, without missing a beat, she shifted the mood. "Let's build the fort," she said brightly, already reaching for the nearest blanket.

We spent the next hour draping every blanket and sheet we could find over chairs and bedposts, transforming the room into our fortress for the night's main event.

Sean insisted we wait until midnight. He claimed that's when the connection to the spirit world was strongest. Liam had already fallen asleep on his bed. We tried not to wake him and planned to lie to him in the morning, saying he'd slept right through it. We couldn't risk him ruining the night.

Once the clock struck twelve, we crawled into the fort and placed a candle in the center to see the board. Connor, being the oldest, took charge.

"Everyone ready?" he said.

We nodded, huddled in close.

"Put your fingertips on the cup—very gently," he instructed, demonstrating. "I'll ask the questions. The cup will move to letters to spell the answers."

He pointed to the board. "You can see it has letters, numbers, and the words hello and goodbye. DO NOT move the cup. I repeat—do not move the cup. Your fingers are just to rest on it. The spirit moves the cup. Got it?"

We nodded and waited, eager to speak with a ghost, though none of us actually believed it was possible. The Ouija board was labeled a "game," so we thought it was all make-believe and good for a laugh.

I leaned toward Olive and whispered, "Hey, maybe Frederick from LaFay Castle will come say hello."

But the moment the words left my mouth, a chill swept over me. The hairs on my arms stood on end. I started to have second thoughts.

"Helen, maybe this isn't such a good idea," she whispered back.

Everyone fell silent. The fort looked eerie in the flickering candlelight, shadows dancing across the sheets like they were alive. Then Connor spoke, his voice low and spooky, adding to the thrill.

"Spirits, we ask that you come to us tonight. We wish to speak with you. Please . . . come to us now."

At first, nothing happened. We waited, glancing at one another, barely breathing.

"This is ridiculous. Let's go back to bed," Prudence whined.

But before anyone could move, the planchette began to shift. If someone was moving it, it wasn't Olive or me. We pinky-promised afterward.

The planchette glided to the word on the left side of the board.

Hello.

We all sat up straighter. My heart pounded, but I reminded myself it was probably a trick. The Hamiltons were just trying to scare us. Still, Connor kept speaking calmly, like he believed every word. I played along, giving Olive a few reassuring nods to show her everything was fine.

"Hello," Connor said. "What is your name?"

The planchette moved again: A . . . D . . . A . . . M. It spelled Adam.

A few of us gasped. I glanced at Olive, whose eyes had widened. But I was still convinced the Hamiltons were behind it.

Connor asked his next question. "How old are you?"

The planchette slid to the number 7, then 2. Connor's face changed. Sweat glistened on his forehead.

"Why are you here?" he asked.

The planchette started moving fast.

I . . . l.i.v.e . . . h.e.r.e.

The moment it hit the last letter, Connor's face filled with terror as he threw the board up, trying to stand. We all screamed, horror-stricken. Then the candle blew out.

Everything went pitch black inside our cloth fort. We all panicked as the sheets tangled around us like the arms of the dead coming to claim their bounty. In the chaos, Liam jolted awake and joined in, screaming bloody murder.

"What on earth is going on up here?" Mr. Hamilton bellowed as he and Mrs. Hamilton burst in with an oil lamp.

We scrambled free from the blankets and told them everything—about Adam, the board, and how the planchette had moved on its own. Mr. Hamilton looked furious. He grabbed the board and warned us never to touch a Ouija board again.

After the parents left, we pushed our beds close together for the night, though I don't think any of us slept a wink.

The next day, Mr. Hamilton destroyed the board. We later discovered that Adam was the name of the previous owner who had lived and died in the house.

The night stayed with me, but not just because of Adam. Because I would come to learn the hard way. Not all ghosts are spirits.

And sometimes, the most painful truths are buried . . . to keep someone safe.

TWENTY-THREE

December 24–May 15, 1914

The holidays arrived, and Aunt Carrie was almost five months along in her pregnancy. Uncle Peter, who hadn't been to the house since my father's visit in February, said he would join us for Christmas dinner.

Similar to last year, Pap, Uncle Will, and I visited Aunt Libby at the hospital on Christmas Day after Mass, the cemetery visit, and breakfast. When we returned home, Uncle Peter was in the kitchen with Aunt Carrie. We could hear laughter from the door when we arrived. I noticed Pap's whiskey bottle and two small glasses sitting on the counter.

Aunt Carrie looked as beautiful as ever, wearing an elegant dress with her apron, hiding any hint of being with child. Uncle Peter's nose was red, which seemed to happen when he drank any alcohol. He nervously flinched when we entered the room, and Aunt Carrie quickly started chopping some herbs at the sight of Uncle Will's jealous scowl.

When we walked in to say hello, Uncle Will fetched the brown bottle. Without saying a word, he put the whiskey back in the cupboard, furrowed his brow, and gave my aunt a cold look.

Aunt Carrie had made a feast for dinner and served the drunk rum cake again for dessert. It had been such a hit last year. After the meal, we exchanged gifts like usual, starting with Uncle Peter's gift for my aunt. Aunt Carrie was gushing as she opened the box, a new hat with a dramatic plume.

I glanced at Uncle Will, biting his lip. Just like last year, he couldn't stand being outdone. He grabbed his gift, set on showing up his brother.

"Carrie, here, darling, open mine," he said, handing her a small box.

Inside was a diamond necklace. Not genuine, of course, but still costly. Aunt Carrie beamed as she clasped it on, assuring him he'd done well.

Seconds later, Uncle Peter disappeared and returned with a grand wicker doll carriage wrapped in a thick bow.

"Helen, I saw it and thought you might like to stroll your dolls around the neighborhood," he said.

"Uncle Peter, it's lovely," I replied, trying not to show my disgust at being treated like a child. I'd be twelve in March, after all. It was a lovely carriage, but I was getting too old for dolls. Of course, I still had Sadie, but I didn't dress her up or fawn over her like I used to.

He handed me another package. I unwrapped it quickly, and a soft bundle of fabric slipped to the floor, revealing a beautifully illustrated fairy tale book.

Without thinking, I blurted out, "Uncle Peter, I'll be able to read it to the babe—"

But it was too late. I clapped my hand over my mouth just as Aunt Carrie jumped in.

"Peter, we were waiting to tell you," she said gently. "After what happened last time, you understand. We're expecting in April."

Uncle Peter was stunned. He tried to force a smile.

"Wonderful. How wonderful for you all," he said, though it didn't sound the least bit believable. He left not long after, complaining of a headache.

When he refused to come for New Year's dinner, I asked Aunt Libby what was really going on.

"You already know he didn't choose the priesthood," she said quietly. "He did it for your grandmother. But Helen, I think he resents what he gave up. A wife. Children. The life Will has now." She paused, then added, "He's a man, not a saint."

In April, Mrs. Fullem, the revered midwife Rosalie Kelly, had recommended, delivered Matthew Albert O'Donnell on the 10th. Pap, Uncle Will, and I waited downstairs the entire time, pacing the floors and reciting the rosary. It was nerve-racking for all of us, especially after losing my mother. We didn't breathe easy until we heard the baby's first cries and were told we could come in.

Mrs. Fullem said the delivery had been short and smooth, and Matthew appeared to be in perfect health. Aunt Carrie was lying in bed, sweaty and exhausted, cradling him against her chest and gently petting his tiny head.

She looked more radiant than I'd ever seen her. She couldn't take her eyes off the baby—until Uncle Will asked how she was doing.

"Do you want to hold him, darling?" she asked.

Uncle Will could only nod, eyes brimming with tears. He

reached out, and after a few awkward attempts, finally settled Matthew into his arms. He gazed at his son with wonder, then bent to kiss the baby's small hands.

Pap stood in the corner, dabbing his eyes with a handkerchief, tapping his chest with his fingers, mouthing, "Thank you, dear God. Thank you!" As he looked toward the ceiling.

The room was brimming with emotions I hadn't known existed. I began to imagine the day I was born, how joyful it must have been, if only for a little while. My parents would've looked at me the way Aunt Carrie and Uncle Will looked at Matthew. They would've loved me with the same kind of love, the love only given by parents.

For a moment, I felt robbed. My eyes filled with tears. I quietly excused myself and walked down the hall to my bedroom. I plopped onto the bed, picked up Sadie, and held her close.

I was ready to have a good cry when I heard a soft tapping at the window. I looked up and saw my little red bird. Cloaked in gleaming scarlet feathers, it tapped the glass with its slender beak. I stared, stunned. I rose and stepped toward the window.

The bird tilted its head and stared at me until I startled it with the palm of my hand on the glass. It felt like the bird was trying to tell me something. *You can't change the past, but you can shape what comes next,* a voice came from inside my head.

And that was all I had. The future.

I made a silent promise to my mother and grandmother that I would be the best big sister ever. I wiped my tears and went back into the bedroom to join everyone else.

When I walked into the room, Aunt Carrie was sitting up and holding Matthew. He was swaddled tightly in a knitted blanket and seemed more like a football than a baby, as he just lay there.

"May I hold him?" I asked.

"Certainly, Helen," Aunt Carrie said. "You'll be a perfect big sister to Matthew as he grows. You'll be siblings."

Siblings. She hadn't said cousins. Yes. I would take care of Matthew. I would love and protect him.

I reached out my hands to hold him, and from that moment on, I loved him in a way I'd never loved anyone. He looked up at me with wise eyes and stared into my soul, as if he already knew me.

Over the next few weeks, if he was crying and I picked him up, he would stop. If he couldn't sleep, I'd rock him gently and sing until his eyes closed and he fell into a deep slumber.

Olive once told me that in the Orient, people believe we live many lives. I started to imagine that Matthew and I had been siblings before in another time, in a faraway land. And that destiny had brought us together again.

Matthew's baptism was set for May 15th. Aunt Carrie asked me to be his godmother, a great honor. It would be my job to help guide his faith and make sure he followed the teachings of Christ.

I wasn't sure if I was ready for such an important job, but I was more than willing to try my very best.

Pap insisted that Uncle Peter be named godfather. I knew Aunt Carrie and Uncle Will didn't want that. I'd overheard the argument in the kitchen.

"What better person to guide Matthew's morality than a priest?" Pap said.

"Pa, it's no secret Peter and I haven't gotten along for some time," Uncle Will replied.

"Peter's stubborn, but he's your only living brother."

"You don't have to remind me of that, Pa. Not a day goes by that I don't think of Albert," Uncle Will said.

"What would people think if you didn't choose him? William, your poor mother would turn over in her grave," Pap pleaded.

There was a long pause.

"Very well, Pa. I'll do it for Mother," Uncle Will said at last, ending the argument.

I often wondered how the phone call between my two uncles went—the invitation, the awkward silence, the forced civility. But whatever was said, Uncle Peter had accepted.

On the day of the christening, Matthew wore a long white gown with delicate eyelets and fine stitching along the hem, a garment Aunt Carrie had sewn herself.

She looked like her old self again. Her short-sleeved, ankle-length dress showed off the dainty shoes from Christmas Eve two years prior, and around her neck hung the gold locket Uncle Will had given her when they were engaged. A wide straw hat, trimmed in lace, ribbons, and a pink rosette, perched atop her head.

Aunt Carrie had bought the hat especially for the baptism, and I was shocked when I saw the price tag of $4.65. I didn't know exactly what their money situation was, but Uncle Will still worked long hours at the factory and played music on weekends. Aunt Carrie brought in a little doing alterations for wealthy women and a few local shops. I knew Pap earned eleven dollars a week delivering coal. I'd overheard him tell Aunt Libby once.

I thought back to the quiet arguments I'd overheard since they arrived. Aunt Carrie worked hard to keep up appearances with the society ladies, though I never understood why. Rosalie Kelly owned only a handful of dresses, while Aunt Carrie had so many that she kept several in my closet.

The baptism itself was one of those rare moments when duty and family came together. Father Reilly officiated, and

Uncle Peter stood beside him throughout the ceremony. At one point, I noticed Uncle Peter's eyes drifting, not to the baby, but to Aunt Carrie and Uncle Will, who stood close together, beaming down at their son. His smile faltered. For a brief second, envy passed across his face. It vanished as quickly as it came, but I saw it.

After the ceremony, Father Reilly and his mother were invited to our home. Aunt Carrie and Uncle Will hadn't invited their friends. The truth was, Uncle Peter didn't approve of any of them, especially Rosalie Kelly, and to avoid conflict, they'd decided it was best to keep the gathering small.

Aunt Carrie had been up since dawn, juggling the baby and the meal. Matthew seemed to nurse every hour, leaving her with little time to rest. The spring day turned unexpectedly warm, and Aunt Carrie opened every window and door in the house, hoping the breeze would offer some relief.

But no amount of fresh air could ease the tension at the table. Lunch was stiff and uncomfortable. Uncle Peter and Uncle Will didn't exchange a single word, and Peter only spoke to Aunt Carrie if she spoke to him first. Pap, Father Reilly, and his mother kept most of the conversation going. At one point, Mrs. Reilly launched into a long, solemn story about her husband's passing and how she'd raised four boys all on her own.

Uncle Peter barely looked at me. I missed the version of him from my younger years, the man who would've lassoed the moon if only I'd asked. Before Gram died, he used to hang on my every word, making me feel like the most important person in the world.

Aunt Carrie got up to fetch more iced tea while Uncle Will slipped out to check on Matthew, who had started crying in the bedroom. I offered to help, but Uncle Will waved me off and disappeared faster than I'd seen him move since the baby was born. I sat quietly, hands folded in my lap, listening to the adults. Until Uncle Peter finally turned to me.

"Helen, I bet you enjoy having a cousin," he said.

A bit insulted by the word cousin, I sat up straighter. "Matthew is my brother, Uncle Peter. Aunt Carrie even said so."

He gave me one of those looks. The kind that let me know I was skating on thin ice. Just then, Aunt Carrie walked in with the iced tea, her voice light as she tried to smooth things over.

"Yes, it's wonderful having Helen's help with the baby. She's so good with Matthew."

From the window, I spotted Rosalie and Mrs. Kelly sitting on their porch, sipping lemonade.

Unfortunately, I wasn't the only one who saw them.

"Is that Rosalie Kelly of the suffrage movement I see next door?" Mrs. Reilly asked.

"Rosalie is our neighbor." Aunt Carrie responded almost proudly.

"The Kellys built their house shortly after we did," Pap added.

Mrs. Reilly leaned into Aunt Carrie and lowered her voice. "I think she is a wicked woman. That girl's headed to Jericho if you ask me. You'd be wise to steer clear."

"Oh? And why do you say that, Mrs. Reilly?" Aunt Carrie asked, her voice much louder than Mrs. Reilly's had been.

Jericho meant Hell. Had she really just said Rosalie was headed for Hell?

The red blotches began to rise on Aunt Carrie's neck, and I worried this celebration might become more memorable than any of us intended.

The old woman adjusted herself in the horsehair chair

and started to say, "She has a—," then stopped, glanced at me, and said, "Let's just say she doesn't have the highest moral standards. You know she was excommunicated from the church? She is fighting to take women away from their families. Despicable. Men and women have roles . . ."

As if on cue, Uncle Will called from the other room. Had he heard the conversation?

"Carrie, I need you! Please come here," he hollered.

Aunt Carrie took a deep breath and excused herself. I wanted to say something, but knew it wasn't my place. Saying anything would have embarrassed Uncle Peter, and I may never have been forgiven for that. It was Pap who, surprisingly, said something.

"I've known Rosalie Kelly for quite some time now, and although she is anything but a demure, typical lady, I don't really know if it is up to us to judge where she will end up."

Uncle Peter quickly changed the conversation and said, "It is very upsetting to see what is happening in Europe."

"Why yes, it is," Father Reilly said swiftly as if picking up the unspoken cue to move the conversation to another topic.

Pap nodded in agreement.

I quietly sighed in relief that the conversation had changed, yet part of me wanted Mrs. Reilly to be put in her place. How dare she say those things about Olive's mother!

"Why, what happened, Uncle Peter?" I asked.

"Germany declared war on Russia," he replied.

Uncle Will and Aunt Carrie walked back into the room. My aunt was holding Matthew, and her neck color was back to normal. The few minutes away had calmed her.

"What does this mean for Ireland, Peter?" Father Reilly asked.

"Great Britain will fight with Russia, and they will get Ireland to fight alongside them. Heaven knows Great Britain will need help, but it's a shame our brethren will be forced to fight with the Brits," Uncle Peter said. He could talk like that because the Reillys were Irish, too.

"I don't like it. All this fighting. It's barbaric. If women were the leaders in this world, we wouldn't allow this." Aunt Carrie gave Matthew a loving squeeze.

"Let's leave the leading to the men. Women need to stay in the kitchen and the nursery where they belong. It's the way it's always been, dear," Mrs. Reilly said to Aunt Carrie.

Aunt Carrie smiled at Mrs. Reilly, and I was sure she was biting her tongue.

"Helen, please sing us another song, won't you?" Uncle Peter interjected.

I started singing "Amazing Grace," and the mood in the room changed within seconds; Uncle Peter sat back in his chair. This put a damper on any possible fight between the two women, which disappointed me a little. I wondered what Aunt Carrie would have said to the crotchety old lady.

When Aunt Carrie tucked me into bed that night, I asked her why she didn't stand up to Mrs. Reilly.

"Helen, I wanted to say something. She got me so angry with what she said about Rosalie, but I respect your Uncle Peter too much to debate with his friends, especially their old mothers. Remember, though, just because someone appears to be in a noble position, it doesn't mean they aren't a person of frail character."

"I don't understand how an older woman would think our place is in the kitchen—only? Why wouldn't she want more for us?" I asked.

"Because she never wanted more for herself, sweetheart," Aunt Carrie said.

TWENTY-FOUR

September 17, 1914–January 1915

Our new seventh-grade teacher, Sister Brigid, arrived at Immaculate Conception like a bouquet of summer flowers, fresh and full of life. She was young and quick to smile, the kind of person who looked you in the eye when you spoke and actually seemed interested in what you had to say.

On the first day of school, I showed her my ring and told her I had a great-great-grandmother named Brigid. Her face lit up like I'd handed her a treasure.

"Ah," she whispered, "then we're kindred spirits, you and I."

After that, I knew I was her favorite.

Most of the nuns we knew were old and traditional, and they taught us by making us memorize long passages from thick books. But Sister Brigid taught with real stories.

Stories full of people and meaning. She asked questions no one had ever asked us before.

"And what do you think Jesus meant by 'blessed are the peacemakers?'" she once asked.

I'd never been asked what I thought in a religion class. I wanted to learn not because I had to, but because something about the way she taught made me feel like I mattered. I looked forward to school every day. The room felt brighter than in years past. We were being allowed to shine, maybe for the first time.

Then one Wednesday evening, Aunt Carrie came home from a suffrage meeting with dancing eyes and a wide grin.

"You'll never guess who was there," she said, practically flying out of her coat. "Sister Brigid!"

"She came to the meeting?" I asked, my pulse quickening.

"Yes, and she signed up to volunteer. She wants to help sew banners and pass out literature. She wants to become a suffragist."

My hand covered my mouth, and a knot formed in my stomach.

"But what will happen to her?" I asked, frightfully concerned. After Matthew's celebration last spring, I knew all too well the church's stance on women's voting rights.

Aunt Carrie sighed and took my hand. "This is the time to be brave, Helen. Living in fear won't get us anywhere."

That fall, Rochester hosted the 46th Annual Convention of the New York State Woman's Suffrage Association. Hundreds of women flooded into the city, and our house turned into a kind of hostel. Between us and the Kellys, we hosted eight suffragists, four each. The women gladly slept on couches and folding cots.

The city came alive with the movement. Parades down

Main Street. Tent talks in Exposition Park. Church gatherings and speeches in Convention Hall. Aunt Carrie told me Mayor Edgerton himself opened the event.

"By the end of his speech," she whispered, "he was nearly converted."

I stayed home with Matthew through most of it. At first, I was disappointed. I wanted to stand beside Aunt Carrie and Olive, passing out flyers and marching in line. But Matthew needed care, and truthfully, I didn't mind all that much.

He and I had grown inseparable. Every morning, I wheeled him down Magnolia Street in his carriage, pointing to clouds in the sky, birds, and the neighbor's silly dog. I beamed when people smiled at us.

In November, my father came for a visit. He brought drawings and handprint turkeys my half-siblings had made, which I tucked away in my drawer and tried not to look at too often. I might've felt sadder about them if not for Matthew. He filled up any empty place left inside me.

By December, Aunt Carrie had taken on extra sewing work, and a quiet strain settled over the house. Something was off. I could feel it, but I couldn't explain what it was.

On Christmas morning, there were fewer gifts under the tree than the year before.

"With two of you now, everything gets stretched," Aunt Carrie explained gently.

Uncle Peter came by late that afternoon, dropped off his gifts, and left before dinner. "Too many commitments today," he said, already backing toward the door.

His gift to me was a statue of the Blessed Virgin Mary, all dressed in blue, with outstretched, welcoming arms.

"This is to remind you that you have three mothers in Heaven," he said. "You are always loved and protected by all of them."

It was better than the babyish doll carriage from last year. Thoughtful, even.

After he left, I kept my eyes on the door, hoping he might change his mind and come back. But he didn't.

As the year turned and the snow piled high against the porch railings, Olive began spending more time away from home. She said it was because I was busy with Matthew, but I knew there was more to it. There was something different about Olive, something I couldn't name yet.

But I'd find out soon enough.

TWENTY-FIVE

April 20–April 21, 1915

By April, Matthew had turned one, and I was still just as devoted to him. Meanwhile, Liam was in fourth grade, Prudence in sixth, Sean in eighth, and Connor in his second year of high school. I had turned thirteen in March, and if not for being schooled at home by her mother and grandparents, Olive would have been in her first year of high school.

One afternoon, we were all playing hide-and-seek, and Prudence was "it." Usually, Olive and I paired up to find hiding spots, but that day, she wandered off with Connor instead. I thought it was odd.

Several minutes later, Prudence found me, and I became the seeker. We regrouped, I closed my eyes, shouted "Go!" and began counting to fifty.

When it was time to look, I checked all the usual spots.

But when I opened the door to the small shed attached to the barn, I found Olive and Connor inside, together.

"You're not supposed to hide together! You both know that!" I yelled.

They looked at each other and smiled, and then burst out laughing. That made me mad.

"Connor, you're it—if I have to decide," I said, arms crossed.

"I love being the seeker!" he said with a smirk, folding his arms and mocking me.

We all parted ways when Connor gave us the cue. Olive and I ran to hide. We could hear him counting and see Prudence, Sean, and Liam scrambling to find good hiding spots.

"Let's hide in the tree fort," Olive said, catching up to me.

"We can't. People aren't supposed to hide together, remember? It gets confusing for the seeker," I said, annoyed.

"Helen, it's just a game," she said.

"That's right. And all games have rules."

She rolled her eyes and ran to the tree fort. I went up to my porch and hid behind a chair.

This is taking forever. Where is he?

After a few minutes, Connor reappeared from behind the house, still "searching." There's no way he missed Olive unless he hadn't been looking. He walked past me and found Liam behind the maple tree.

"Got you!" he yelled.

We all came out when we heard him. Liam started counting next, and the rest of us scattered again. I saw Olive and Connor run off, laughing, and duck into Nell's stable. I was piqued. Olive knew the rule about hiding together.

The game dragged. Liam was a slow seeker. Eventually, he found Prudence behind the bush near the house. We called for Olive and Connor, but they didn't answer. I marched into the stable and found them standing there.

"What are you two up to? Prudence, is it," I said, my voice sharper than I meant it to be.

"I don't want to play anymore. Connor and I are going to walk to McGregor's and get a Coke. You want to come, Helen?" she asked.

"Really? In the middle of the game?" I asked.

"This game is boring," Connor said.

"Olive, you know I can't go with you. I have to watch Matthew like I do every Wednesday when your mother and Aunt Carrie go to their meeting," I snapped.

"Okay then. We'll see you later. Bye!" Olive said, completely unbothered by my tone.

"Tell Mom I went to get a Coke, Prudence!" Connor called.

"She won't be happy," Prudence muttered. "You'll be late for dinner."

I watched the two of them walk down the street, alternating between silent moments of looking at each other and the ground. I had never seen this behavior from either of them before.

A week and a half later, I went to Olive's house. She had been busy with her work with Dr. Young and her studies, and I had been preoccupied with school, watching Matthew, and attending choir practices. We were in the bedroom, taking turns brushing and braiding each other's hair.

"You've been acting strange lately. Is everything okay?" I asked.

"Yes, of course. Everything's fine," she said, too quickly.

I didn't believe her.

"Is something going on with you and Connor?"

"What do you mean?"

"You know what I mean. Do you like him or something?"

"Well, he is kind of cute. Don't you think?"

"Don't I think? No! Positively, absolutely not. He's a stinky boy!"

"Helen, he's a nice boy. Actually, he's more of a man than a boy. He told me he wants me to be his girl and that he dreams of kissing me. What should I do?"

"My goodness. That's horrible! You tell him you're a good girl."

"Helen . . . would it be bad if I kissed him?"

"Olive, that's how girls get pregnant. Stay away from him! Ya hear?"

I was so upset that I left her house and went straight home after she finished braiding my hair. What was she thinking? She was my friend. Connor was the boy who used to bully and tease us.

The next day, in church, when I looked down from the chorus balcony and spotted Olive with her grandparents, my mouth dropped open. There stood Olive, once the neighborhood tomboy, looking ravishing in a new dress that accentuated never-before-seen feminine curves, with her long hair pulled up in a hat and wearing white gloves.

Heavens! When had Olive become a woman?

My resentment simmered, low and hot, jealousy running through me like an illness. Resentments I'd tried to stuff down since I'd met her began coursing through my veins. Olive was just right, her height, her smile, her weight, her everything.

And me? Homely. Awkward.

She won contests, worked with Dr. Young, and had a poise I could only dream of having.

And now Connor? My Connor? The boy I grew up with wanted her to be his girl?

By the time church was over, my jealousy had twisted itself into something deep and dark.

Evil thoughts crept into my head. Thoughts that made me hate myself a little, but that refused to leave. I imagined telling Connor about Olive's father and him being shocked, maybe even angry. Maybe when he'd realize Olive had lied to him, he wouldn't want her to be his girl anymore. Over my dead body would Connor Hamilton take Olive away from me.

The Kellys hadn't come home yet, so I went straight to the Hamilton's house after Mass. Prudence looked surprised when I showed up asking for Connor without Olive by my side.

He hesitantly followed me out back, and for a second, I wavered. But then it came spilling out. I told him that Olive's mother had been raped and that Olive didn't even know who her father was.

The words felt ugly the second I said them.

I waited for Connor to react. Waited for that cold look of disgust. But instead, his face changed in a way I didn't expect. He looked stunned, yes, but angry too. And not at Olive.

He jumped to defend her, like I'd insulted someone sacred. And just like that, I knew my plan had backfired.

"Why would you tell me this? I thought you and Olive were best friends. Helen, get on home."

I slunk back to my room and picked up the framed poem Olive had gifted me a few years back for Christmas.

"You're a complete idiot, Helen. What did you just do? You pinky swore!" I scolded myself.

My heart sped up when I heard a knock at the door. I peeked out the window and saw Olive cradling a tiny kitten against her chest. I opened the door, convinced she hadn't yet spoken to Connor. Her expression was far too pleasant.

Olive excitedly told me how one of Doc Young's friends had found the sickly kitten in a tree and brought it to him, hoping he could save the little thing. Not knowing what to do with it, he brought it to Olive to nurse it back to health.

Here was Olive standing on my porch holding a kitten that looked uncannily similar to the one Gram had shooed away all those years ago. The irony hit me like a hard slap. As a child, all I had wanted was a friend.

My heart skipped a beat.

We walked over to her grandparents' home and into the room she shared with her mother. Olive had made a little bed for the baby cat, and together we bathed it, washing away the dirt, grime, and fleas.

"Nana and Granddaddy said I could keep him. They said they would watch him when Mom and I travel for marches. Helen, you'll help me name him, won't you?"

The name Judas immediately came to mind.

"What about Oscar for Oscar Wilde?" Olive asked.

"Who is that?" I asked.

"He was one of the greatest writers and poets to ever live, and Irish, too. Surely, you've heard of him? He wrote "The Selfish Giant," "The Happy Prince," and many other books. He was put in prison for loving a man," she said.

"Loving a man? Like husband and wife?" I blinked.

"Yes," Olive said.

"I've never heard of such a thing," I said, suddenly choking on a swallow.

"The church forbids it, but Oscar taught people that love is love. He was brave, and I shall call the kitten Oscar because it, too, is brave."

"But if the church forbids it, it's wrong, Olive," I said.

"Helen, why would God care if two people love each

other, no matter who they are?"

I didn't have an answer except that it was in the Bible. But that never worked with Olive. She didn't read the same Bible the rest of us did. She and her mother followed *The Woman's Bible* by Elizabeth Cady Stanton, a book I was pretty sure the church didn't approve of.

We went back to doting on the kitten, now officially named Oscar. Olive spoke sweetly to it and began brushing its fur with a small silver brush, the kind meant for babies. We had one just like it for Matthew. As we sat there, a knot twisted in my stomach. The guilt was too much. I had to excuse myself, running to the outhouse as fast as I could.

For the next three nights, I couldn't sleep. One night, I had a nightmare that the Sadie look-a-like doll that Uncle Peter gifted me came out from under the bed and attacked me. I had forgotten about this doll. At the time, I believed playing with her would make me an unfaithful friend. A cheater, a pretender, or a phony. But the truth was far worse. I had been an unfaithful friend to my only flesh and blood friend in the world. My best friend. And I felt deeply, horribly ashamed.

After the third sleepless night, Olive came knocking at the door.

"Mrs. O'Donnell, is Helen here?" I heard her ask.

Her voice was tense, and she sounded like she could cry at any moment.

"Is everything okay, Olive?" my aunt asked.

"No. It isn't, but I need to speak to Helen, please."

"She's upstairs in her room playing with Matthew. Here, I'll get Matthew, and the two of you can talk."

Aunt Carrie knew something was wrong. I could hear it in her voice. I braced myself, hearing the two of them coming up the stairs, and picked up Matthew and kissed him. Aunt

Carrie knocked, then pushed the door open.

"Olive is here, darling. Let me take Matthew so the two of you can talk," she said.

One look at Olive and I knew I was done for. Her face looked ugly for the first time.

"Why on earth would you ever tell Connor about my father?"

"I . . . I shouldn't have done it. I'm sorry," I said.

"Sorry? That was a secret. You pinky swore! I didn't want the Hamiltons to know that. Why would you do that?" she screamed.

"I don't know. I truly don't. It was wrong," I cried.

"Helen, I thought we were best friends. A real friend would never have done such a thing. I don't ever want to be friends with you again. Do you understand? You are a selfish, immature little girl, and our friendship is over!"

Tears rolled down her cheeks with every word. In minutes, she was down the stairs and out the door. The slam echoed through the house, and the quiet that followed was crushing.

I grabbed Sadie, whom I rarely played with anymore, and sat on my bed. Her porcelain face stared up at me, blank and calm, offering no judgment.

I knew I'd crossed a line that couldn't be uncrossed, one no apology could fix.

The word selfish stirred uneasily in my chest, but I tucked it away.

Instead, I fixed upon the word immature.

How dare she?

I told myself I'd be fine without Olive. After all, I still had Matthew. I still had my family.

TWENTY-SIX

June 8–June 27, 1915

The night Uncle Will returned from his business trip to Chicago, I was up late reading when I overheard an important conversation between him and Aunt Carrie. The tone of her voice made me sit up.

I slipped out of bed and crept to the top of the stairs, straining to hear.

"They have a house for us," Uncle Will said, his words tumbling out in a rush of breathless excitement, something I hadn't heard from him since he moved back.

"It's near the club, and Mr. Carthage said we can buy it eventually if we'd like. Of course, we'd visit first to make sure it suits us. Chicago is right on Lake Michigan, Carrie. It's beautiful. There are Catholic churches and good parochial schools for Helen. Downtown is thriving with restaurants, hotels, museums, libraries, shops of every kind. And as you go further out, there are these gorgeous houses, tree-lined streets. It's like nothing you've ever seen."

Aunt Carrie must have been pacing because I could hear her footsteps moving across the floor. "Tell me more," she pleaded.

"Mr. Carthage owns a clothing store downtown," Uncle Will said, his voice lighting up. "He told me if you wanted to continue sewing, he could give you as much work as you wanted. But the best part, darling, you don't have to work."

Aunt Carrie let out a small laugh. "I wouldn't mind having some of my own money. Ten hours a week would be perfect. When I need to pick up or drop off work, Helen could watch Matthew." There was a pause, and her tone shifted. "William, what about Pap? And your music? Are you really ready to give that up?"

Uncle Will's voice grew firm. "Carrie, I can't live under Peter's thumb anymore. We're his pawns. This is his town. I need to make my own name for myself, and if that means giving up music for a while, then so be it."

"I know," Aunt Carrie said softly. "It's been difficult, having Peter watch and judge our every move. But what about your father?"

"Pap will be fine, Carrie. Who knows? Maybe eventually, he'll come live with us. But this—this is our chance. We have a family now. We have to give Helen and Matthew as many opportunities as possible." His voice rose with conviction.

"Carrie, I'd be making ten times what I make now. No more dirty factory work, no more breaking my back for scraps. We could finally have our own house. An automobile. A real future."

All went quiet. Then Aunt Carrie asked, "What does a floor manager do at the Fort Dearborn Club?"

"I'd make sure the men are happy," Uncle Will explained. "That everything runs smoothly, the music, the food, the cigars. I'd oversee the staff and handle the books. It's respectable work, Carrie."

She took a deep breath. "It sounds impressive, darling. When would you start?"

"August 17th. So . . . what do you think?"

She hesitated, and for a second, I thought she might say no. But then she sighed. "I'll miss Rosalie, Aunt Lib, and Pap. I'll worry about your father. But I know how miserable you've been since we moved back here." She paused, "William, if this is what you want, we should do it."

I sat on the edge of my bed and thought about what it all meant. I had lived in Rochester my entire life. After what happened with Olive and Connor, I didn't feel comfortable playing with Liam, Sean, or Prudence anymore, and I didn't have any friends at school. I liked Sister Brigid, but she would only be my teacher this year.

Certainly, I would miss Aunt Lib, Pap, and Uncle Peter, but Matthew, Aunt Carrie, and Uncle Will were my family, and I was very clear in my mind that wherever they went, I would go, too.

How exciting. We were moving to Chicago.

The next day, Uncle Will and Aunt Carrie sat me down and told me about the move.

"Helen, of course, you would come with us. What do you think about all this?" Aunt Carrie asked while bouncing Matthew up and down on her hip.

"I can't wait to move to Chicago!" I shouted at the two of them.

Aunt Carrie and Uncle Will both seemed surprised at my eager response.

"You didn't happen to hear us talking last night, did you?" Aunt Carrie had a smirk on her face.

"I don't know what you're talking about," I replied with the innocence of a babe.

Later that day, I overheard Aunt Carrie speaking to Pap on the front porch about the move.

"Carrie, I wouldn't assume Peter will let Helen go. Peter is a funny bird sometimes, and since he is Helen's legal guardian, he could put a kink in your plans."

"Pap, don't be ridiculous. Why would he ever separate Helen from her brother? He barely even sees her anymore. And besides, we could never leave Helen. That would mean we would have to stay, and Will would have to continue working at the factory. That would be awful."

Her voice tensed up as she realized what it all would mean if Uncle Peter disapproved.

"All I'm saying is, don't underestimate Peter, and don't leave him out of this plan," Pap said.

I had never considered that Uncle Peter wouldn't let me go to Chicago with my family. The thought was so absurd, I put it out of my head.

Aunt Carrie and Uncle Will went to Chicago the following week to explore the city, meet the club owner, and view the house where we would be living. I stayed home with Pap and Matthew and studied from home for a few days. I waited on pins and needles for that week to pass and to find out what my aunt thought of Chicago. If she said yes to the move, then it was a go.

When Aunt Carrie and Uncle Will arrived home, they were happier than I had ever seen them. They announced we were leaving for Chicago at the beginning of July. The cheerful Uncle Will I had seen when he first moved into Magnolia Street was back. I hadn't realized how unhappy he had been until I heard the conversations about Chicago.

With only a week left of the school year, Sister Brigid approached me at the end of the day.

"Helen, your mother, I mean your aunt, told me you are all moving to Chicago this summer. I wanted to tell you how overjoyed I am for you," she said.

"Sister, thank you so much. I'm very excited about it all. It'll be a big change, and I'll certainly miss seeing you next year."

"I shall also miss seeing you, Helen, but it all sounds wonderful. And nice job on your Beatitude assignment. It looks like another 'A' for you," she said, adjusting the belt of her long robe. "Your writing has improved tremendously since the beginning of the year. Keep up the good work. Go on now, and I'll see you tomorrow."

I knew I needed to be a good writer if I ever wanted to become a professor, and this information thrilled me.

About a week later, Uncle Will came home looking completely distraught.

"Carrie, get Helen to watch Matthew. I need to speak with you."

I knew Uncle Will well enough to sense that something was dreadfully wrong. From the kitchen window, I watched as he and Aunt Carrie stepped outside. They were arguing. I couldn't hear the words, but their gestures said enough.

Moments later, Aunt Carrie rushed back into the house in tears.

"Helen, darling. I just need a moment," she hollered as she ran to her bedroom.

Uncle Will came in from the backyard, looking worn from their conversation.

"Uncle Will, is everything all right?" I asked.

"No, Helen. It's not. My brother has made it clear you won't be moving with us."

I stared at Uncle Will, stunned. Had I simply misunderstood him?

"Excuse me, what did you say?"

"Your uncle is your legal guardian. I met with him today to discuss our plans, and he told me that you would never leave Rochester, that Rochester would always be your home. He said he would pursue legal action if we took you."

"My home is with my family, with Matthew, Aunt Carrie, and you. How could he think otherwise?" I yelled.

He pulled out the spindled wooden chair and sat down.

"I don't want to get you in the middle of this, Helen. I will have Pap talk to him tomorrow. I just want you to prepare yourself for the possibility of staying back."

"Staying back? You mean . . . you would leave me here?" I asked, barely able to utter the words. I felt that I might fall limp to the floor.

This shut Uncle Will down quickly. He put his head in the palms of his hands and shook his head back and forth.

The next day, Pap came back from speaking with Uncle Peter. Uncle Will wasn't home from the factory yet. He told me to go to my room so he could speak to Aunt Carrie. Try as I did, I was unable to hear them from upstairs. I was surprised when Pap came knocking on my door.

"Helen, can I talk to you?" he asked.

I opened the door to see a sullen-looking Pap. His gray face was pasted with a dim, forced smile. As he walked into my room, I noticed the coal still underneath his fingernails from work. However, his clean shirt made me believe he'd gone to visit Uncle Peter at the rectory.

"Helen, your uncle isn't going to let you go to Chicago

without a battle. Yes, Aunt Carrie and Uncle Will could hire a lawyer. Maybe they would even win, maybe they wouldn't. But at what cost? Having a family that doesn't speak anymore? I can't have my two only living children fighting. I ask that you just stay here with me."

Pap gave me a big hug and left before I could respond. It didn't feel real. As I watched him walk out the door, I could almost feel all light leave the room with him. My head began to spin.

Pap wants me to stay? And not be with my family?

I grabbed Sadie and a blanket off the bed and wrapped us both up. Within seconds, I was rocking back and forth on the floor, crying like a baby.

In my mind, I saw the train pulling away. Aunt Carrie holding Matthew. Uncle Will tipping his hat.

And me, standing on the platform beside Pap, forgotten.

Eventually, the tears stopped. As I placed Sadie back on the bed, my eyes fell on my garnet ring. Brigid Hogan's ring. This was the ring of a strong and brave woman from County Clare. I had fierce blood in my veins. I couldn't forget that. I was a Hogan. A Conlin. An O'Donnell.

I would speak to Uncle Peter myself.

The next day at school, I asked Sister Brigid if I could speak with her. I told her how shattered I was at not being able to move to Chicago with my family. Sister Brigid would never be called a worldly person or even a person with street smarts, but she had a heart of gold. Her eyes moistened as I poured out my story. I was sure she hated my uncle almost as much as I did by the end of it.

I convinced her to write a letter to Uncle Peter sharing her thoughts on the matter. She said the whole thing was incomprehensible, and that, as someone who worked with children every day, she knew my emotional well-being was at stake. I'd never heard the phrase "emotional well-being" before and had no idea what it meant, but I was thrilled she was willing to help me.

I watched her pen glide across the paper and imagined the convincing words landing on one page and then the other. Unfortunately, she sealed the envelope as soon as she finished. I would never know the contents.

After Pap got home from his coal runs, he agreed to take me to see Uncle Peter. He washed up, changed his clothes, and with "Saint" Brigid's letter in hand, we headed to Immaculate Conception Rectory, where Uncle Peter was expecting us.

Talking to Uncle Peter about anything he didn't already agree with was not something I had ever been successful at, and the butterflies in my stomach sent me running to the outhouse more than once before we left.

Upon arrival at Immaculate Conception Rectory, we were greeted by Annabelle, the housekeeper, who led us to my uncle's office. His door was open, and he looked up, then quickly back down to his papers, appearing busy.

I noticed the pretty new canary in the cage hanging from the corner of the room. I winced. I couldn't help but compare myself to the poor, jailed thing. Why did it have wings, after all, if it was never allowed to fly?

"Pap, I'd like to speak to Helen alone," he said, not looking up from his papers.

"You sure, Peter? I think Helen could use me in here," Pap said.

"Pap, I'll take care of this. Please go outside."

And like a dog being commanded by his master, my scared grandfather left the room without another word.

I had wished Pap would stay to support me, to help bolster my defenses, but onward I would go, to fight this battle alone. I had no choice. I had to stay and fight for myself and my future.

"Close the door, Helen, and sit down."

He looked so stern in his black frock and white collar, I worried my churning stomach might erupt.

With my heart racing, I summoned all my courage, walked further into his office, and sat down as I was told. Pap will be waiting in the carriage. Uncle Peter isn't going to bite me. I can do this, I told myself.

As I sat there, waiting for him to finally look up, I noticed how clean and kept his hands were, so different from Uncle Will's and Pap's. My eyes drifted to the small bird who had started singing for me.

"She's so lovely, Uncle Peter. When did you get her?" I asked.

"Two weeks ago. So, Helen, what is this about?" he asked abruptly, uninterested in small talk.

"Uncle Peter, this is a letter from my teacher telling you I should go to Chicago with Aunt Carrie, Matthew, and Uncle Will. Please read it," I said, handing the letter across his desk.

My uncle's brow furled as he quickly opened the letter.

"Ah, how delightful . . . Sister Brigid," he said. I couldn't tell if he was being sarcastic.

He read the two-page letter with a few nods of the head and some awkward smiles. He certainly took his time, as if studying her words. Finally, he calmly spoke.

"I see. You think I'm the problem here. That I won't let you go with my brother and his wife. But you're wrong, Helen. It's my brother who's trying to flee from you. He just isn't man enough to say so."

"What?" I asked, completely stunned.

"Helen, this goes back to when your father came knocking. Who do you think contacted him and told him to come?

It was William. Your aunt and Pap were in on it, too."

As he spoke, my head went light trying to understand his words.

Uncle Will contacted my father? Aunt Carrie and Pap knew?

"Your uncle wanted you gone so he could go back to Buffalo and reclaim his life. Carrie just wanted William to be happy again. Pap was tired of all the complaining. He thought the best place for you was with your father. William contacted him right after the funeral. It was all staged—like a play. I had no idea until later. I was furious. I'm the one who's been protecting you, Helen. Just like I'm doing now."

"What?" I said, my head about to burst.

"It's true. And now that they have a baby, they want a fresh start. They could stay here. They know this is your home. I'm not the bad guy here."

It was unimaginable. My denial started as soon as the shock began to fade.

"No, Uncle Peter. You must be mistaken. That can't be true," I said, pleading.

"I'm sorry, Helen. Your aunt and uncle aren't as first-rate as they seem. Why, they even fooled Sister Brigid, apparently."

His words numbed me. The denial vanished, and in its place came rage. They never wanted me. I thought they loved me. I thought Aunt Carrie loved me. I'd been fooled.

The air seemed to fade away. The room felt smaller by the second. I couldn't breathe. I stood up, unsure even how to find the door.

"Helen. I love you. I'll always be here for you," he said as I tried to escape.

Somehow, I made it to the carriage. Pap looked at me and asked if I was alright, but I couldn't speak. Not a word. I stared out the window to avoid looking at him. He was in on it, too. They were all liars. Aunt Carrie and Uncle Will had made me believe I was loved. Wanted. But in reality, I was just a nuisance. A pest.

As we reached Magnolia Street, I finally turned to Pap and said, "I don't want to go to Chicago. I'm staying in Rochester."

Matthew's little face came to mind the moment I said it. And I felt like I died inside.

TWENTY-SEVEN

August 4–August 20, 1915

I stopped talking to Aunt Carrie and Uncle Will once it became clear they weren't going to change their plans. I started to hate them both.

Being without my brother felt unimaginable. Matthew had become the sun, moon, and stars in my world. Now he would grow up without me, learning to talk, to walk, to skip rocks and play hide-and-seek, all without my help. One day, he'd become a young man, and I wouldn't be there to see it.

Those moments were being stolen from me. Would I even be his sister anymore, or just a cousin like Uncle Peter had said at the christening? Then came the worst thought of all—what if Matthew forgot me entirely?

Aunt Carrie seemed upset after learning I wouldn't be going with them, but I had no sympathy for her tears. She could stop the move with a single word. She could tell Uncle Will that keeping our family together mattered more than any job or paycheck. She had that power, and I resented her for not using it. Her silence told me everything.

So, when she finally said, "You'll come to live with us someday, sweetheart. In two and a half years, when you're sixteen, you won't need a legal guardian anymore. You'll be free to do whatever you want, wherever you want, with whomever you choose."

It didn't bring comfort. It only made me angrier. I didn't believe her. Not anymore. I went numb. The sadness that settled over me was heavier than anything I'd felt at the Allens. Sometimes, I wondered what the point of it all was. I felt sorry for myself constantly. I was a girl without a mother, without a real family to catch me when I fell. And now, not even Olive. I missed her terribly. I started to believe again that I was simply unlovable. How could I have done what I did? I wondered whether she and Connor were still friends or if the truth about her father had broken that, too.

Uncle Peter had even made me question Pap's love. I wanted to be angry at him for keeping me here, but whenever those feelings crept in, his words echoed in my head.

"Helen, they all knew your home was here, yet they tried to have your father take you away. They arranged this whole move, knowing full well you could never leave Rochester. They did this while all I did was take care of you and do my righteous duty to keep you here, with your school, friends, Pap, and me."

Uncle Peter was the one in the family who was closest to God. I could almost hear Grandma say, "Trust him, Helen."

But still, a small part of me wondered if this was truly what was best for me, why did it feel so awful? If only I could talk to Aunt Libby and tell her how I was feeling. I missed her terribly and wished she lived closer so I could visit her on my own.

During those last couple of weeks before Aunt Carrie and Uncle Will left, I started pulling back even from Matthew. I was preparing myself. I didn't think I was strong enough to say goodbye. Rosalie had taken Olive on the road with her and had been gone since mid-July. Aunt Carrie was upset she didn't get to say a proper goodbye to her dear friend. Although Rosalie and Aunt Carrie were disappointed that Olive and I weren't friends anymore, they didn't try to push us back together. The split between us didn't seem to change their friendship, at least, not that I knew of.

Uncle Will's band had fallen apart after two of his bandmates joined more prominent bands out of state. Mr. Hadder and his wife had moved to Boston, and Jay and Ruth Bolder had gone to New York City. So Uncle Will wasn't leaving many friends behind.

Pap and I were the only ones being left.

On moving day, I stayed in my room the entire morning while they packed the truck with several large wooden crates. Bill Roberts Furniture and Piano Movers was written in giant letters on the side of the vehicle Uncle Will had hired to bring them to Bragdon Station.

When the time came to say goodbye, Aunt Carrie and Uncle Will both wept, although I questioned their sincerity. I gave each of them a cold, unfeeling kiss and thought I might get away without crying. But I was wrong. When I leaned down to kiss Matthew, my heart melted. I realized this could be the last time I'd see my little brother for a very long time. I struggled to stay upright, to hold back my tears. Matthew just looked up at me, confused, his lip trembling like he knew something was terribly wrong. When he began to cry,

I couldn't hold it together anymore.

Aunt Carrie wept and promised she would write, but I didn't want her to. I wanted to forget we ever had this time together. To forget I ever knew what it was like to belong. It would have been easier if I had never known how wonderful it could be. How being part of something gave me a sense of wholeness, a place in the world.

Pap and I stood on the front porch, and I sobbed as they drove away. I'd never felt so completely abandoned in all my thirteen years. My ground had dropped out from under me.

As the truck turned the corner, it kicked up a soft cloud of dust that hung in the summer air. I began to wail. I'd been left, yet again. Pap held me, and I wondered if some part of him felt abandoned, too.

A week after the move, Uncle Peter came over after Sunday Mass and threw another bomb into my lap.

"Helen, Dr. Brian McClatchy, and his wife have moved back to town from Scranton with their two little boys. Do you remember visiting them after my mother died?' he asked.

"Yes. I remember them," I said. Of course, I remembered them. Dr. Brian had left an uncomfortable imprint on me.

"I am most excited to tell you that I have arranged for you to go live with them. Mrs. McClatchy needs help with the boys. This will be a wonderful opportunity to learn some useful womanly skills," he said with a giant grin.

"Uncle Peter, you mean I'm to go live and work there?"

Good grief, an indentured servant had more freedom than I.

"Yes, you can learn to be a lady and a mother. Two very important skills, all while being able to stay at Immaculate Conception. As you know, Dr. Brian is one of my closest friends, and I will be able to keep a watchful eye on you. Pap and I will be able to see you whenever we please," he said.

As angry as I was at Aunt Carrie, I was certain she was both a mother and a lady. So what exactly was my uncle implying?

He cleared his throat and began rearranging the mantle without looking at me.

I was wrestling with the idea of living with the McClatchys. It felt wrong, but I knew it was only a matter of time before Pap started drinking again. Without a strong woman keeping him in line, he never lasted long. I knew that as well as anyone.

"You'll have a shorter walk to school, and Magnolia Street is only thirty-minutes away," he said. I thought about going back to school and seeing Sister Brigid's familiar face. Boy, it would be nice to talk to her.

I had only met the McClatchys that one time after Grandma died. We'd taken the *Black Diamond to* Scranton to stay with them. I remembered Mrs. McClatchy being very nice, but there was that evening in the parlor when Dr. Brian and I were alone.

Nothing that happened felt right or normal, but the doctor hadn't done anything bad to me. I would have remembered that. The angel on my shoulder whispered that Dr. Brian was an old, dear friend of Uncle Peter. It was wicked to think anything unsaintly of him. I decided my memories of discomfort weren't reliable. After all, I'd been distraught over Grandma's death, and I was only nine years old.

"Uncle Peter, when would I go?" I paced around.

"You can see them and meet the boys after Mass on Sunday, and then we can move you in the following Saturday." He had a pleased smirk on his face.

That Sunday, after Mass, Pap and I went over to see Uncle Peter, who was talking to a gentleman I instantly recognized as Dr. Brian. He wore an expensive-looking suit with wire-rimmed spectacles perched on his rosy nose.

Mrs. McClatchy and the boys were nowhere in sight. I later learned she'd gone to fetch them from the children's area. Pap stood beside me, eager to see Peter's old friend again. Across the hall stood Dr. Brian. His belly was much larger than I remembered, and I couldn't help but joke to myself that maybe it was he who was pregnant this time.

As we got closer, I noticed perspiration building on his forehead. When he saw us, he removed his hat and blotted his brow and nose with his handkerchief.

"Hello, Doctor," my grandfather said, shaking Dr. Brian's hand enthusiastically.

"Tom, good to see you."

"You remember Dr. McClatchy?" My uncle said, turning to me with a bright smile.

"Well, what do we have here? It's been a long time since we've seen the likes of you," the doctor said.

"Yes, Dr. Brian. It was four years ago. I'm thirteen now," I said, giving him a polite kiss on the cheek.

"Look at you, all grown up," he said. "Mrs. McClatchy and I are just tickled at the thought of you living with us and helping with the boys. We have a dog. Do you like dogs?"

"Yes, sir. What's its name?" I lied. The only dog I'd ever known was Harlequin, the Hamilton's dog, and she was such a nuisance that my feelings about canines were a bit soured.

"His name is Zeus, and he's a Doberman Pinscher," Dr. Brian said, straightening his tie.

"Ever seen a Doberman?"

"No, sir," I said.

"Let's just say," he chuckled, glancing at Pap and then at me, "he was worth every penny."

I had no idea what a Doberman Pinscher was, but I

hoped Zeus was like one of the cute little dogs I had seen walking in the park, and that the name Zeus wasn't symbolic of his size.

Two young boys came barreling towards Dr. Brian. One was hardly old enough to walk.

Mrs. McClatchy walked over. "Now, children, how many times have I told you not to do that to your father?" Then, noticing me, "Helen? Goodness, look at how you've grown. Your hair is so beautiful, you've taken good care of it," she said as she kissed my cheek.

"Mrs. McClatchy, what a pleasure to see you again," I said.

I thought back to our visit in Scranton when she had combed out the nest of snarls that had accumulated under my hair after Gram had died. It pleased me that she noticed how nice my hair looked. I was frequently reminded that I wasn't a pretty girl by all the stares landing on Olive and not me when we walked downtown. However, my long, red hair drew attention, and after the Scranton trip, I took meticulous care of it. A beautician had even offered me four dollars to cut it off. I laughed, knowing I'd rather die than lose my only redeeming feature.

Mrs. McClatchy wore a fashionable, high-waisted dress with a large, matching hat, but the eyes that had once been so warm and welcoming now seemed a bit cold and vacant. Her full, pregnant belly and healthy-looking cheeks from the last time I had seen her were now concave and painfully thin. Uncle Peter had said the family needed help. Maybe motherhood or the move back was too much for her.

"Let me introduce you to these two little goblins. This is Timothy." A cute boy of three or four approached me and shook my hand. "And this is Michael." The toddler tugged at his mother's dress until she picked him up.

When they were ready to leave, Mrs. McClatchy said,

"Helen, we so look forward to you coming to live with us."

That week, I readied myself for another departure from Magnolia Street. Again, I asked in my prayers—what would become of Pap in my absence? How would he survive without Aunt Carrie or me? I thought about Olive, too. I wanted to tell her I was leaving. Losing her friendship haunted me. Would I ever forgive myself? Would she ever forgive me?

The night before I left, I lay tossing and turning. The unopened letters I'd stuffed in my drawer kept tugging at my thoughts. Even after everything, I couldn't get Aunt Carrie out of my head.

Finally, I hopped out of bed, lit the lamp, and opened the drawer. One letter had a Cleveland postmark from August 4th. She must have mailed it from the train. The other was from Chicago, dated August 8th.

I admired Aunt Carrie's pretty handwriting and held the letters to my chest. But when a tear slid down my cheek, I blurted, "I hate you! I hate you! I don't need you in my life!"

Then I tore the letters to pieces. And tossed them in the trash.

TWENTY-EIGHT

August 21–September 6, 1915

Pap, Uncle Peter, and I headed to the Corn Hill area to the McClatchy's new home. I remember my uncle telling me that Dr. Brian's grandfather, an Irish immigrant, had made a fortune in the steel industry. We'd driven by Dr. Brian's old childhood home on East Avenue. Uncle Peter always pointing it out like a landmark.

It had a brick façade, Greek-inspired white columns, and an observatory porch roof for stargazing. He bragged about the grand staircase and how he and Dr. Brian used to sleep on the roof in summer. The place had electricity, plumbing, and everything else that screamed success.

I didn't know what their new home would be like, but I imagined something just as impressive. At the corner of Clarissa and Atkinson Streets, I spotted a grand two-story house with a massive, curved porch wrapping around the entire Atkinson Street side.

"This is your new home." Uncle Peter's words felt like a sharp jab in my gut.

New Home?

This was an upper-society house, unlike the Allen's or even the McClatchy's previous home. It had a kind of grandeur, though on a smaller scale than the LaFay Castle. Scalloped siding adorned the peaks of the many jutting rooflines, and intricate porch detailing gave the house an almost dollhouse quality.

Most people I knew would have been impressed at the thought of living in such an exquisite house, but as thoughts of Aunt Carrie, Uncle Will, and my dear Matthew filled my head, the whole situation made me want to gag.

We waited at the door for so long that I began to think we were at the wrong house. Finally, a very frazzled and out-of-breath Mrs. McClatchy answered the door.

"Michael just broke something. Please come in, Father," she said, then disappeared upstairs in a flash.

The spacious foyer boasted a sweeping staircase and dark wooden walls, framed by towering stained-glass windows that stretched up two stories. I was delighted to see a large grand piano tucked into the corner of the music room when we stepped inside. I remembered Mrs. McClatchy being a fine player.

Through the adjoining room, I glimpsed a fire glowing in the hearth and boxes and wooden crates stacked every which way, signs of a home still being put in order. We waited in the parlor for Mrs. McClatchy to return. She appeared with Michael on her hip, while Timothy led the way ahead of her.

"Hello, boys!" Uncle Peter said.

Timothy walked up to him and shook his hand in a manner befitting an adult.

"Hello, Father O'Donnell. It is a pleasure to see you again," he said. Then he turned to his mother.

"Was that right, Mama?" he asked, embarrassing the woman.

My uncle smiled and quickly changed the topic to the gleaming piano.

"This must be the new addition to the family Brian told me about."

"Yes, it fits the room perfectly, don't you think?" Mrs. McClatchy's tired face became peart.

"Absolutely! I look forward to hearing you play again, Kate," Uncle Peter said.

When we stayed with the McClatchys four years ago, Uncle Peter yelled at Mrs. McClatchy quite harshly for dressing me up in makeup and her clothes. I wondered if she still remembered it like I did.

I had my own bedroom now, and it made my room at home look like a pauper's closet. The bed had a massive decorative headboard, a matching footboard, and a dressing table with a mirror and washbasin. My new drapes cascaded from the tall ceiling to the floor. The house had all modern luxuries, hardly a surprise, including electricity and plumbing.

Mrs. McClatchy mentioned I'd be sharing the bathroom with the two boys, and as we passed the tiled room, I imagined being treated like a queen, soaking in hot, clean water in the glistening white claw-foot tub.

Uncle Peter and I headed downstairs.

"Goodness, where is Kate?" Dr. Brian asked in a stern voice.

"I believe she's with the boys," my uncle replied.

Dr. Brian made a face. "That woman. What shall I do with her?" he teased.

Zeus was nothing like I'd imagined. He was a large black-and-orange dog with a sleek, shiny coat, a stubby tail like a sausage, and ears sharp and alert, like a big cat's. He sat, waiting for his next command.

"Zeus, say hello to Helen and my good friend, Father O'Donnell," Dr. Brian said.

My uncle shook Dr. Brian's hand while I cautiously patted Zeus on the head. The gesture made me nervous. The dog carried himself with a strange kind of arrogance, if that was possible for an animal. He didn't even react to my touch.

Immediately, my thoughts of Harlequin became less harsh as I thought about the few times I dared pet that old, stinky dog and the wagging tail that would follow.

"I know Kate's prepared a meal for us all. Go on into the dining room, and I'll fetch her," Dr. Brian said.

A short while later, Mrs. McClatchy entered the room, looking frail and flustered. She carried a roast, with vegetables and a bottle of whiskey.

"Best whiskey you'll ever try. A farmer in Scranton made it for me," Dr. Brian said. Mrs. McClatchy brought out two glasses, and Dr. Brian poured the amber liquid.

My uncle took a small swig. "Woo-wee, that is good," he said.

Dr. Brian and Uncle Peter spoke of two new Irish immigrants from the church who would be coming next week to work for the McClatchys. A man named Shamus would help with house and garden maintenance, and a young lady named Maggie would be their full-time maid.

"Peter, thank you for finding us help. God knows we can use it." Mrs. McClatchy sighed.

"It is a good opportunity for these young immigrants. Immaculate Conception sponsors as many Irish as we can, giving them lodging and a job so they can get on their feet,"

Uncle Peter said with a mouthful of cheese. "I am so happy that you decided to move back, and what a fabulous opportunity for Helen."

I nodded, smiling politely as I sat at the table, with my legs crossed at the ankles, dabbing my mouth with my napkin as I ate my soup daintily. I kept trying to convince myself that my new situation would be fine. I would show Olive, Aunt Carrie, and Uncle Will that I didn't need them. I would live here and be happy, happier than they could imagine. I didn't care if I ever saw them again. At least, that was the plan.

During my first couple of weeks at the house, I helped Mrs. McClatchy in preparing for the large party that would take place in two weeks' time, introducing Dr. Brian to the community as a family practitioner. This was a significant gathering, and many community members were expected to be in attendance. With the new help not starting for another week, I had plenty to keep me busy.

The McClatchys still had unpacking to do from their move, and empty wooden crates that had safely stored glassware and plates were now strewn out back, soon to be burned in the fire pit. Mrs. McClatchy had things Grandma would have fancied, and as I held the objects to clean, dry, and put away, I was struck by the elegance, the vibrant, colorful designs, and how fragile everything was.

Shamus and Maggie showed up at the door the week before the party. Maggie was much younger than I expected, about Olive's age, and Shamus told me he was twenty-seven. Maggie did all the laundry, mending, ironing, cooking, and cleaning, while Shamus was primarily responsible for the gardening and things that Maggie couldn't do. I watched the boys, and Mrs. McClatchy often stayed in her room.

On the night of the celebration, the house looked as if

President Wilson himself could have shown up. The flowers and food, not to mention the alcohol and cigars for the men, were downright impressive. The boys and I were allowed to sample some of the tasty treats for our evening meal before the guests arrived, and then we disappeared upstairs, hidden from view. Children were to be seen, not heard, and seen only when desired, as I'd learned from my time with the Allens.

I was reading to the boys in the bedroom they shared when Mrs. McClatchy came in looking rattled. She asked, "Helen, quickly, can you help with my hair?"

Mrs. McClatchy was arrayed in an exquisite cream-colored, short-sleeved gown made of satin, lace, and chiffon, featuring a hobble skirt and cummerbund, which was the latest fashion in Paris. I knew this from Aunt Carrie. The dress looked so small that I thought it would fit me, as thin as I was. But after our dress-up fiasco when I was nine, I was certain Mrs. McClatchy wouldn't be dressing me up again.

Just three days earlier, the seamstress had come to the house for final alterations and said, "Mrs. McClatchy, this fit you last week. Are you forgetting to eat?"

That night, Mrs. McClatchy wore a three-strand sparkly necklace, a large, brilliant sapphire and diamond ring, and dangling diamond earrings. She now needed help placing the hair ornament, a band of shiny crystals stitched onto a silk ribbon, into her pinned-up hair.

When she was ready, I couldn't help but look at her in awe. "Mrs. McClatchy, you look absolutely stunning," I said.

"Honestly, Helen? Do I?" she asked.

"Yes, ma'am. You look spectacular."

She stood up, looked at herself in the large mirror, and smiled. "You are to take care of the boys, and when they go to bed, you can also retire for the night. In the morning, I will need help cleaning. Maggie will come after Mass to help."

"Of course, ma'am. I hope you have a nice time tonight," I said.

The company began arriving, and I got excited watching all the fancily dressed people from the stairs. My uncle arrived and came to say hello for a minute, but quickly left to join the festivities. I saw women wearing expensive long dresses and men in suits with tails, similar to the attire I saw at the LaFay Castle for the suffrage event. I desperately wanted to be part of it.

I tried my darnedest to get the boys to sleep, but with all the noise coming from downstairs, it was taking longer than expected. Mrs. McClatchy was playing the piano, and after each song, the guests clapped loudly.

Once I finally got Michael and Timothy down, I went to my room like I was supposed to, but I couldn't stand being left out. I wanted to be part of the fun, even if I had to sneak.

When Mrs. McClatchy started playing Moonlight Sonata, all the talking stopped. I figured everyone was gathered in the parlor, listening. It felt like the perfect chance.

With Sadie in my hands, I crept down the stairs, slipped into the room, and dove under the dining table, unseen. I was too old to play with dolls, but with so little good company these days, Sadie had reclaimed her place as friend and confidant. If I got caught, I figured her moral support might come in handy.

While hiding under the table, I overheard a conversation about a secret rendezvous at the Hotel Rochester, scheduled for Wednesday at noon. As the man whispered the details, a woman with a smoky voice leaned in and hissed, "Keep your voice down. No one can know about this. Do you understand?"

Later, I heard Mrs. McClatchy speaking with a woman about the suffrage movement.

"Mrs. Smith, I was a member of the National Association Opposed to Woman Suffrage while we lived in Scranton. Do you have a local chapter here?" she asked.

A cold rush swept through me. *The National Association Opposed to Woman Suffrage?*

"We don't have that particular group here," Mrs. Smith replied. "But I belong to an organization you might find more fitting. We're always looking for young mothers who understand a woman's place in the world, not like those nutty suffragists."

I could feel my face burning. I bit the inside of my cheek, furious and stuck in silence.

I had assumed Mrs. McClatchy supported the movement. However, it became clear that the women in her circle liked suffragists as much as the devil liked holy water. Married Catholic women were instructed to believe their place was solely in the home, caring for their husband and children. Anything other than that was an abomination to God and his plan.

When so many women saw themselves as housecats, how could anything ever change?

I must have fallen asleep under the table, because I woke to the bickering voices of Mr. and Mrs. McClatchy. The jovial noise of the party was gone, replaced by Dr. Brian's shouting.

"Every time I turned around, you were talking to Daniel Clarkson. You're a whore. A no-good whore," he yelled.

"Brian, you're drunk. I only spoke to that man once," she pleaded.

"I give you everything a woman could want, and this is

how you repay me? Embarrassing me at my own party, you bitch."

"Brian, stop it, please! You're hurting me," she cried as he shoved her into the dining room table.

"Kiss me! Why won't you kiss me?" he bellowed.

"Stop it!" Mrs. McClatchy sobbed.

They were now in a full struggle. From the sound of it, he was hitting her. I wanted to leap out from under the table and protect her, but I stayed put, frozen, like a deer in a hunter's sights. I told myself I'd only make things worse if I were discovered.

The struggle dragged on. Then I heard fabric tearing. My mind jumped to her dress. How radiant she'd looked earlier, preening in the mirror before the guests arrived, proud as a peacock. Now, torn.

She cried out and ran upstairs. Dr. Brian followed seconds later. The bedroom door slammed.

As quietly as I could, I slinked out from under the table, crept up the stairs, and climbed into bed. I wasn't there two minutes before I realized I'd left Sadie behind. I'd have to get her in the morning.

The shadows of the tree outside cast jittery figures on the ceiling. I stared up at them, my heart still pumping fiercely. What had just happened?

I knew couples argued. But this? This was something else.

I didn't think Mrs. McClatchy had flirted with anyone. But even if she had . . . did that mean she deserved to be yelled at, hit, and called that word?

That word. Whore. I'd heard it before. I knew it wasn't for polite mouths. I thought of all her work preparing for the party. How lovely she looked. Was her dress ruined now?

And something else troubled me: Did Uncle Peter know Dr. Brian hit his wife?

The next morning, I came downstairs and spotted Sadie sitting on top of the dining room table. My heart sank. Someone had found her. Someone knew I'd been under the table. I snatched her up and rushed her back upstairs, hiding her under the bed.

Then I walked, as calmly as I could manage, back down to the kitchen. Mrs. McClatchy sat alone at the table. When she turned around to greet me, I saw she had a white, powdery face. It masked some of the swelling and bruising, but there was no hiding her puffy, red eyes.

"Good morning, Helen," she said.

"Mrs. McClatchy, are you okay? I asked gently.

"Silly me. I fell off the porch last night while saying good-bye to some guests."

I knew this wasn't true, and wondered why she was lying.

"Helen, won't you fetch some flour and eggs from the larder? We'll make pancakes," she said, forcing a smile.

Mrs. McClatchy moved as though every part of her body ached. I was baffled by her lies and wanted to scream.

What are you talking about? That horrible man you call a husband beat you up last night!

But I said nothing. Instead, I set the flour and eggs on the counter, my insides burning. I knew too well that adults cared more about appearances than they did the truth. She limped to the icebox and pulled out some sausage, then turned toward the griddle with trembling hands. Watching her hobble around the kitchen was more than I could bear.

"Mrs. McClatchy," I finally cried, "you must go lie down."

"Helen, I'll be fine. I just fell down the stairs. Do you understand? I fell down the stairs. That is what happened! We won't talk about this anymore to anyone. Are we clear?"

"Yes, ma'am," I said, startled by her sharp tone.

Mrs. McClatchy didn't go to Mass, and when Maggie arrived after the service and saw her, she gave me an odd look. I knew better than to say anything, and Maggie was smart enough not to ask.

Mrs. McClatchy never mentioned finding Sadie under the table that day, or ever. In the months that followed, she sometimes limped through the house with bruises on her face or arms, pretending, as she had the morning after the party, that everything was fine.

Like everyone else in the house, I learned it was best not to ask questions.

TWENTY-NINE

September 7–November 12, 1915

I knew eighth grade was going to be trouble the moment I saw Brother Gene walk into the room. When I blurted out an answer on the first day, he nearly bit my head off. But after finding out I was Father O'Donnell's niece, he softened. Not for the others, though. Some of those girls were twice as smart as me, and he didn't give them the time of day. It made my stomach ache.

Not long after school started, I went looking for Sister Brigid. I checked downstairs in the seventh-grade class-room where she used to teach, hoping to tell her about Uncle Peter keeping me in Rochester and about the beatings.

Instead, I found Sister Francesca, by far the oldest nun in the school, sitting behind Sister Brigid's desk, grading papers. She glanced up over her glasses, then went right back to work like I wasn't even there.

"Well, what is it, Helen?" she asked, obviously annoyed.

"Good afternoon, Sister Francesca. Is Sister Brigid here?"

"Sister Brigid is no longer with us."

"What?" I uttered.

"She was transferred to a school in New York City at the end of last school year," she said with all the emotion of a toad.

Shock, denial, and something close to horror rushed through me. "I don't understand. She didn't even say good-bye."

"She left quickly. That's how transfers go sometimes." She adjusted a paper on her desk without looking at me. "She's with more like-minded people now. Everyone will be happier, I'm certain."

Then she scrawled a large red *C* at the top of a paper and waved me off with a flick of her hand.

I left in a fog and wandered out of the building, only to realize I'd gone the wrong way. My feet had taken me toward Magnolia Street—toward home. I stopped, turned around, and retraced my steps to the school's stone stairs.

From my pocket, I pulled the folded map Mrs. Mc-Clatchy had drawn that morning, directions to my new place of residence.

I would never call Atkinson Street home.

I sat in stunned disbelief. Heavens, Uncle Peter had gotten rid of Sister Brigid. He sent her away because she tried to help me.

Poor Sister Brigid. Caring, compassionate, and beloved by her students. Gone. I felt sick. I had no allies now. Then my thoughts turned to Aunt Libby. I hadn't seen her in months. I missed her wisdom and support. She always had the answer. I needed to get to the hospital, somehow.

On the way to the McClatchys, I heard the singing of a cardinal and noticed the brightly colored bird following me. I had seen it several times since moving to Atkinson Street and was comforted that my little winged friend had found me.

When I arrived, Maggie was in the kitchen making dinner, and Mrs. McClatchy sent me upstairs to care for the boys. She was moving normally by now, and her bruises were almost gone, but her dull, hollow shell was painfully evident. She was a completely different person from the kind, pregnant woman I remembered from Scranton so many years ago, and the hopeful smile she greeted me when I first arrived was gone without a trace.

One day, while we were in town, we passed a group of suffragists holding signs. Several of them recognized me and waved. Mrs. McClatchy turned to me and said, "Oh, Helen. You must stay away from those women. Women were put here on this earth to be mothers and wives. Voting is something only the men do."

My response flew out before I could stop it. "Why can't women be mothers, wives, and part of our election process?"

As soon as I said this, I knew I'd made a big mistake. Mrs. McClatchy's expression soured, like I'd just rubbed a cactus across her face.

"Helen, that isn't God's will. You certainly don't agree with the suffrage movement, do you?" she asked.

I was cornered. I was a suffragist through and through, and to say otherwise would be a lie, but telling my new caretaker I wasn't on God's side, according to our church, was probably foolish this early in our relationship.

"It just seems that women have a different way of looking at things, and we might bring more nurturing and peaceful ideals to our government if allowed," I said, speaking the truth but not going overboard.

Her lips pressed together, but she said nothing. *Phew!*

I assumed Uncle Peter hadn't mentioned that my aunt was a suffragist or that I had attended a suffrage march in Albany. What would happen if the McClatchys found out? Would they send me away? Uncle Peter would never forgive me if that were to happen.

I thought the beatings were the only thing breaking Mrs. McClatchy, making her walk around like one of the zombies Olive taught me about, but I was soon to realize it was so much more. One Sunday, after Mass, she took the boys upstairs while I stayed in the kitchen to check the turkey in the oven.

The doorbell rang, and I answered it. A mysterious, well-dressed man in a dark suit, hat, and tie stood there.

"Is your father home, young lady?" The man said, straightening his tie.

"Oh, you mean Dr. McClatchy, sir?" I asked.

"Yes," he grimaced, his voice getting firm.

"May I tell him who is—?"

Abruptly, Dr. Brian pushed me out of the way, told me to go to my room, and walked outside to speak to the man.

I ran to the open window in the den, eager to see if I could hear any of the conversation.

"What are you doing coming to my house like this and on a Sunday?" Dr. Brian hissed.

"You think I wanted to come here? Tony wasn't happy he had to send me. He's been very patient. Where's the two grand?" the man asked coldly.

Dr. Brian's voice faltered. "I'm working on it. I'll have it soon."

"You have until Saturday, Doc. Trust me, you don't want me coming here again. Capisce?"

"Yes, I understand," Dr. Brian said.

One evening, about three weeks later, I heard Mrs. Mc-Clatchy yelling to high heaven as she prepared for the opera.

"Helen! Have you seen my sapphire and diamond ring? The one I wore the night of the big party? Have you seen it?" she asked, close to hysterics.

"No, Mrs. McClatchy. I know the ring you're talking about, but I haven't seen it," I said.

"Jesus, Mary, and Joseph! Where could it be?" she cried, running back to her room. Then, quickly tore down the stairs into Dr. Brian's office. I scampered to the top landing to listen.

"Brian, my diamond and sapphire ring is gone!" she cried.

Dr. Brian sounded calm, too calm. "I'm sure it'll turn up, Kate. You probably just misplaced it."

"Brian, this is my diamond and sapphire ring I'm talking about. The one you gave me for our fifth anniversary. I know exactly where I keep it. What could have happened to it?"

"I certainly hope Maggie didn't take a liking to it. You know, sometimes people like her want what people like us have."

It was no coincidence that Dr. Brian needed money, and now her most expensive ring had gone missing.

"Do you think she actually could have stolen it?" she asked.

"If it doesn't turn up, we'll have to let her go. I'm sure she'd just deny it if we confronted her," he said. "I remember her saying she wished she had the money to bring her family from Ireland. That ring could easily make that happen."

"Brian, I knew that ring was too expensive to keep in the house. We should've stored it at the bank."

"Don't go blaming me it's gone. You're the one who lost it."

"I didn't lose it! It was in the box in my drawer. I am

positive. I can't believe Maggie would have stolen from me. She seems like such a nice young girl. I just can't believe it," Mrs. McClatchy said.

"Let's not get the police involved. That wouldn't be good for my new practice or the church, since they sponsored her. Hopefully, it will turn up."

Mrs. McClatchy started up the stairs, and I dove into my room.

"Now, Helen, you are sure you didn't take the ring or see it anywhere?"

I paused momentarily, wanting to tell her that her husband most likely took it and sold it to pay that scary man who came to the door looking for his boss's money, but I knew better.

"No, ma'am, I haven't seen it," I said.

That Wednesday, when Maggie showed up in the morning to clean the house, Mrs. McClatchy asked her about the ring. I peered down the stairs and saw panic fill the girl's face. I suppose this was a maid's worst fear, having something go missing while employed.

"No, ma'am. I've never seen the ring."

The look on Maggie's face tore me up. She had no money or family and had recently arrived in our country. Even if the police didn't get involved, she would instantly become unemployable in the area. People who could afford servants and cleaners were part of a different social sphere, where they all knew each other and interacted. What would become of her?

"Look for it today while you're cleaning. It better turn up," Mrs. McClatchy said sternly.

The next morning, Maggie wasn't making breakfast like usual. When I asked Mrs. McClatchy about her, she told me that her services were no longer needed.

Things became even stranger one night after I put the boys to bed and drew myself a bath. I was soaking quietly when I heard a noise outside the door. I glance over at the keyhole, a large one, the kind you could see straight through.

All the keys in the house had been hidden, fearing the boys might accidentally lock themselves in a room. Now, as I stared at the keyless hole, my blood ran cold seeing the unimaginable.

I gasped, shot up from the water, grabbed my towel, and flung opened the door. No one was there.

My chest pounded. I tiptoed to the boys' room. They were fast asleep.

And in the chair, seemingly asleep, too, sat Dr. Brian.

Just then, I heard footsteps on the stairs.

"Helen! What on earth are you doing?" Mrs. McClatchy snapped. "Get back in that bathroom this instant and get dressed. And clean up that wet floor. You can't be half-naked with Brian and the boys in the house!"

I wanted to tell her what I'd seen. That someone had been watching me through the keyhole. But what would she think? That I was accusing the men in the house of something unholy?

Instead, I lied.

"I thought I heard one of the boys scream," I said. "It's fine, ma'am. I checked on the boys, and Dr. Brian is sleeping with them in there. I'm not sure what I heard."

Thoughts flooded me as I lay in bed that night. I felt scared, hopeless, and homesick, for Olive, for Aunt Carrie and Uncle Will, and most of all, for Matthew. I'd tried not to think about my little brother because the pain was too great. But tonight, I piled on the agony.

I pictured his smile, his laugh, his soft blue eyes. I imagined holding him, hugging him. But when I closed my eyes and squeezed, I found myself clinging to my cold, lifeless doll instead.

Matthew, Aunt Carrie, and Uncle Will were so far away, and I longed to be with them desperately. I hadn't seen Olive or Rosalie around town and assumed they were still traveling. I missed Aunt Libby too—missed hearing her voice, missed feeling seen.

I didn't want to live in the McClatchy house anymore. I didn't like or trust Dr. Brian, and Mrs. McClatchy had become a shadow of her former self, a fading woman, weaker with each passing day.

Like so many nights before, my thoughts circled back to the lie. Aunt Carrie and Uncle Will had deceived Uncle Peter about my father. They'd tried to give me away, just to be rid of me. They could have stayed in Rochester. Uncle Peter was right.

There was a horrible fight going on inside me, and most nights, it ended the same way, where I'd beat my fists into my pillow until the goose feathers flew, then cry myself to sleep.

One day after school, as I took Zeus for a walk, he pulled me toward the backyard and into the bushes. Catching the scent of something, the large dog suddenly lunged, yanking the leash from my hands. He disappeared behind the shrubs, then reemerged seconds later, proudly carrying a dead red bird in his mouth.

My beautiful songbird. Lifeless. Still. Never to sing or fly again. The sight of it made my knees go weak. I swayed for a moment, then screamed and bolted into the house to find Mrs. McClatchy. The dog had killed my bird, my friend.

Mrs. McClatchy said I could bury her in the backyard and that the boys could help. We dug a small hole and collected several rocks to put on top of the grave, and then the three of us said a short prayer. I feared that my grandmother would not be able to communicate with me now, and I became distraught.

At dinner that night, as soon as the boys sat down, they excitedly told their father how we'd buried the red bird Zeus had killed.

Dr. Brian looked at his wife and said sharply, "You what? What kind of sissies are we raising? That pesky thing woke me up every morning. I killed it with Timothy's BB gun."

Mrs. McClatchy and the boys hung their heads. My blood boiled.

"You killed the bird? You killed my bird? How could you?"

Dr. Brian reached across the table and grabbed my hair, knocking a glass of milk to the carpet. "Don't you ever talk to me like that, you little brat."

I couldn't move and was hunched over the table in severe pain until he let go of me. As soon as I was released, I ran from the table, up the stairs, and slammed the door to my room. I leaned against the door, ready to cry. But within seconds, I heard footsteps pounding up after me. I dove to the side of my bed, heart pounding.

Dr. Brian swung open my bedroom door like a wild animal. He grabbed me by the hair, yanked me up, and dragged me to the chair. He threw me across his lap. My scalp burned, but that was only the beginning.

"You will never disrespect me like that ever again. Do you understand?"

He struck me hard, again and again. When he pulled my dress up and hit through my bloomers, the pain worsened.

When he yanked them down, I started screaming.

"Stop! Stop! Please, Stop!"

He kept going. No one came. After what felt like forever, he shoved me to the floor.

"Don't ever disrespect me again. Are we clear, Miss O'Donnell?"

I couldn't speak.

"Are we clear?" he bellowed.

Between sobs, I whispered, "Yes . . . sir."

He left me there, face wet, bloomers at my ankles, body burning in pain.

Uncle Peter had hit me before, after the suffrage march. But no one, not even Grandma, had ever struck my bare bottom. I was almost a woman. He'd left me broken. Or so he thought.

The next morning was a school day, and as usual, I was expected to get the boys dressed, then bring them down for breakfast before walking myself to school.

I was awoken by a slight knock on my door. Before I could say anything, it opened, and Timothy walked in.

"Helen, you okay?" he whispered. "I got all dressed by myself today, and I can get Michael dressed too if you need me to."

I reached out to hug him, the movement making me realize that my head and my bottom were still sore. Timothy's kindness made me think of my beloved Matthew and how much I missed him. Tears welled up in my eyes.

"Timothy, you are such a good little boy. Thank you." I sniffled. "I am fine. I will be fine." I tried to convince myself.

"I don't like it when Father hits me. It hurts," he said.

"Yes, Timothy. It does hurt."

That morning at breakfast, Mrs. McClatchy acted as

though nothing had ever happened. I wondered what I would do. Uncle Peter and Pap were taking me to visit Aunt Libby in a week. I was looking forward to this with great anticipation. Uncle Peter thought it would be best for him and Pap to not visit me for a month or two, while I got "cemented" into the McClatchy family. I didn't understand this at all.

The Saturday after Samhain, Pap and Uncle Peter came to pick me up in Uncle Peter's automobile. It came as no surprise that the McClatchys didn't celebrate Samhain, and I thought about my dear Aunt Libby and the fun we had on my first Samhain when she lived with Pap and me.

I squirmed when I heard Dr. Brian belying the events of the last two months so earnestly to Uncle Peter and Pap. When we were leaving, Dr. Brian asked if I could come into his office quickly to retrieve something. Mrs. McClatchy followed my uncle and Pap outside.

I stepped cautiously into Dr. Brian's office. At first, his hands were gentle as they settled on either side of my head, almost tender. But then, I felt pressure building as he pushed. "What happens in this house stays in this house," he said.

He yanked me closer, so close I could smell the sharp stink of whiskey on his breath. His eyes bored into mine. "Clear?"

I desperately wanted to break free from his hold. "Yes, sir," I said.

He let go of me, and his temperament changed instantly. "Now make sure your uncle takes you to the candy store on me," he said. He grabbed some loose change from his desk and handed it to me with a smile that was anything but believable.

I ran from his office and past Mrs. McClatchy on the sidewalk, who was talking to my uncle. Pap was already in the automobile, and I quickly opened the door and hopped to safety in the backseat.

Pap turned around, took one look at me, and chuckled, saying, "Helen, you look like you've seen a ghost."

Neither of them noticed my blank stare or shallow breathing in the back seat. When they asked questions about school and my new "home," I didn't say much. I couldn't say much. I had just been scared to death and could still feel Dr. Brian's hands on my head.

When we got to the hospital, I ran up to Aunt Libby and hugged her soft, fleshy body tightly. Her embrace comforted me like never before, and I didn't want to let go. She cradled me and kissed me multiple times, sensing my longing. Within minutes of arriving, Uncle Peter left to bless the people on Aunt Libby's floor. Eventually, Pap went off to talk to an old friend, and finally, Aunt Libby and I were alone.

She immediately asked me why I hadn't responded to any of Aunt Carrie's letters.

"I ripped them up before I left for the McClatchys. I never read them."

"Ripped up Aunt Carrie's letters? Why on God's green earth would you have done that?" she asked.

"Well, I . . ." I stammered.

"Oh, dear. Aunt Carrie wrote to me, so upset that she hadn't heard from you. She's worried sick."

"They are off living happily without me," I said indifferently.

"Helen, stop that. Your aunt told me she's written you a letter a week since they left."

"A letter a week? That's not true, Aunt Lib. I only received two letters," I said, bewildered.

"Then something's wrong. Maybe ask the McClatchys? Your aunt is heartbroken. You must know how much she loves you.

I hesitated. "Aunt Libby, I don't know if Aunt Carrie loves me. They did leave me here," I said.

"Helen, you need to stop being so selfish."

I sat back in my chair, the word hitting like a slap. I struggled to keep from saying something I would surely regret. Selfish? After everything? She had no idea.

"Things were difficult for your aunt and uncle moving back here. They were so good to you. I also know it wasn't easy with your uncles not getting along. Helen, they had an opportunity to have a better life. You can't fault them for that. Your uncle should have—"

"What are you two talking about?" Uncle Peter said, startling us.

Just like that, the door slammed shut. There would be no more conversation with my aunt.

There was so much I needed to tell Aunt Libby, but not nearly enough time. The truth was, I would've needed a whole day, maybe longer, to explain everything that had happened to me over the past couple of months.

On the way back to the McClatchys, I wondered what Aunt Libby was about to say.

Your uncle should have—what?

And was it true that Aunt Carrie had written me multiple letters? What if Aunt Carrie and Uncle Will had no choice but to move?

Aunt Libby was a wise woman, and I trusted her, but I was angry at my aunt and uncle. I still blamed them. Deep within me, though, I hoped it was true. I hoped Aunt Carrie and Uncle Will did love me.

I desperately needed Olive to help me sort through this mess. I thought about my friend daily and how I betrayed her.

She would never forgive me, I knew, but maybe she would take pity on me and help me. My frazzled brain brimmed with the thought of going to her house and knocking on her door, but I decided I could never do that.

Olive had every right to slam the door in my face. I imagined the advice Olive would give me instead. She would tell me to search for the letters.

When we returned to the McClatchys that evening, I asked Dr. Brian and Mrs. McClatchy at the dinner table if they knew of any letters that had been addressed to me.

Dr. Brian looked at Mrs. McClatchy, then back at me.

"I haven't seen any letters. Have you, Katie?" he said, sipping his whiskey, the ice clinking in his glass.

"No. I haven't," she said, her eyes searching her plate. Had she looked at me when she responded, I may have believed her. I had no idea why they would lie to me or why they'd keep my letters from me, but in my gut, I knew they weren't being truthful. Hidden somewhere were Aunt Carrie's letters. I was positive.

I didn't know where they were or if I'd ever see them, but the mere thought of their existence was enough to give me hope.

It took a few days for me to be alone in the McClatchy house. On that day, instead of attending choir practice, I snuck back early, knowing no one would be in the house.

As soon as I walked in, Zeus greeted me, then returned to his parlor rug and sprawled out like usual.

I headed straight into Dr. Brian's office. I wasn't allowed in there, and if I got caught, the punishment would be severe. I carefully opened the door and had one foot in the dark room when Zeus came in, startling me. I yelped. He lay down in front of the cold fireplace, his eyes studying me. It was almost as if he were warning me.

You don't belong here.

Books lined the shelves, and a portrait of Mrs. McClatchy hung above the mantel, the same woman I'd met in Scranton four years ago, on that trip with Uncle Peter after Grandma died. One shelf held a photo of the family when Michael was a newborn.

On the far wall, another showed Dr. Brian standing proudly on the carcass of a black bear, one boot pressed to its neck. His rifle glinted across his chest, like the killing had made him a hero. I stared at the animal's glassy eyes, then down at the plush fur rug beneath my feet. My bird came to mind, and my stomach turned.

I went to the desk and opened the top drawer. No letters. I opened the second and froze. A pistol rested inside, all black and shiny. It looked just like the ones I'd seen policemen carry in town. But Dr. Brian wasn't a policeman. Hunters used rifles, long ones. This was different. Small enough to hide. And the fact that he kept it here, in the desk, terrified me.

I couldn't tell if it was loaded, and I knew better than to check. I thought about hiding it somewhere else, but what if it went off in my hands? What if the boys found it? And what would happen when Dr. Brian realized it was missing?

In the end, I left it in the drawer. And that choice haunted me.

Feeling shaken, I went to get Zeus, but he was fast asleep on the bear rug. I nudged him, hard, but he only lifted and lowered his head, refusing to move. Did he want me to get caught? He was too big to carry. I pushed him again and again, panic rising in my throat. Someone could walk in any minute.

I darted to the pantry and grabbed the dried salami, holding it out like bait.

"Come on," I whispered through clenched teeth. "Move."

At last, Zeus rose and lumbered toward the kitchen, just as voices echoed from the porch. I flicked off the light, eased the office door shut, and sprinted to the pantry. When Timothy came bounding in, I was already stepping out, Zeus by my side.

Timothy took one look at the slobbering dog and laughed, "He's hungry!"

I wiped Zeus's drooling mouth with the hem of my skirt and forced a smile. "Yes, I think he is."

But I was still shaking inside.

And the image of that pistol, black and gleaming, refused to leave my mind.

THIRTY

November 18–November 19, 1915

I wrestled with the idea of writing to my two aunts, but each time I started a letter, I tore it to pieces. It all sounded so incredible. What was I to tell either of them?

Things went from dire to horrible in mid-November. Since Maggie had been let go, I had taken over her duties. Dr. Brian insisted we would be fine without a maid and that we needed to "make do." Shamus, the maintenance man for the house and grounds, had found another job on the other side of town and left shortly after Maggie. He hadn't been replaced either.

I was growing increasingly resentful of my uncle for placing me with these people. Then, one Friday morning, two weeks after the visit with Aunt Libby, something shifted.

Mrs. McClatchy greeted me at the bottom of the stairs.

Her left eye was blackened, and bruises ran down both arms. I'd seen her like this before, but this time felt different.

"Helen, I'm asking you to miss school today. My father is ill, and I must go to Ithaca to be with him." She spoke calmly, without meeting my eyes. "You're to care for the boys entirely while I'm gone, including meals from today through Sunday night. On Monday, Mrs. Bell, a woman from church, will arrive at seven to make breakfast and stay with the boys until you return from school. My train arrives late on Monday night. Understood?"

I mumbled, "Yes, ma'am," and went to my room, where I closed the door and punched my pillow until my arms ached.

The thought of being left alone with that man all weekend made my stomach turn. Her father wasn't sick. I knew that. She and Dr. Brian had fought again, and once more, I was left wondering why adults insisted on pretending. A part of me, deep down, was glad she was going. Maybe she was finally learning to stand up for herself. But my common sense feared for the boys. And for me.

A vision entered my mind of going to school today and never returning. Reality brought me back when I realized I had to care for the boys. Running away wasn't an option.

That evening, I changed into my nightgown, grabbed Sadie, and knelt by my bed. Uncle Peter had brought the Blessed Mary statue he gave me last Christmas to the Mc-Clatchys, and I prayed before her for protection.

I lay awake well after midnight, holding Sadie tightly until Dr. Brian returned home. My heart sped up as I heard him put his coat in the closet and head up the stairs. I closed my eyes and said a quick prayer when he paused at my door. The door opened. I hoped he was just checking on me, but then I heard the door close. He slowly walked over to my bed.

Why would he shut the door?

I pretended to be asleep. My heart was beating so loudly that I was certain he could hear it. My breathing became strained, and I wondered if I would pass out. The thick smell of alcohol filled my room. I could feel his eyes on me.

"Mother Mary, help me!" I prayed silently.

Then, as though he had been poked with a diaper pin from up above, we heard Michael scream bloody murder.

My first reaction was to jump up and check on little Michael, but I stayed still, playing asleep, as Dr. Brian rushed out and into the boy's room. Within minutes, the screaming stopped. I heard him consoling Michael, telling him it was just a nightmare, urging Timothy back to sleep. I pulled my sheets up to my chin and started praying again while listening to Dr. Brian scold Michael about how "big boys don't cry." Eventually, the crying ended.

I didn't sleep a wink that night. Thankfully, Dr. Brian didn't come back into my room. By the next morning, I was exhausted. A full day of cooking and caring for the boys kept me busy. I thought about going to Pap's, or to Olive's, or Uncle Peter's, but there was no way to sneak off without being noticed. Dr. Brian was home all day, glued to the chair in his office. Had he left, I would've called someone. Anyone. But I couldn't risk it. I just had to make it one more night. Tomorrow after church, I'd tell Pap everything.

That night, once the boys were in bed, Dr. Brian's old childhood friend, a man named John, came over. The two of them sat in the parlor drinking. I crept downstairs, hoping to hear something useful.

"Buffalo could win, but my money's on U of R. I've got $300 on it," Dr. Brian said.

"Too rich for me. Hope it works out for ya, doc," John slurred.

"You've got to take risks in life. That's the only way to get ahead, John."

"Nice to have you back in town, doc. We used to have some good times." He chuckled. "Hey, I saw that pretty Kelly girl in town the other day. The older she gets, the more I see the resemblance. She's got your eyes."

"Rosalie Kelly is a whore," Dr. Brian snapped.

His words made me flinch. What did he mean . . . she's got his eyes?

"You and me know that woman ain't no whore, doc," John mumbled. "She's one of them broads that don't like men." His words blurred together, his tongue heavy from drinking.

"That girl's father could be anyone in town," Dr. Brian said, his voice rising.

"I remember that night like it was yesterday. You got that bitch good and drunk..." John went on, oblivious to the growing tension. "Butch and I were rootin' you on. O'Donnell left early. Too straight and narrow for my taste."

The clunk of a bottle rang out.

"I think you've had enough." A chair scraped the floor. Someone slammed a glass hard on the table.

I needed to get upstairs.

"I don't need you coming here and bringing up old crap."

"Didn't mean nothin' by it, doc. Just talkin' about the good 'ole days. Didn't mean no harm."

"Get out." Dr. Brian's voice cracked with fury.

I slipped up the stairs, quiet as I could, shut the door, and let the tears come.

Dr. Brian had raped Rosalie Kelly.

That monster was Olive's father.

"The good 'ole days?" My head spun. I climbed under the covers and cried into my pillow.

My tears dried, but my anger burned. I thought about

how Uncle Peter had always been so critical, so judgmental, of Rosalie and the Kellys. How he'd poisoned Gram's opinion of them with his warped version of morality. His friends had called Rosalie a whore after that night, and Uncle Peter had believed them.

But they were the ones who got her drunk. They did the unthinkable to her body. Then condemned her for having loose morals. I wasn't allowed to befriend Olive because she came from a family of "immoral people."

But now my thoughts shifted to my situation. I'm living in a house with a rapist. I'm not safe. I have to get out.

Mrs. McClatchy wasn't due back until Monday afternoon. Dear God, I couldn't leave the boys alone with that man for that long. How could I guarantee their safety? I would tell Pap everything after Mass. He would help me and the boys. We could make it until then. We had to.

Sleeping in the boy's room seemed like the safest choice. I didn't think Dr. Brian would try anything in front of them. I'd make it look like I'd nodded off while reading.

I crept into their room, the two of them fast asleep, grabbed *Grimm's Fairy Tales* from the bookshelf, and settled into the rocking chair. A crocheted blanket lay folded nearby, which I pulled over myself.

The next thing I knew, daylight poured in, and Michael was standing beside me, laughing.

"Miss Helly, here all night?" he asked in his adorable two-year-old talk.

"Michael, I must have fallen asleep. How silly of me."

Timothy stirred and sat up.

"Helen, you slept here?"

"Yes, boys. I did. It isn't a horrible thing," I said.

"When is Mama coming home?" Timothy asked.

"Tomorrow," I said, and as I spoke, I wondered what Mrs.

McClatchy would walk into. Would we all still be here?

"Yay!" the boys cheered.

"Today we have Mass. I think we have time for some soda bread and eggs first," I whispered. "Let's see how fast you both can get dressed!"

I put on a fake smile for Dr. Brian when he came down to take us to church. The sound of his voice and the smell of him nauseated me. I looked at the front door and was tempted to run, but I held onto hope that Pap would rescue me.

At Immaculate Conception, I slipped into the choir loft. Sister Teresa greeted me. I nodded, put on my cloak, and sat down.

Uncle Peter was assisting with the Mass. My insides raged thinking of the pain he'd caused for Rosalie, the Kellys, and me. What would he do when he learned the truth about his closest friend? He was always so protective of Dr. Brian. I doubted he'd believe a word I said.

From the loft, I scanned the congregation. My eyes froze when they found Dr. Brian, front pew, head bowed in pious silence. My gut twisted.

Rosalie Kelly hadn't been allowed in church for having a child out of wedlock, yet the man who raped her was sitting there in the front pew of the church as if his soul were clean and pure. The injustice of it all was criminal. What would people do if they knew who Dr. Brian really was? What would Uncle Peter do?

Each time we stood, I searched the pews for Pap. But from the loft, I couldn't see under the overhang at the back of the church. When I didn't spot him, I told myself I'd find him after Mass in the greeting line for the priests.

At the end of our final hymn, I slipped off my choir cloak and crept downstairs before Sister Teresa could stop me. I had to reach Father O'Donnell before Dr. Brian did.

I moved quickly through the side aisle, heart hammering, and joined the line forming in front of my uncle.

"Where's Pap?" I asked, trying to keep the panic from spilling out of me.

"I stopped by to pick him up for Mass this morning, but he wasn't feeling well," Uncle Peter said.

"Oh no." Pap rarely missed Mass. Images of him nursing an intense hangover flashed through my mind.

Dr. Brian appeared from nowhere and stood next to me. When he touched my arm and grinned, I became queasy.

With him there, I couldn't say a word to my uncle, not that I knew how to even begin.

"Father O'Donnell, how are you today?" Dr. Brian shook my uncle's hand with too much enthusiasm.

"Fine, Brian. Everything okay in the McClatchy house?" Uncle Peter asked, patting his friend's back.

"Oh yes. Kate's off visiting her father. He's ill, but Helen's taking wonderful care of the three of us."

He winked at me. My stomach was coming up into my throat.

"I'm sorry to hear about Kate's father, but glad that Helen's there to help," Uncle Peter said.

He turned to me. "You look thinner than usual. You getting on okay?"

My eyes flicked to Dr. Brian, then back to my uncle.

"Yes, Uncle Peter. Everything is just fine."

"Glad to hear it. I'll try to stop by sometime this week, if I can."

"Dr. Brian, I'll get the boys," I said, as usual. But panic pooled in my veins as I walked away, my steps unsteady.

How could I survive one more night with him? Would I be so lucky next time? Should I grab the boys and run? Where would I even go?

Aunt Libby was a good hour away on foot, so I couldn't get to the hospital. I regretted not saying something to Sister Teresa, but she was already gone by the time I looked back up at the choir loft.

I missed Olive. If she'd been in church, I would've begged her forgiveness and asked for her help. But neither she nor her grandparents were there today. I remembered what that disgusting friend of Dr. Brian had said. That he'd seen Olive in town recently. The Kellys must have left for another event. Otherwise, they surely would've been in church. They always were.

Thoughts turned to my grandfather. Why was he so weak? I needed him desperately now. I needed my family. Aunt Carrie, Uncle Will, Pap, Aunt Libby, Uncle Peter, someone needed to help me!

I realized that Aunt Libby had been right all along. Aunt Carrie did love me. I had been selfish. Never once thinking about what they might have needed. And the more I sat with it, the clearer it became. Uncle Peter had created all of this. He poisoned Grandma's mind against the Kellys. He drove Aunt Libby out of our home. He turned me against Aunt Carrie and Uncle Will and made me believe they didn't love me. He made life so difficult for them that leaving Rochester felt like their only way to find happiness. He separated me from my brother. He's the one who put me in that house with a monster. Did he convince Gram and Pap to steal me away from my father, too?

Uncle Peter always said he loved me to the moon, but the truth was, he'd never cared about what I wanted. It had only ever been about what he wanted.

The one time Dr. Brian left the house that day, I seized my chance. I picked up the telephone, just as I'd seen adults do, and in my most adult voice, told the operator I needed to be connected to Mrs. Carrie O'Donnell in Chicago, Illinois.

"Ma'am, I have over one hundred O'Donnells in the Chicago area in my directory. Do you have the correct address?"

Again, like a fool, I had thrown away the letters with that information. Feeling thoroughly discouraged, I hung up the receiver and sat there, staring at the phone, weighing my options. I'd wanted to call Aunt Libby next. She would've had Aunt Carrie's address. But before I could place the call, Dr. Brian came home.

I was making Sunday dinner, peeling turnips, potatoes, and carrots, when images of bedtime came to mind. Terror seeped into my bones.

My thoughts turned to the lock on my bedroom door. I needed to lock myself in. About a month ago, I'd seen Mrs. McClatchy open the attic door with a skeleton key. Keys were supposedly hidden for the boys' protection, but I had no idea where.

I'd already searched every drawer and cupboard downstairs, even Dr. Brian's office, while looking for the letters. I knew where the key wasn't. That left upstairs. Most likely, the McClatchy's bedroom.

After dinner, Dr. Brian sat down at the piano, something he'd taken to since his wife had been away. He had a long way to go before catching up to his wife's talent. That was certain. While he pounded out wrong notes and the boys played quietly in their rooms with trucks and little soldiers, I crept into the McClatchy's bedroom.

I started with Mrs. McClatchy's nightstand. I opened the top drawer. No key.

Still hearing the banging of keys from downstairs, I figured it was safe to check the other side.

I crossed the room slowly, careful not to make a sound. I

reached for Dr. Brian's nightstand, fingers just about to open the drawer, when I heard—

"Miss Helly, potty."

I jumped.

Then quickly grabbed Michael's tiny hand and led him to the bathroom. When I returned, the piano was still groaning. I slipped back into the bedroom, crossed to the doctor's nightstand, and opened the drawer.

There, beneath a stack of papers, I found it!

The skeleton key.

I snatched it, dashed to my room, and slumped onto the bed, breathless with relief.

We ate dinner, talked about Mrs. McClatchy coming home the next day, and then played a game of hide-and-seek. Later, while I was bathing the boys, Dr. Brian came into the bathroom.

"Helen, I don't know what we'd do without you. You take such good care of the boys. I've got a special treat for you all tonight. I made hot cider," he said.

"Thank you, sir," I replied.

Once the boys were dried and dressed, we went down to the kitchen, where three steaming mugs waited on the table. Under normal circumstances, I would've slurped mine up without a second thought. But the brain in my stomach told me to be wary. Dr. Brian never did nice things. I knew better than to trust him. And needed a way to empty the mug. I wasn't sure about letting the boys drink theirs, either.

"Now, boys, don't drink too much," I said gently. "It might make you wet the bed."

"Don't be ridiculous," Dr. Brian snapped. "The boys will be fine. All of you. Drink up."

He watched us closely as we sipped. I lifted the mug to my lips, pretended to take a sip, and told him how marvelous it was. As soon as he stepped out to check on Zeus, I rushed to the sink and dumped the cider, unnoticed. The boys, however, drank every last drop.

Dr. Brian returned to the kitchen.

"Helen, you've been working so hard. You must be tired. Go on up to bed, you hear? I'll take care of the boys tonight."

He had never tucked them in. Never told me to go to bed early or made warm drinks. His sudden generosity felt highly suspicious. I glanced at the boys. Their eyelids drooped. Their heads appeared heavy. Too heavy. Something wasn't right.

Not knowing what else to do, I kissed the boys goodnight and went to my room. My skin crawled at the thought of leaving those sweet boys with that man, but I had only my prayers at the moment to help them.

I entered my room with the plan to lock my door. However, when I reached for the key, I stopped. What if he tried the knob and found it locked? What if he started banging, shouting? Or worse?

What would I do? Whether I locked the door or didn't, either choice felt dangerous. All that effort to find the skeleton key, and now I was too afraid to use it.

I couldn't return it to the McClatchy's bedroom, not with Dr. Brian nearby. Instead, I slipped it into my bookshelf beside my door, vowing to return it in the morning before school.

I changed into my nightdress, climbed into bed, and stared at the door. I wanted to push my chair against it, to fortify it somehow, but I knew that could backfire. I longed to sleep in the boys' room again. But that wasn't possible tonight.

Tomorrow, Mrs. Bell would arrive at seven to make breakfast and care for the boys until Mrs. McClatchy returned in the afternoon. I knelt before my Blessed Mary statue and prayed. Then I hugged Sadie close, slipped beneath the covers, and turned out the light.

The boys must've fallen asleep right away. I didn't hear a sound from them after they went upstairs. I lay there for what felt like half an hour. Then, the door creaked open.

And Dr. Brian's voice, low and sickening, cut through the dark.

"Helen? You awake? . . . Helen?"

I didn't move. I pretended to sleep.

Dear God, please help me.

His footsteps crept closer. Then, he pulled the covers off me. I kept my eyes shut, wanting him to believe I was asleep.

He turned me onto my back. And climbed on top of me. I opened my eyes. His massive, naked body hovered over me.

"Get off me! Get off me!" I shouted into his stunned face.

He grabbed my nightdress and yanked it upward as my shouting turned to screams.

"Relax, Helen. Girls like this," he whispered, pressing a firm hand over my mouth.

"I won't hurt you."

Then I felt his hand—

And I sank my teeth into his palm, harder than I ever thought I could. He recoiled with a grunt, clutching his hand, blood blooming between his fingers.

I shoved him off the bed.

"You little bitch! Why, you . . . !" he roared, enraged.

I scrambled to my feet, grabbed Sadie, and struck him as he crouched, moaning, holding his blood-drenched hand.

He lunged again. But I raised Sadie one last time and hit him on the head. The blow made him stumble out of my room, giving me just enough time to slam the door shut. I locked it fast, grabbing the key from the shelf and turning it with my shaking hands. Then I dragged the chair under the handle, wedging it tight.

When I turned on the light, blood smeared across the floor in a gruesome trail. Dr. Brian was howling in pain. I feared he'd wake the boys, but I never heard a sound from their room.

I grabbed a sweater from my closet, threw on my shoes, and stuffed Sadie into a pillowcase.

Then I heard him storming back down the hall.

"You little bitch. You ungrateful little bitch," he snarled. "Is this how you treat the hand that feeds you?"

I rushed to the window, but it was stuck. He was at the door now, rattling the knob, shouting horrible things. He sounded like he wanted to kill me.

I yanked at the window, frantic. It refused to move. Then there was silence. The rattling stopped. Was he going for the gun? Panic gripped my throat. I threw myself against the window one last time—it gave way.

I tossed my pillow with Sadie, inside, onto the ground below. As I started to climb out, I heard him return.

Terror rooted me in place as I listened to him fumble with the lock. He had another key!

"Thought you were so clever, didn't you?" he sneered.

The knob turned. When the chair held it fast, he let out a roar.

"Helen!"

The chair was still braced beneath the handle. And now he was furious. My body moved before I could think. I grabbed the branch hanging outside the window. For a breathless moment, I dangled, my legs swinging in open air.

Then, I heard the door crash open behind me.

I let go.

The drop was long. I prayed the November snow had left more than a dusting. Unfortunately, I hit the ground like a bag of bricks. The unyielding earth knocked the breath from my lungs. Pain shot through both my legs. I couldn't move. Not at first. Then something deeper, will, fear, survival, kicked in.

Run! I forced myself up. My legs ached. My lungs burned. Every muscle I had was now braced to flee.

I turned and looked up. Dr. Brian stood at the window, still naked, a towel wrapped around his bloodied hand.

"Get back here! Come back to this house. Now!" he hissed through clenched teeth.

"Quickly, before someone sees you."

I took one last look. Then I grabbed my pillowcase and ran as fast as I ever had down Clarissa Street, headed home.

THIRTY-ONE

November 19–November 20, 1915

I looked back every few minutes to make sure Dr. Brian wasn't following me. The full moon lit my way, and I found some small comfort in its glow. All was quiet except for the crunch of my footsteps on the white powdery sidewalk, the rush of my breath, and the distant yelping of a neglected dog.

I was tired. I needed to rest. But I didn't dare. I had to get as far away from the McClatchy house as I could.

I could still feel Dr. Brian's hands on me like I'd been branded, like cattle. The taste of his blood lingered in my mouth, vile and metallic. I gagged every time I swallowed. I felt dirty. All I wanted was to wash it away.

My thin nightdress and sweater were no match for the frigid November night, but I welcomed the cold. I craved it. I had to dull the memory of his touch.

When I saw the sign for Columbia Avenue, I sprinted toward Magnolia Street, spending the last of my strength. I raced past the Hamilton's house. And there it was, waiting for me with open arms.

My old home. What a beautiful sight.

I ran to the front door and knocked hard, but it was locked. Pap didn't answer. Was he sleeping? Panic began to rise in my chest.

I was frozen to the bone, and the fear that Dr. Brian might be behind me had my heart speeding like a runaway train. With no other choice, I decided to break in.

I ran to the back, to the window with the rusted old latch. I found a crate to stand on and hoisted myself up. My fingers were stiff, useless from the cold. I groped the lock as my breath hovered before me.

Finally, the window gave. I pushed it open just enough to squeeze through. I dropped my pillowcase into the kitchen and pushed myself up into the opening like a thief, raking my stomach on the rigid casing. I landed on the wooden floor with a thud and sat for a moment, looking at my red hands and legs. I rubbed my palms together, begging for warmth. That's when I saw Brigid's ring on my hand. The sight of it stirred something within me. I found the strength to stand and shut the window. I then searched every room, calling for my grandfather, but he was nowhere to be seen.

What if Dr. Brian came through the door, looking for me? I couldn't stay here. Not alone. It wasn't safe.

Not knowing what to do, I climbed the stairs to the safety of my old bedroom, clutching the pillowcase to my chest. I sat on the bed. I reached into the cotton sack and pulled out my loyal companion.

Sadie. My brave protector.

She had saved me from the big, bad monster. Now her

face was cracked. Her head crushed, held together only by her short hair. Her right arm was broken. Several fingers on her right hand were broken off, and her velvet shoes were missing.

"Sadie, no!" I cried.

Her wounds were fatal. I knew no repairs could fix her. My dear old friend, who had been with me through the toughest of times, was gone. I started to sob.

I was really on my own now.

Still afraid Dr. Brian might be after me, I gathered myself. I needed to think clearly. I couldn't stay here. In the corner, I saw Sadie's old carriage, right where I'd left it. I laid my beautiful friend inside gently.

"Sadie, I'm going to be okay. You made sure of that. Sleep now."

I bent down and kissed her broken face, then tucked her in beneath the tiny quilt my grandmother had made her, a Christmas gift from long ago.

When I turned, the mirror caught my eye. A wet-faced, swollen-eyed version of myself stared back. And there, streaked along my chin, was Dr. Brian's blood. I was still thirteen. My face hadn't changed much. But the child inside was gone . . . vanished . . . slipped away somewhere in the dark. Like a Victor Herbert song, I'd wandered past the gates of *Toyland* tonight, and I knew I'd never return.

Damn my uncle. Damn him for putting me in that house, for trusting that man. Damn him.

But I didn't have time for anger. Not now. I had to think.

Olive's house. She must not be in town. Otherwise, she would have been at Mass. I could sneak into her room, keep warm, and plan my next move.

I'd been so childish. So petty. I couldn't blame Olive for turning away from me months ago. Friends didn't do what I did. Heck, even a doll knew what true friendship was. Sadie knew that in the end, it all comes down to taking care of one another—protecting, supporting, loving each other.

I looked out the window to be sure the coast was clear. Then I slipped downstairs and out the back door. Olive's bedroom was on the far side of her grandparents' house. As I crept through their backyard with the moon lighting my way, I glanced behind me at the trail of footprints I'd left in the snow. Hopefully, no one would notice the straight line from my old house. I placed the same crate I'd used earlier beneath Olive's window and started having second thoughts.

Should I go back to Pap's? No. Not without him there. It was too dangerous. I couldn't risk Dr. Brian finding me.

I twirled my great-great-grandmother's ring twice and whispered a thank-you to her for helping me. Then I climbed onto the crate, pushed open the window, and slipped through. Pain shot through my side as I scraped my stomach again. I winced when my elbow hit the hard floor.

Now face down on the warm wooden boards, I took a deep breath and rejoiced in the familiar smell of the room.

Thank God Almighty. I'm safe.

Then a voice rang out.

"I have a gun, and I know how to use it!"

THIRTY-TWO

November 20, 1915

"Olive, it's me!" I whispered, my breath catching in my throat.

Olive lit a lamp and turned, gripping a thick stick like a club. Her eyes went wide.

"Helen? Is that blood on your face?"

I rushed forward and blew out the lamp. "Don't! He might see the light."

"Who might see the light?" she asked.

I fell into her arms. She caught me without a word and held me tight. And just like that, I broke. The sobbing and shaking lasted for several minutes as Olive tried to calm me.

When I could breathe again, she pulled back and whispered, "What happened?"

I went to sit on the bed, then yelped when something squealed beneath me.

"It's just Oscar," she said, scooping the cat into her arms. "You sat on him."

"Helen, please. Tell me."

I looked at her. Then at the cat. And somehow, I found the words. I told her everything.

When I finished, the room was so quiet I could hear Oscar's soft purring. Then Olive's fists clenched. Her whole body seemed to shake.

"That son of a . . . what a savage."

"Olive, he's sick," I said, barely able to get the words out.

She placed Oscar gently on the bed and grabbed my hands.

"He can't get away with this," she said, her voice trembling. "Let's call your Uncle Peter."

"I need to wash up. I can't—" I couldn't finish. The sensation of his hands seemed to be fused to my skin.

"Of course," she said quickly. "Come on. We'll get you cleaned up."

She disappeared down the hall and came back with a basin, soap, and a towel.

"Here. Take those off," she said softly, pulling a cozy nightgown from her drawer.

When I'd scrubbed myself almost raw with the ice-cold water, I dressed and climbed into her welcoming bed.

"Pap's not home," I whispered. "I didn't know where else to go. I thought you'd left town since you weren't at church. I didn't mean to break in . . ."

"You did the right thing," she said, handing me a handkerchief. Her eyes were wet, too.

Oscar nudged her side, and she picked him up, cradling him like a baby.

"He's gotten so big," I said, reaching out to scratch his head. "You've taken good care of him."

"He's a good cat," she murmured. Then she looked at me. "Helen . . . I've missed you."

I looked away. "I'm so sorry I hurt you. What I did was wrong. The truth is . . . I was so jealous. Will you ever forgive me?"

She didn't hesitate. "Of course I forgive you, silly. I've missed you something gargantuan."

I couldn't help but smile, just a little. Leave it to Olive and her ridiculous vocabulary to sneak light into the darkest room.

I continued to tell her everything I could. The beating. The man who came for money. The missing ring. The girl who got fired. The dead bird. The keyhole. Everything right up to the present—Monday, November 20. Everything except the conversation I'd overheard between Dr. Brian and his friend John.

We both agreed that Dr. Brian put something in the cider. It explained everything. The look on his face when he saw I was still awake. The boldness. The way he—

"I'm worried about the boys," I said, my voice cracking. "I had to leave them, Olive. I didn't have a choice."

Her face tensed. "Are they safe?"

"I think so. Mrs. Bell's coming early, and Mrs. McClatchy's supposed to be home tomorrow—or today, I guess." I glanced at her clock. 3:30. I couldn't believe this was real.

"You have to tell your Uncle Peter. He'll do something. And we should talk to your grandfather. He's been out late, more than usual. And we have a telephone now. We can call your uncle tonight."

"Olive . . . I don't know if he'd believe me. He and Dr.

Brian go way back."

"Then, your uncle keeps bad company," she said flatly.

I hesitated. "You don't know the half of it. Saturday night, one of Dr. Brian's old friends came over, and I overheard something, something awful."

"Go on."

Oscar purred as Olive stroked his fur, but her shoulders had gone still.

"The man talked about that night," I said.

"What night?" Her hand froze mid-pet. She gently placed Oscar at the foot of the bed.

"The night your mother was . . . well, you know. The night she was—"

"Raped?"

"Yes." I met her eyes, unsure whether to continue.

"Helen, tell me," her voice calm but pressing.

I blurted out, "The man who raped your mother was Dr. Brian."

Her eyes widened. She slapped a hand over her mouth. It took her a moment to find her voice. Then—

"Jesus, Mary, and Joseph!"

"I'm sorry, Olive."

She shook her head slowly, like the words didn't make sense.

"That monster is my father?"

I moved toward her. This time, I held her. She cried but only for a moment. Then something changed in her face. Her chin lifted. Her eyes filled with fire.

"I won't cry for him again," she said. "He's not my father. He's the man who raped my mother. That's all he'll ever be."

She looked at me. Her voice was steady now, but even in the dark, I could see the shimmer in her eyes.

"Helen, do you think your uncle knew?"

"I don't think so. I don't think he ever believed your mother was raped. He believed whatever lies his friends told him about her."

We held each other tightly until Olive kissed my forehead.

"Helen, you've been through so much. I'm sorry," she whispered.

She looked at me again, and somehow, she was already thinking about me. Not herself. Me.

"What are you going to do?" she asked. "You should be in Chicago with your aunt and uncle. That's where you belong. Why aren't you there?"

"It's complicated," I scowled.

"My mother said your uncle wouldn't let you go. She said your aunt was heartbroken. She wrote and never heard back."

"I miss them so much," I said, my throat tight. "I didn't know. I only saw two letters when I was still with Pap. Nothing after that. Aunt Libby said Aunt Carrie wrote every week."

Olive's eyes narrowed. "Helen, I wonder what happened to Aunt Carrie's letters?"

"When I asked the McClatchys about the letters, it felt like they were lying. I think Uncle Peter told them to hide them. He wouldn't let Pap visit for the first two months either, said it would help me 'adjust.'" I rolled my eyes.

"That's so wicked. Would your Uncle Peter really do that?"

"Olive, he's stubborn and selfish. He'd rather I stay with the McClatchys than live in a loving home with my brother and aunt, and uncle. I'm ashamed. I believed him. I let him convince me they didn't love me."

"Oh, Helen," Olive shook her head. "That's an evil thing to do."

"I believe my aunt and uncle would come for me, but I'm scared Uncle Peter will drag them into trouble too. He's made it very clear I'm not allowed to leave Rochester, even threatening to get the law involved."

I lay back on Olive's bed and stared up at the dark ceiling.

"What am I supposed to do? I can't go back to the Mc-Clatchys. And if I return to Pap's, Uncle Peter will just send me back to Dr. Brian's. He has legal guardianship. He holds all the power, and he'd never believe what his friend did to me."

"I won't go back. Not ever!" My voice cracked.

Olive sat beside me, thinking hard. "My mother is in Washington, D.C. this month, working on suffrage legislation. She could have helped us." She hesitated. "Maybe . . . maybe we should tell my grandparents."

"No. They go to my uncle's church. I can't put them in that position. What if he does something to them for helping me? He got rid of my teacher last year just for writing a letter saying I should go to Chicago."

"Sister Brigid?" Olive grabbed my arm.

"Yes. He had her transferred."

"The suffragists always wondered why she left," Olive muttered. "What about your father? Would he help?"

"My father is a kind man, but he's no match for my uncle. That was obvious when he tried to take me with him to Cleveland."

"Hmm," she paused. "It's too bad your grandfather drinks so much."

I gave a bitter laugh. "If Pap had been stronger. If my mother hadn't died. If Gram hadn't died. If I hadn't been stolen from my father," I sighed. "I'm sorry. I'm just feeling sorry for myself."

Olive reached for my hand. "You can't change the past, Helen, but you can change what happens next."

Her voice became firm. "What happened tonight proves it. You fought back. You survived. You're stronger than you know."

I managed a smile.

"The best place for you is with your aunt and uncle. What if you ran away to them? Maybe the laws are different in Illinois. Maybe Uncle Peter won't be able to stop you."

"I want that more than anything," I whispered.

Olive turned toward a small dresser illuminated by a glimmer of moonlight and started digging through the drawers.

"I know it's here somewhere . . . yes!"

She lit up as she held up a folded piece of paper, tracing a line of numbers with her finger.

"A one-way ticket from Rochester to Chicago is forty-four dollars."

She looked elated, but the number made my heart sink. I shook my head, already feeling defeated.

"The train leaves at 10:30 this morning and gets in around 8:00 tonight," she continued. "I'll contact your aunt and tell her you're coming!"

"Well, I don't have forty-four dollars," I said, too sharply.

She didn't flinch.

"We can't let something as silly as money keep you from your destiny," she said, marching to her closet.

She pulled down an old brown urn, popped off the lid, and dumped a cascade of coins onto the bed. "I've been saving. It's not much, but it's yours."

She held up two silver coins. "These? I got paid for a story I had published in a paper two months ago."

"Olive, that's wonderful. I'm so proud of you." I hesitated. "But I feel awful taking your money."

"Four dollars and twenty-three cents," she announced. "Not enough. Not even close. How much do you have?"

"Nothing. The only thing I have is my great-great-grandmother's ring and . . . my hair," I mumbled, instantly feeling foolish.

"Your hair?" she repeated, raising an eyebrow.

"A woman I met downtown told me she'd give me four dollars for it. Said it's hard to find true red hair, so long and lush."

"My, my," Olive said, folding her arms.

"We don't want to go cutting your hair unless we absolutely have to. You already look a bit like a boy, and without it—hmm—"

She tilted her head, thinking. Then her eyes lit up.

"Wait! Maybe you *should* cut it. You're too young to travel alone. They might not even let you on the train. But if you looked like a boy . . ." Olive held her chin, which now held a devilish grin.

I shuddered and ran my fingers through my hair, the long strands falling over my shoulder.

"Now . . . clothes," she said, glancing toward her closet.

She stretched her legs and nearly launched poor Oscar into the air, but caught him just in time. I scooped him up and sat on the bed, trying to make sense of her plan to disguise me as a boy.

"What about that suit in your grandparents' closet? The one that belonged to the uncle who died before you were born?"

I remembered it well. We'd been rummaging in Pap's closet, looking through some of Gram's old things. We found Uncle Albert's confirmation suit, mothballs stuffed in the pockets to keep the pests out. I'd always been told never to take it off its hanger.

"Uncle Albert's confirmation suit? I can't take that out of the closet. Gram would be furious," I said louder than I should have.

"Helen, hush!" Olive whispered, giving my arm a sharp smack. "You'll wake my grandparents. Don't you think your grandmother would give you her blessing, just this once?"

I wrinkled my nose.

"I suppose. Maybe . . . it'd be all right," I said.

"Helen, I'm certain even your departed kin are doing their bit to see you safe," she said, her eyes wide and beaming.

A momentary flutter of hope filled me, but that was until Olive added very matter-of-factly, "We'll need to sell your ring."

I swallowed hard and held my ringhand tightly to my chest.

"I'll go first thing in the morning and sell it. I'll bring your hair, too. Between that, the ring, and my $4.23, we might have enough."

I didn't want to cut my hair, as being even more homely wasn't exactly appealing. But I realized, if Sadie could do it, so could I. I would cut my hair. It would grow back. The ring, now that was different. Once it was gone, it would be gone forever. No passing it on to future children or grandchildren. It would be out of our family, never to return.

"Olive, I can't sell this ring. It's like a protective talisman from my ancestors. I really feel like Brigid is watching over me. How can I possibly sell it?"

Olive leaned forward, her voice low and serious.

"Helen, didn't you hear yourself? Brigid is watching over you. How do you know that's not the exact reason you have this ring? Maybe it's to help you find the life you deserve? And if money is the only thing standing in the way, don't you think your ancestors, past, present, and future, would bless you for using it?"

She paused, her eyes shining.

"Maybe, just like Uncle Albert's suit, all your ancestors are helping you right now. Trying to get you to your proper home. To your true family. I think you deserve that. And I'm sure they do too."

It comforted me to think they might want me to be happy, safe, and prosperous. I was part of them, after all. I carried their blood within me. Maybe, just maybe, they were helping me now.

I twirled the ring twice, one final time, and recited Grandma's prayer aloud. Olive closed her eyes reverently as I spoke:

> "May you see God's light on the path ahead
> when the road you walk is dark.
> May you always hear, even in your hour of sorrow, the gentle singing of the lark.
> When times are hard, may hardness never turn your heart to stone.
> May you always remember when the shadows fall, you do not walk alone."

I whispered a quiet thank-you to all my ancestors, then slid the ring off my finger and placed it in Olive's hand.

"Here, Olive. Now . . . let's go cut my hair."

THIRTY-THREE

November 20, 1915

Olive slipped out of the room and returned quickly, undetected, with her grandmother's shears in hand.

"It's way too dark to see what I'm doing. I'll need to light the lamp."

"I suppose if Dr. Brian were going to barge in, he would've by now. Go ahead. I just don't want you accidentally cutting off my head!"

I tried to make light of it, but when she turned on her kerosene lamp and I saw the size of those metal blades, I began to wonder whether I was about to have a haircut or an amputation.

Olive handed me a ribbon.

"Here, tie your hair up. It'll be easier to cut that way. Now sit and don't move."

She gave my shoulders a firm push and guided me into the chair.

I clenched my hair tightly. *I couldn't do it.* The mirror across the room caught my eye, and I walked over to it, drawn to my reflection.

Aunt Libby's voice echoed in my mind. "Helen, would it matter if you were ugly?"

I admired my long, red locks one last time, then tied them up like a horse's tail and eased back into the chair. Then I took a deep breath and closed my eyes.

"I'm ready. Go ahead."

The scissors struggled to make it through my thick hair. I sat there bravely, focusing on the image of my family, welcoming me. Within a minute, my head felt much lighter. Olive, with a mix of sadness and reverence, held up the sheared-off tresses.

The sight made me gasp.

"Dear Mother Mary, what have I done?"

I stepped toward the mirror, trying not to cry as I stared at my new reflection.

"It's kind of cute, Helen. You really do look just like a boy now," Olive said, wearing a smug little smile.

"Thanks," I muttered, lifting my chin and willing myself not to cry.

I sat on Olive's bed and ran my fingers through the blunt new edges. It felt strange—rough, and boyish.

"Helen, it'll all be worth it. Don't forget that."

Olive put on her coat and scarf and held my hair in a bag and my ring in her pocket.

"We'll see how much I can get. Be careful sneaking in and out, getting that suit. If you hear my grandparents coming, hide in the closet. I'll be back as soon as I can."

She opened her door and blew me a kiss. "Say your prayers, Helen."

I stood and peeked through the curtains. The morning light stretched across the sky, and I let out a quiet breath of relief. For the second night in a row, I hadn't slept. Exhaustion embraced me, pulling me to lie down. But something inside me kept pushing. This wasn't the time to be tired. I could still make my life good again. I just had to be strong. I couldn't give up.

Somehow, by some miracle, it would all work out. Olive would come back with enough money. I'd sneak into Pap's closet, take Uncle Albert's suit, and spend the next several hours on a train, passing as a boy.

I closed my eyes and prayed.

Soon, I saw Pap and Nell leave for work. For a moment, excitement filled me. Finally, I could fetch the suit. But the feeling faded fast as I watched them disappear down the street.

I realized I'd be leaving my grandfather, a man I loved very much. I desperately wanted to take him with me so we could all live happily ever after, but I knew it wasn't possible.

Perhaps life would be kind and unite us again.

I'd call him the moment I reached Aunt Carrie and Uncle Will. I'd tell him everything. I'd help him understand that I belonged in Chicago with my family.

I crept out one window and snuck into another. Once inside, I went straight to Pap's room and into his closet. There, in all its glory, was Uncle Albert's confirmation suit. My ticket to freedom.

"Thank you, Uncle Albert," I said respectfully, pulling the wool suit from the wooden bar. The smell of the mothballs hit me hard, but there wasn't one single hole in the fabric.

On the top shelf, I spotted several caps and picked one that looked old and worn. Hopefully, Pap wouldn't be too upset when he noticed it missing.

The only thing I still needed was the right pair of shoes. My girlish ones would surely give me away.

Olive returned within a few hours and walked into the room, eating some jerky. When she saw me, she froze.

"Mother Mary!" she exclaimed.

Slowly, Olive removed the scarf covering her head. We both stood silent, taking in the strange sights before us. This wasn't the same girl who had left a few hours ago, standing before me.

"Olive! Your beautiful hair—" My eyes became hazy as I studied her.

"I wasn't about to let two dollars get in the way of your fate," Olive shrugged.

Her hair was just as short as mine. She didn't look ugly, though. She had never looked more beautiful.

I wiped my tears. Her generosity had undone me.

"Here, eat this," she said, handing me a strip of jerky, seemingly oblivious to her selfless act.

As I chewed, she recounted her morning's adventure.

"I went to two places to see how much they would give me for your ring. The first store would only give me twenty-five dollars, but when I went to the second place, he offered me thirty-five, saying he could tell it was well made. It was getting late, and by the time I walked into Lacey's Salon, before I could pull your hair from the bag, the lady was already touching and smelling mine. Thought I was there to sell it!"

She smirked, "When I asked her how much for yours, she said three dollars. But five for both. Helen, it's only hair. It'll grow back."

The thought of her doing this for me, of all people, overwhelmed me. I cried again. Without a word, Olive dumped the money onto the bed and started counting. Like a proud pirate over her bounty, she grinned.

"Forty-four dollars and twenty-three cents! We did it, and luckily, my grandparents still have no idea you're here."

I could hardly believe it. After everything, I was finally going to be with the people who truly loved me. And it was Olive who made it possible.

"I'll get you some food for the trip. You can use my old tote. You can give it back next time I see you," she smirked and then started shaking her head, looking me up and down. "Golly . . . you really do look just like a boy."

I looked down at myself, trying to see what she saw.

"What about my feet? My shoes won't pass for men's shoes."

"My mother has those boots from the New York City to Albany march," Olive said. "They're a bit worn, but they'll work. I'm sure she'd give them to you if she were here."

She reached into the closet she shared with her mother and handed me the perfect pair to complete the disguise. I pulled them on and turned to the mirror. I reveled in our work for a moment. We'd done it. A young man stared back at me.

"One more thing." Olive went to her desk and pulled out a leather-bound journal. She tore out several ink-scrawled pages and grabbed two sharpened pencils.

"You can write on the train. Write your story, Helen. Write it all down."

She tucked the journal and pencils into my sack, then glanced at the clock. Her smile faded.

"We need to go," she said. "You can't miss that train."

"Olive . . . there's one last favor." My voice cracked.

A covered bundle was on the floor, tucked away near Olive's dresser. I walked over, picked it up, and gently peeled back the small blanket, exposing Sadie's broken face. When I saw that my friend now only had one eye, I paused, struggling to speak.

"She was a good soldier, Olive. She has too many injuries

to be repaired. I would be so grateful if you could bury her in my backyard. She needs to be buried at her home. Magnolia Street will always be her—" I stopped, unable to get the rest of the words out, and gave Sadie a tight squeeze.

"Oh, Helen. Poor Sadie. Of course, I'll give her a proper burial. I'll put her right here next to Daisy for now." She reached out her arms as I gave my dear old companion, Sadie, one last tender kiss. Olive carefully held her like a baby and walked over to a small doll's bed. Daisy, long forgotten now that Olive was a girl of fifteen, lay there in her dress and bonnet, both of which were beginning to fray. The two dolls had once been playmates—like us.

Olive arranged Sadie gently. I looked at them one last time. I was losing my two best friends today.

At the train station, we gave each other a long, tearful embrace as nosy strangers looked on. We must've been a sight. Me in boy's clothes with butchered red hair, and Olive, just as cropped, radiant in her grief.

"I love you, Olive Kelly. Promise you'll write?"

"I love you, Helen O'Donnell. I faithfully promise to write you every week. Miles will never separate us."

And with that, I boarded the train and turned one last time to wave goodbye to my best friend. We were friends for life. No matter what happened next, we would always be there for each other. In this unpredictable, complicated world, that was everything.

As the train rumbled beneath me, Olive's words from earlier came back. "Like my Nana always says, Ar scáth a chéile a mhaireann na daoine. It's through the shelter of each other that we survive."

I've turned that old Gaelic proverb over in my mind more times than I can count. Helping others is good and holy. It's what makes the world turn and the sun rise each morning. None of us can survive without the embrace of another, without someone standing beside us inspiring us to get back up when we trip or falter.

When I look back on my life, I see all the courageous people who have sheltered me with kindness, strength, and unwavering arms. I don't know where I'd be today without the women who shaped me. Many of them suffragists. All of them fearless in their own way.

Olive. Rosalie. Aunt Carrie. Sister Brigid. Aunt Libby. Mrs. Kelly. Grandma. My mother. And great-great-grandmother Brigid.

Because of them, I learned I could do hard things. Because of them, I now knew the meaning of sisterhood.

Toward the end of the nine-and-a-half-hour ride, exhaustion claimed me. My head sagged, my eyelids surrendered. I fell asleep.

In my dream, Uncle Albert appeared, a bright-eyed, smiling boy no older than Connor Hamilton, dressed in his crisp confirmation suit. He waved. I waved back, full of gratitude.

The train lurched.

"Last stop, Last stop!" a man called.

I made it!

I tossed the journal and pencil into my bag, adjusted my cap, stood, and straightened my jacket. At the window, a sea of people blurred past. My chest tightened.

How will I find them? What will I do? I went to twirl my ring, but it was no longer there.

Panic almost overtook me.

I remembered Olive's words, ". . . when your wings become tired, and you feel you can't go another foot, go higher anyway. And when you really can't go another inch, stop and look in your pocket, have a butterscotch . . ."

I reached into my pocket, relieved I hadn't yet eaten the sweet candy. I unwrapped the crinkly gold treat and popped it into my mouth, and closed my eyes. I immediately felt better.

Breathe, Helen. Breathe, I reminded myself.

I opened my eyes and stood, finding myself shoulder to shoulder with anxious travelers hurrying to get off the train. From the corner of my eye, I saw something familiar. Before me stood a woman holding a magazine. On the back cover was a bright red cardinal.

Of course. I was going to be okay. God, Grandma, my mother, Brigid, and Uncle Albert they were all with me.

I took a deep breath and stepped off the train. The night was crisp, the sky clear. The crowd swallowed me, backs and elbows pressing in. One wrong move and I'd be trampled.

Fear gnawed at me until I heard what sounded like the voice of an angel calling my name.

Was I imagining this?

I pushed through the crowd and climbed onto the base of a light post to find where the voice was coming from. A cold November wind sliced through me, but the chill disappeared when I heard it again. My name rising clearly over the crowd.

There.

A woman stood on a platform, scanning the crowd. "Helen!" she shouted again.

It was Aunt Carrie.

She looked right at me, but didn't recognize me. I jumped down and ran. She was here. Olive had reached her.

I pressed forward, tugged at her dress. She flinched, startled, and slightly kicked at me. "Aunt Carrie! Aunt Carrie—it's me! It's Helen!"

She looked down, and this time, she really looked into my eyes.

"Helen!" she cried.

She rushed down from the platform and wrapped her arms around me, tighter than anyone ever had. She kissed me again and again, tears streaking down her cheeks.

And at that moment, I remembered how Rosalie Kelly had looked at Olive after the march. How I'd once told myself, no one would ever look at me that way. Not with that kind of love.

But I was wrong. Because now, I was being looked at with a love so deep and mighty, it could have lifted me to the moon.

"My dear Helen, you poor girl," Aunt Carrie whispered between kisses.

Through the blur of it all, I saw Uncle Will and Matthew pushing through the crowd.

"Helly, you boy." Matthew giggled.

He remembers me.

Uncle Will pulled me into a firm hug, his voice thick with emotion. "You look just like my little brother, Albert." He paused to collect himself. "Helen, your uncle has agreed to let you live with us. No one will ever hurt you again. Not while I'm alive."

"It's true," Aunt Carrie said, her eyes brimming. "He's giving up guardianship. He and Pap are coming next week with your things. Helen, it's happening. You're going to live with us."

She tried to say more, but her voice wavered. She kissed me again, tears falling freely.

At first, their words struggled to find space in my battered heart. I paused to look at them both as the beautiful music of what they were saying began to settle in.

And then, I became giddy with joy, knowing I wouldn't be forced to go back.

I, Helen O'Donnell, was finally home.

EPILOGUE

Five Years Later

August 27, 1920

Yesterday, the 19th Amendment was ratified. Today, Rochester's Main Street erupted with joy. Thousands gathered, including me, Olive, Rosalie, Aunt Libby in her wheelchair, Aunt Carrie, Uncle Will, Matthew, and the Kellys. We marched, danced, and sang with joy, our heads held high, knowing that seventy-one years after Seneca Falls, daughters, mothers, and grandmothers will finally cast their votes in the upcoming November election.

As we cheered in the streets, I couldn't help but remember the girl I once was. The past five years have brought many changes to our country and to my life. It feels like only yesterday I ran away to Chicago disguised as a boy.

Later, I learned that Olive had gone straight to Uncle Peter and told him everything about Dr. Brian's attack. She stood her ground, even when he refused to believe her.

When Uncle Peter and Pap arrived at the McClatchy's house, they found Mrs. McClatchy's father and brothers packing clothes and toys. Word had reached them that Dr. Brian had not only been abusing his wife, Kate, but had also been sexually molesting young girls at his medical office in Scranton.

It all came to a head that day, when Mrs. Bell, alarmed and uncertain, phoned Dr. Brian. He arrived at the house to find Uncle Peter waiting for him. The moment my uncle saw the bandage on Dr. Brian's hand, exactly as Olive had described, something inside him snapped.

Presumably fueled by betrayal and anger, Uncle Peter struck with all his might, breaking Dr. Brian's nose. The doctor collapsed in a heap of blood and denial. He shouted his innocence—about me, about his patients, about his cruelty to Kate.

But the truth had found its voice.

After the brawl, Timothy and Michael left for Ithaca with their grandfather and uncles, belongings in tow. It would be the last time their precious young eyes would see their father alive.

Days later, the newspapers reported Dr. Brian's arrest for his crimes. But before his case could go to trial, his body was found in Canandaigua Lake. An accidental drowning, they said. Others said justice found him by other means.

A week after I arrived in Chicago, Uncle Peter and Pap came with my things. Uncle Peter wept. I'd never seen tears from him. Not once. When he asked for forgiveness, there wasn't a dry eye in the room. My uncles promised Pap that the feuding was over for good.

I forgave my uncle that day. It was what Gram and my mother would have wanted, and I found deep down that I loved him. Maybe not past the stars as I once had, but high enough to the far-away place where birds fly. My love would no longer be blind to his imperfections, though. He was a flesh-and-blood human, just like me. No better, no worse.

Within two years, Uncle Peter left the priesthood, something no one could have predicted. The news shocked the Rochester community and everyone who knew him. He moved to Ithaca, took a job as a high school principal, and married Kate, choosing a life far from what anyone had expected.

Although his choices were seen as scandalous, his eyes are now filled with joy. He's found purpose as a devoted husband, a father to Timothy and Michael, and a respected leader in his new community. According to Uncle Peter, he had been pushed into a life he hated, a life that was slowly destroying him.

When he left Rochester, we returned to Magnolia Street to care for Pap, who had refused to move to Chicago. And we were happy to come home. We'd missed Pap, Aunt Libby, and all our friends.

Aunt Carrie and Uncle Will opened O'Donnell's, a lively place full of good food, non-alcoholic drinks (thanks to the recent passing of the 18th Amendment), and music to honor our Irish roots.

Pap, retired now from delivering coal since Nell's passing, delights in greeting every guest and sampling the food. Prohibition has squelched his spirit. He moans often, but he's carrying on despite it.

In fact, he's become something of a local legend, polishing up his singing, dancing, and storytelling skills for the delight of everyone who walks through the door.

I occasionally perform at the restaurant with Uncle

Will, singing classic Irish pub songs that get the whole place swinging their mugs full of cider in time.

As for Rosalie and the other suffragists, I do wonder what they'll turn their energy toward now that the vote has been won. But something tells me there's still plenty of work to be done.

Olive is currently studying to become a doctor at the University of Rochester, with a dream of establishing a clinic for women and the underserved. She says it's the injustice and suffering of others that drives her and that no man or woman should ever lack safe, skilled hands to turn to, no matter their status or means. I still see in her eyes the lingering sorrow for Connor Hamilton, her fiancé, who never returned from the war. His loss, along with the flu epidemic, has scarred us all.

As for me, I have found my place. I have grown from an awkward child to a confident and well-adjusted woman. I'm dating a handsome law student who shares my passion for women's rights. Ed came into the restaurant one night when I was singing and called me a songbird. As my ears were pleasantly vibrating from the purr of his words, I looked into his eyes and saw a future, my future, something I'd never experienced before.

I'm finishing high school and will soon start at the University of Rochester, determined to become a history professor. I believe that positive societal growth can only occur when its members can clearly and critically examine their past. We must be able to study and understand our mistakes to become a society that values all people, regardless of gender or skin color.

On this historic day, I find myself reflecting on what it truly means to be a woman.

Womanhood is no mold into which we are meant to be pressed, nor a road laid out by another's design. It is not a story authored for us by others, nor a cage, however gilded, meant to display our beauty, our humility, our delicacy, or our silence.

It must not require the swallowing of words for the sake of harmony, nor the emptying of ourselves so that others may feel whole.

It must call us to speak the truth, even when the cost is high. To nurture without duty and to love freely, deeply, and without obligation. For such love is not our burden; it is our gift.

It means having the courage to defy what has always been, to journey beyond what we were told we could do and be, and to know, without question, that we were created in equal measure to men.

It means standing in solidarity with other women. Lifting. Inspiring. Strengthening. Passing the torch of courage from hand to hand, until no wind, no matter how strong, can blow it out.

Because power isn't only in the roar of the ferocious, mighty lion. It's in the uprising of a brigade of house cats who will never stop believing, marching, or fighting for justice.

Unite.

Break your cages . . .

And FLY

Author's Note

The character of Helen is inspired by my grandmother, Helen Dowd Gretchen. In 1976, she wrote a twelve-page memoir for her eight grandchildren—a simple yet powerful reflection on her life as a young girl in early 20th-century America. That memoir, along with her 1915 eighth-grade school photo from Immaculate Conception Elementary School, became my constant companion as I wrote this book.

Many elements in this novel were drawn from real events and cultural tensions of the era, though most of the characters and the storyline are fictional. Like the women in these pages, the real Helen lived through a time of profound change. She and countless others celebrated the signing of the 19th Amendment in 1920, never knowing it would take another forty years for *all* women in the United States to fully gain that right.

This book is a tribute to the brave women (and men)

who fought for truth, equality, and justice. Because of their perseverance, courage, and passion, women today have the power to vote on issues that matter to them, many of which only women may fully understand.

Even as of this publication (105 years later, to be precise), some politicians have expressed a desire to repeal the 19th Amendment. In a world where so much remains uncertain, I urge you: never take the right to vote for granted. It took blood, sweat, and tears to get us to the voting booths. Educate yourself on the issues. Find candidates who reflect your values. And then—vote. Or, if need be, march. Complacency will not carry us forward.

If this book has moved you, I'd be deeply grateful if you could share it with someone else, whether through a recommendation, a gift, or a thoughtful review. Word of mouth means everything to authors, and your voice can help stories like Helen's find their way into more hearts.

You can follow my journey on social media and stay in touch at www.aimeespring-author.com. Also, please consider gifting my children's book, *The Little Butterfly: For Young Hearts Who Have Experienced Loss,* to a grieving child, available at Online bookstores or on my website.

Acknowledgments

Thank you to my husband, Rob Cecil, and to my children, Hollee and Bray, for listening to many versions of chapters, offering suggestions, and encouraging my writing even when it meant time away from them. I'm confident our entire family grew because of *The Girl from Magnolia Street.*

Melissa Cristallo helped me realize I could write when she asked me to co-author a book years ago. Although that project never came to fruition, we learned a great deal about novel writing together. Melissa has always believed in me, my writing, and Helen's story. The best friend/sisterly bond between Helen and Olive was inspired by our fifty-plus-year friendship. Words cannot express my deep gratitude to her for being my lifelong best friend and one of my biggest cheerleaders.

The pandemic reignited my desire to finish this book, and the stars aligned when I took a writing course at the

Gardiner Library in New York, taught by Laurence Carr. When the class ended, Mr. Carr graciously agreed to become my writing coach. I credit him with helping me turn a half-finished manuscript into a completed first draft. His gentle spirit, patience, and writing wisdom were precisely what I needed. Laurence Carr is a writer and editor living in New York's Hudson Valley. He writes fiction, poetry, non-fiction, and plays, and is the publisher of LightwoodPress.com, an arts and culture magazine.

Through Laurence, I met Penny Freel, a retired SUNY New Paltz lecturer and all-around extraordinary human. Penny volunteered countless hours to help me with this novel. Her intelligence, generosity, and insight shaped the book in vital ways. I will forever be indebted to her for her patience, encouragement, and belief in Helen's story.

Thank you to Hollee Candido and Cassandra Dunn for their insight and editing skills, as well as to my beta readers: Andie Vaaler, Melissa Cristallo, Wendy Hatoum, Susan Keeler, Dave Young, Jennifer Spring and also my advanced readers. Through their support, I found the courage to believe in myself and realized that others wanted to hear Helen's story.

Further Reading

While this novel is a work of fiction, many of its themes and historical elements were inspired by real people, places, and movements. For readers interested in exploring the social currents and cultural atmosphere of the suffrage era, as well as some of the deeper roots behind its characters and customs, the following works were especially helpful during my research:

The Woman's Bible: A Feminist Perspective by Elizabeth Cady Stanton (Dover Publications, 2002; originally published 1895–1898)

Votes for Women! American Suffragists and the Battle for the Ballot by Winifred Conkling (Algonquin Books of Chapel Hill, 2020)

The 1910s: American Popular Culture Through History by David Blanke (Greenwood Press, 2002)

Women WILL Vote: Winning Suffrage in New York State

by Susan Goodier and Karen Pastorello (Cornell University Press, 2017)

The Woman's Hour: Our Fight for the Right to Vote (Adapted for Young Readers) by Elaine Weiss (Random House, 2020)

Irish Customs and Rituals: How Our Ancestors Celebrated Life and the Seasons by Marion McGarry (Open Press, 2020)

Samhain: The Roots of Halloween by Luke Eastwood (The History Press, 2021)

www.ingramcontent.com/pod-product-compliance
Lightning Source LLC
Chambersburg PA
CBHW020238010826
48973CB00006B/1565